HOSTILE ASSET

A DANE WINTER THRILLER

SAM COGLEY

Boldwood

First published in Great Britain in 2025 by Boldwood Books Ltd.

Copyright © Sam Cogley, 2025

Cover Design by Head Design Ltd

Cover Images: Shutterstock, iStock and Alamy

Every effort has been made to obtain the necessary permissions with reference to copyright material, both illustrative and quoted. We apologise for any omissions in this respect and will be pleased to make the appropriate acknowledgements in any future edition.

A CIP catalogue record for this book is available from the British Library.

Paperback ISBN 978-1-83703-797-1

Large Print ISBN 978-1-83703-796-4

Hardback ISBN 978-1-83703-795-7

Trade Paperback ISBN 978-1-80656-017-2

Ebook ISBN 978-1-83703-798-8

Kindle ISBN 978-1-83703-799-5

Audio CD ISBN 978-1-83703-790-2

MP3 CD ISBN 978-1-83703-791-9

Digital audio download ISBN 978-1-83703-793-3

This book is printed on certified sustainable paper. Boldwood Books is dedicated to putting sustainability at the heart of our business. For more information please visit https://www.boldwoodbooks.com/about-us/sustainability/

Boldwood Books Ltd, 23 Bowerdean Street, London, SW6 3TN

www.boldwoodbooks.com

1

The small Mexican city of San Yetaxa was famous for many things. Mostly bad.

However, what made it most memorable were the rolling hills cradling it. Rodrigo Vargas had lived there his entire life, and he appreciated the hills' beauty like everyone else. What he enjoyed more, though, were the roads carved upon it.

As he steered his car through the twisting corners, he glanced over at the growing stack of folders which lay on the passenger seat. Every day he went to work, he vowed to halve the pile, yet somehow it only grew larger.

He chuckled and turned up the incline of a sharp hairpin. It was one of the key features of the infamous path known as the Camino Sin Vuelta Astras, or "The Road of No Coming Back". He drove it every day between home and work, and as somewhat of a motoring enthusiast, he enjoyed the challenges it presented.

Two cars rapidly approached from behind. Vargas slowed and hugged the right-hand side of the road as best he could, allowing the two black Mercedes-Benz sedans to pass by on the narrow straight. The speed demons took the opportunity and disappeared from sight at the next bend. Vargas shook his head. While he was no shrinking violet, he was far from an idiot.

His cell phone buzzed from the dock affixed to his dashboard and he checked the caller ID. It was Karina. With a smile, he swiped the small screen to accept the call.

"Hey, baby."

"You're late," she said, her tone cheerful but laced with frustration.

Vargas noted the time. He was running two hours behind schedule. "I'm sorry. I got caught up. You know how it is."

"Your dinner's gone cold."

It was the same way their conversation had gone every night since he had started working for Gilberto Sanchez. "It couldn't be helped. I'll make it up to you tomorrow, okay?"

Radio silence permeated from the end of the line. Karina was no fool. She knew it was a promise he could not keep. "Your daughter's about to go to bed. I thought you'd like to say goodnight."

"Of course. Hello, Lilia, it's Daddy. Can you hear me?"

"Hi, Daddy!" his five-year-old squealed.

Vargas smiled at the infectiousness of her tone. "Did you have a good day?"

"I did."

"What did you get up to?"

"Just things."

"Things, eh? Sounds like fun."

"It was."

"Listen, Lilia, I'm going to be late, but—"

"Again!"

"I know." Saying the words broke his heart. "I'm sorry. I promise that once I'm home I'll come in and give you a big cuddle, okay?"

"Okay."

"That's my girl. Can you put Mommy on, please?"

"Okay."

"Goodnight."

There was a clatter through the speaker, along with the sound of a door shutting.

"You there, Karina?" Vargas asked.

"I'm here," she said. "Listen, Rodrigo, I know when we decided that you'd start working for—"

"Hold on a second, baby." Vargas pressed the brakes and slowed at the sight ahead of the Camino Sin Vuelta Astras' main tunnel section. There before him, parked in front, blocking his path, were the two Mercedes-Benz sedans which had passed him earlier. "I'll, uh, call you back shortly. I'm just about to move out of cellular range."

Before Karina could say a word, he swiped the phone and brought his car to a halt. He tried to make eye contact with the sedan drivers, but the tinted windows were almost as black as the cars' paintwork.

Then their doors opened from all sides. Eight men in total stepped out wearing light gray suits, with white shirts and shiny black shoes. Four were holding compact assault rifles, the others pulling back their jackets to reveal sidearms nestled in their holsters.

Vargas's heart sank. He immediately shifted his car into reverse and went to plant his foot. As he craned his neck behind in an attempt to flee, two more vehicles, matching the others, barreled up the hill and stopped to block his path. Their doors flung open, revealing another group of impeccably well-dressed and well-armed men.

One was more distinctive than the others. Tall and wiry. His hair was jet black, slicked, and tied into a ponytail. His face, though young, was covered in dark tattoos down one side. While the rest stood back, he walked toward Vargas's car, coming to a stop at his door. He knocked on the window three times and gestured for him to get out.

Vargas obeyed, wrenching the door open slowly before hopping out. He peered up at the ponytailed man, who was a foot taller than him, his eyes void of any emotion. Without a word, he frisked him, obviously finding no weapons.

"Follow me," he instructed Vargas.

He complied, and they walked to one of the sedans at the rear. His tattooed escort opened the passenger-side door and revealed someone sitting in the back seat.

Unlike the others, the gentleman wore a tan outfit and a Panama hat to match. He tossed his feet from the footwell and stepped out. He was no taller than Vargas, both men dwarfed by the goon standing between them. His leathery face exposed someone not necessarily of age, but a person who enjoyed the sun. His eyes were dark, his stare cruel. Take away the nice suit and he might have passed as some random person on the street. Vargas knew better.

"Alfonso Berrera."

The older man raised an eyebrow. "You know my name?"

"Of course I do. Who hasn't heard of San Yetaxa's most illustrious 'businessman'?"

Berrera smiled, his devilish lips curling at the edges. "Well, I suppose it's a day of coincidences. Because I know your name too, Rodrigo Vargas."

Vargas held his stance, doing his best not to show any fear. "Is that supposed to impress me?"

"Come now, there's no reason for us to get our relationship off on the wrong foot."

"I find it hard to believe you're too concerned about that."

Vargas gestured to the cars which surrounded him and the men who could shoot him at any second. "I know what this is about. My boss has the ability to complicate matters for you. Because of that you need to make a statement. So you've come here to kill me."

"You think of me as barbaric. I'm not going to kill you. Quite the opposite, in fact. I'm willing to give you a chance to live."

"I don't understand."

"Come with me." Berrera ushered him away from the vehicles to the edge of the road. "Have a look down there. It's a long way, isn't it?"

Vargas glanced past their position, his gaze settling on the steep embankment that separated them from the city of San Yetaxa. His gut churned at what was being suggested.

"One hundred and thirty-one people die on average driving the Camino Sin Vuelta Astras every year," Berrera continued. "Do you know how many survive?"

"I have a feeling you're about to tell me."

"Three. Three out of one-hundred and thirty-one. A survival rate of 2.3 percent. That is the opportunity I'm giving you, Mr. Vargas."

Vargas scoffed. "You want me to drive off the edge?"

"I told you I'd give you a chance to live. Here it is." Berrera pulled a phone from his pocket and dialed a number. "And just to show you I'm serious..."

He activated the speaker function.

"Hello?" came the confused voice on the other end of the line.

It was Karina.

Berrera ended the call.

"You son of a bitch!" Vargas went to lash out, but the tall, tattooed thug put a hand on his shoulder, his grasp stopping him.

Berrera pocketed the phone and placed his hands behind his back. "I'd advise you to get in your car, Mr. Vargas."

Vargas studied the man, searching through the cruelty. There was no pleasure in his eyes, no hint of sadism. To him, it was business—San Yetaxa style. "How do I know you won't kill my family?"

"I told you, I'm not a barbarian."

Vargas's hands balled into fists. What choice did he have?

The tall goon remained clasped to him and turned him toward his car, slowly marching him to the driver's side. Before tossing him in, he grabbed Vargas's cell phone from the dock and crushed it under his boot. With one final thrust, he threw Vargas into his seat and slammed the door behind him.

All of Berrera's men stood back and allowed Vargas a path. He put on his belt and turned the key, the engine sputtering to life. He shifted the car into drive and moved across to the other side of the road. Through the windshield, Vargas found Berrera standing with his Panama hat in hand, his stare boring into his own.

Vargas closed his eyes and steadied his trembling hands on the steering wheel. When he opened them, the view of San Yetaxa greeted him—a city on the edge of fate, just like he was. Two-point-three percent. Not impossible odds.

He exhaled, forcing his foot onto the gas, his leg a quivering mess of nerves. With a firm press, he guided the car to the embankment of the road, the tires gripping to the tarmac beneath him.

Then the world fell silent, the noise swallowed by the rush of gravity. His vision blurred, the ground below rushing up to greet him. As he plunged, tears ran down his cheeks, and the images of Karina and Lilia appeared in his mind.

If this was the end, at least he would meet it with them in his thoughts, carrying their love to wherever or whatever came next.

2

Dane Winter rode down the endless stretch of road on his motorbike, the wind hissing past him in warm gusts. It was hot, but the occasional breeze carried just enough to make it bearable. Occasionally, the weather reminded him of his childhood in Hawaii. In Nevada, though, there was no ocean or Mauna Kea creating a spectacular backdrop. Instead, the ragged peaks of the Ruby Mountains rose in the distance, a sure sign he was closing in on the Camp Redwind Training Facility.

He slowed and pulled into the main entrance of the huge plot, flashing his ID to the security staff, who in turn lifted the boom gate. He gave the motorbike some throttle and rode further into the heart of the complex, down the path that split a series of structures. One might have mistaken it for an old army base, the buildings on either side housing barracks, an administration hub, an infirmary, and various training compounds. But Redwind Security was not the army. At least not in the traditional sense.

Colonel Dawson had gathered a well-trained group of men and women, mostly former soldiers, ready for deployment anywhere in the world at a moment's notice. They were qualified to implement rescue operations, perform protection details, conduct investigations, and many other such functions. Winter was proud to consider himself as one of the team.

He moved past the population center of the facility and skidded up a dusty incline by the sniper-rifle range. He took the bend at the top and arrived at what appeared to be little more than a large shed. Bringing the bike to a halt, he tossed his leg over the side and brought his foot down on the kickstand to prevent it from falling.

Winter removed his helmet and walked over to the shed, opening the door and entering. The pistol range was much cooler on the inside, the AC working overtime to keep those training within it cool from the elements. Laid out before him were twenty shooting lanes. At one end stood the shooters, and at the other, their targets. A dozen of his colleagues were taking the opportunity to hone their skills, the smell of burned gunpowder filling the air.

He grabbed a set of earmuffs and safety glasses and placed them on, walking by the rear of the shooters, who were deep in concentration, unloading their guns. Along the way he gave mock-salutes to those he knew and continued on until he reached the far end of the range where four familiar souls stood. All were typically locked in serious competition, one standing at the line and firing her Glock into the target.

Middleton was the tallest, slender, and covered with tattoos. Every time Winter saw her, it seemed she had added a new one to the collection. Her dark hair cascaded down to her shoulder blades, the black coloring a reminder of her youth when she dabbled as a goth. Her shooting was impeccable. Each round she fired either hit the middle of the silhouette or just missed off-center.

Middleton shot her last bullet and turned to the others, removing her earmuffs in victory. "That's what I'm talking about!"

Lynch pressed a button on the panel to the side, bringing her target back their way via the motorized pulley in the ceiling. Winter's large, bearded colleague handed it off to Sidhu, who tallied up the hits, comparing it to the others who had already competed.

"Well, look what the cat dragged in." Watts, the youngest and shortest of the group, turned to Winter, removing his earmuffs. "I thought you were on vacation."

"So did I." Winter shrugged, joining the others in taking off their earmuffs. "The colonel called me back."

"Any idea why?" Lynch asked.

"Couldn't tell you."

"He'll have a job for you," Middleton said.

Winter nodded. She was likely right. It was not Dawson's style to cut short someone's vacation unless he had a very good reason.

Middleton shifted her attention to Sidhu. "Well, did I win or what?"

The softly spoken man turned and nodded. "You pipped Lynchy by three points."

She gave Lynch a playful nudge. "Suck it!"

Lynch rolled his eyes while everyone else had a chuckle. As the banter rippled through the group, Winter tiptoed over the spent shells and took one of the Glocks sitting on the shelf next to the silhouette targets. He found a full magazine and loaded it into the sidearm.

"Put up another one." Winter placed on his earmuffs and turned to the others. Sidhu grabbed a fresh silhouette target and clipped it to the pulley, sending it down to the other end of the shooting lane.

Winter stood at the line, his feet shoulder-width apart in his preferred Weaver stance. He did a mental note of the distance to his target and drew a breath, gripping the gun just enough to remain in control.

Then he squeezed the trigger.

Round after round pelted into the paper target. Before he realized it, he had spent the entire magazine.

Lynch thumbed the panel, and the silhouette returned. Everyone removed their earmuffs, and Middleton's glee transformed into a scowl. She knew it. Winter knew it. Everyone knew it. Sidhu refrained from doing the math. He simply unclipped the target and tossed it on the pile.

"You know, I much preferred it when you were on vacation," Middleton said.

The group of four laughed. Winter had been gone a week, but it was as if he had never left. Suddenly, Watts tapped him on the shoulder and nodded toward the door of the firing range.

"Don't look now, here comes Mr. Bean," he said.

The happiness in the air vanished and Eric Bridges approached. He was even shorter than Watts, the scrawny man somewhere in his fifties, his hair jet-black from a horrible dye job. Bean was his nickname. Not that he knew it.

Yes, he held a passing resemblance to one of Rowan Atkinson's most beloved characters. Yes, he could come across as a bumbling fool at times. But the name was more due to the fact he was Redwind's new financial officer—the bean counter. Unlike most of Dawson's employees, Bridges was not ex-military.

The job itself had been a revolving door of men and women for the years Winter had been at Redwind. Winter could not say whether they disliked working for Dawson or simply hated the Nevada heat. He preferred to leave such questions to those with paygrades higher than his.

Bridges stopped before the group and pulled an earmuff from his ear. "Welcome back, Mr. Winter."

"Thanks, Bridges," he said.

"The colonel has been informed of your arrival and wishes to see you."

"Fair enough." Winter laid the gun in Middleton's hand and gave her a wry smile.

"You owe me a rematch," she declared.

"You know where to find me."

Winter stood in Bridges' office, unsure why he had been ushered into the smaller confines. Unlike the colonel's workspace, the room felt stuffy. There were no personal touches. There were not any family photos, no snapshots from reunions with old comrades, and none of Dawson's antique muskets which had been passed down through the generations.

There was a plain black desk, an ergonomic chair, and a double-screen computer setup. Bridges had been here three months, but it gave the impression he was yet to move in.

As Winter waited, he paced the small room. What little he could find seemed to tie in with Bridges' role as Redwind Security's financial officer. Ledgers stacked on the filing cabinet, performance charts plastered to the wall, and a payroll register atop the desk. There was no wonder it felt different to Dawson's office. The space was designed to process numbers, not people.

Winter stopped near the rear window, which had a perfect view of the training ground. He spotted something unusual next to the timber frame. On the wall in the corner, hidden from sight, was a small glass case, and within it, a medal. A Bronze Star. He did a double-take, finding the item out of place compared to the rest of Bridges' office. It was definitely the real deal. He would know. He had one himself.

"Dane!"

Winter jolted at the sound as if he were still a Marine. He turned to find Dawson entering with a file folder under his arm. While not intimidated easily, Winter could not help but be awed by the man. Tall as an oak and just as wide, his former superior officer had a presence about him which had not diminished with time. If it were not for the gray hair, one would think he was still in his forties.

"What gives, Colonel?" he asked. "You don't get the morning sun in this office."

"I got kicked out of mine. They're giving it a new lick of paint." Dawson rounded the desk and took a seat. "Believe me, I don't plan on staying here for long."

At the colonel's invitation, Winter sat down in front of the desk.

"You look good, Dane." Dawson placed his folder down and smiled. "I was going through my old diaries this morning. Have a guess what day this is."

Winter shrugged.

"It's been three years since you started working for me."

Winter raised his eyebrows. "Has it been that long?"

"Apparently so."

"Time flies, doesn't it?"

"You know I had reservations when you started here? I thought perhaps you were beyond saving. Wasn't sure if you were going to work through your... issues. I'm proud of how far you've come."

Winter cleared his throat, preferring not to dwell on darker times. "I assume you didn't call off my vacation because you wanted to celebrate?"

"No." Dawson shook his head. "I'm sorry about that. A job got tossed on my lap at the last minute. One I'd like you to take point on."

"Where am I going?"

"Mexico. San Yetaxa, to be more precise. It's located in one of the smaller Mexican states, Tlapetla."

"San Yetaxa? Cartel country?"

"The region is known for being somewhat of a funnel for the cartel to ship drugs from the south to the north. The DEA has suspicions there may even be a full-blown meth production site somewhere there." Dawson opened his file folder and revealed a color photo of a man waving to a crowd in a sharp black suit, his hair dark but thinning.

"This is Gilberto Sanchez. He's making a run for the governorship of Tlapetla. He, along with his rival, are both promising to clean up their state and kick the cartel out."

Winter chuckled. "That mustn't be winning them any friends."

"It's a popular stance with the people, but not so much with the cartel." Dawson revealed another image, this time of a smashed SUV and a corpse being dragged from the wreck. "This was Sanchez's campaign manager, Rodrigo Vargas. Three days ago, he died on his way home from work. He drove his car over an embankment. Coroner said he was dead on impact."

"An accident or the cartel?"

"I don't think there are many coincidences in San Yetaxa." Dawson leaned back in his chair. "Gilberto Sanchez has requested our services. He's putting on a posh fundraiser for his campaign tomorrow night at his house. Wealthy businesspeople, local sports stars, and TV celebrities from all over Tlapetla will be there."

"And he wants security?"

"Vargas's death has spooked him. He's worried the local cartel might make a move."

Winter crossed his arms. "What's wrong with the city's law enforcement?"

"Sanchez doesn't trust them."

"Corrupt?"

"He has his reservations." Dawson stood from his chair and walked to the window, pulling down the blind as a team in training ran by, hauling assault rifles. "Before you arrived, I was on the phone to the DEA office in Mexico City. The current climate in San Yetaxa is tricky, to say the least. It's believed the cartel activities down there are overseen by a man known as Alfonso Berrera. They've never managed to pin anything on him, but the suspicions are strong. However, it's also suspected that Berrera might only be a front, and that there's a bigger player behind the scenes."

"Any proof?"

"Not exactly. In some of the scant surveillance the DEA has been able to get away with, a name constantly comes up—El Maestro."

"The Master?" Winter smiled. "Sounds like a person with an ego."

Dawson returned to his chair and sat down. "Suffice to say Sanchez trusts no one. For all he knows, El Maestro has every officer in the San Yetaxa police department on his books. Hell, El Maestro could even be the police chief himself. That's why he wants someone from the outside to oversee his fundraiser. Redwind has a small contingent of local security that you'll take command of."

"Have you got a blueprint of Sanchez's house?"

Dawson reached into the file and pulled out a floor plan.

Winter looked over the immense size of the estate. "Not a bad little pad he's got here. I'm going to need more than local security to keep this place locked down."

"I thought you might. The usual suspects?"

Winter placed the document in front of him. "That is, unless you've got them heading out on other jobs."

"They're yours."

"I'll need some firepower and cars."

"Put a list together and have it to me within the hour."

Winter stood. "And your plane. Don't think I'm going down there in economy class."

Dawson closed his folder. "I'll make sure it's fueled."

"Good." Winter walked toward the exit and stopped just as Dawson was booting up his computer. "Oh, and Colonel?"

"Yes?"

"I hope you know you owe me."

"Don't I always." Dawson averted his eyes from Winter, forcing down the smirk curling on his lips. "Get the hell out of here, Dane."

4

The photo was creased, folded and unfolded so many times the lines had become part of the image. Though it was worn and faded, he could still make out the shape of her face and the curve of her smile. Her green eyes. Her hair as bright as fire.

Captain Dane Winter remembered the day the photograph had been taken. He and Sara had just returned from Coney Island. Only hours before he'd had to ship back out to the sandbox.

One more mission, I swear...

"Thirty seconds!" rang out the voice of the pilot over the comms.

Winter placed the photo in his pocket, securing the flap so that it stayed close to his chest.

The chopper banked hard toward the Taktur Mountains, hovering low over the sand, kicking up the grit in the darkness of the early morning. Winter wasted no time, jumping from the cabin and hitting the ground running. His team of Raiders trailed behind, the fourteen men vanishing with him into the shadows of the surrounding rock formations.

Prior to the drop, recon drones had tracked the movement of ten to fifteen targets inside the cave ahead. If the intel fed to them was accurate, it housed the leader of a regional ISIS cell, which had become a serious thorn for local and American forces over the past months. Their mission was straightforward: flush out the enemy and come home in one piece.

They broke into groups of two, moving fast and low, hugging the canyon until they reached the cave mouth. Winter froze, spotting a flash of something in his night vision goggles.

A sentry.

The enemy had repositioned the machine gun that they were expecting on the other ridge.

He raised a fist to bring both teams to a grinding halt.

A roar shattered the silence as the scream of the old Soviet PKM echoed around them, the weapon spraying gunfire on the team of Marines below.

"Contact left!" Winter yelled out.

The gunfire tore into rock and sand, stirring up a storm. Everyone in its path scrambled for cover. On the other side of the narrow canyon, a wail burst from one of his men.

"Collins is hit!" a nearby operator shouted.

Winter cursed under his breath. He turned to the others behind him, signaling them to draw fire away from the second team. Peering across the terrain, he mapped their exact location in his mind. With another motion, he ordered his gunnery sergeant to his side.

"I'm going up there," he said to Cooke. "When I get close, unleash hell."

Cooke nodded and took up a position with two others, ready to let fly when the time came. Winter scaled the incline to high right and surged toward the machine-gun and the ISIS fighter squeezing the trigger.

So far, Winter had not been spotted. But he knew that would not last.

He broke into a sprint, bursting across the ridge under the cover of the long shadows provided, his HK416 locked and loaded.

Then his target saw him.

Right on cue, his gunnery sergeant's suppressing fire hammered the machine-gunner's position, forcing him back from his PKM on the rock's edge. Winter took the window of opportunity and fired his weapon. The muzzle lit up the night, the bullets slashing his target's chest.

The impact threw the enemy combatant backward, his body slamming into the exterior cave wall. Just as Winter turned, another figure emerged from the shadows, as if appearing out of thin air.

He swept an old AK toward Winter. Before he could pull the trigger, Winter batted it from his grasp with his own weapon. The ISIS fighter recovered quickly, taking hold of Winter's Heckler and Koch, the two men struggling over it, getting caught in a duel of strength. His opponent did enough to wrench it from his grip, sending it scattering to the ground.

Winter shoved him backward, and the pair slammed into the rock. They struggled until finally his enemy got the upper hand as Winter clipped a crevice under his boots. The ISIS fighter reached for his belt, where grenades and a combat knife hung. His fingers wrapped around the blade and he unsheathed it, lunging at Winter.

Winter ducked as it slashed over his head, the knife scraping the cave wall. Another thrust followed, the arc too wide and too slow. Winter seized the opening and grabbed him by the wrist, clamping down his fingers like a vise until the blade broke free. He removed it, flicked it in the opposite direction, and drove it into the man's chest.

No scream. Not even a whimper.

His body sagged, but Winter held on, keeping him upright.

A burst of Arabic echoed from the hidden cave entrance behind him, where the ambush had begun. Two more enemy combatants emerged, their eyes locking onto the rock ledge. For a split-second, they stared at Winter, fully exposed and ripe for the kill.

Their rifles swept his way, and they moved their fingers over the triggers. Winter glanced at the body next to him, still holding the man up with the handle of the knife. He shot a hand to the man's belt and yanked a grenade free.

He let go of the blade and pulled the pin, hurling the grenade at the two fighters. As if in slow motion, it spun through the air. The fighter's eyes widened in terror and they attempted to scramble for cover.

It was too late.

The grenade fell at their feet and detonated, the blast tearing them apart. Shrapnel shredded flesh and bone, what remained of them slumping to a crumpled heap.

Winter retrieved his fallen rifle, while his gunnery sergeant and four other operators appeared up the incline.

"Sir," Cooke said. "We've taken out two more targets in the canyon. We've got a clear path forward."

"How's Collins?"

"He didn't make it." Cooke shook his head. "We lost Sergeant Hicks too."

Winter gritted his teeth, the pain of the loss running deep. It was as if a piece of him had died, too.

"What are our orders, sir?"

Winter steadied his grip on his rifle. "We complete the mission."

* * *

Winter rarely got to travel in the company aircraft. It all came down to the job, where it was, and what was required. Since Gilberto Sanchez's request had come at short notice with little opportunity to plan, it made sense to expedite the trip to Mexico in Dawson's Gulfstream. After putting his crew together, and ensuring the colonel could supply them with their needs, it was wheels up the next morning.

Arrival time at the tiny San Yetaxa Airport was marked before midday. There they would gather their supplies and make their way to Sanchez's house to get a better look at the security required so that his fundraiser would go off without a hitch.

Winter had been a part of many such operations with Redwind. Most went as planned. Some were more difficult. What he had learned in his years was not to expect the unexpected, but to anticipate all likelihoods. He had studied up on Sanchez and the situation in San Yetaxa back at Camp Redwind. The man's promises to wipe the cartel off the map had created a powder keg in Tlapetla. It would take a mere spark for it to blow.

Winter, from his previous times working in Mexico, knew the cartel's capacity for extreme brutality firsthand. Luckily, he had always kept his head. This trip would be no different.

"How long until we reach San Yetaxa?" he asked the pilots, resting a hand on one of their shoulders.

"We'll touch down in a little over two hours," came the reply.

Winter peered out at the view before him. There was barely a cloud in the sky, the blue matching the azure shores of the Mexican coastline. It reminded him of the southern Californian beach he'd been sitting on before he'd got the call from Dawson to report back to Camp Redwind. A glutton for punishment, he was.

"At least the colonel pays well," he muttered.

The pilot turned. "Sir?"

"Sorry, I was just talking to myself." Winter left them to their work and returned to the cabin.

The scene before him was exactly what he expected whenever he traveled with the four he had handpicked for the job. The lavish interior had been transformed into the set from an early

2000s teen movie, the Bluetooth speaker on one of the tables blasting System of a Down.

Lynch sat in the plush chair in the back corner, his hands clasped around his phone, no doubt attempting to figure out his fantasy football lineup for the coming weekend. Opposite him, Watts was also on his cell, likely looking to buy another old car to put in his shed.

Middleton was seated closest to the pilots' door, one leg hitched over the other, reading a book by some philosopher who Winter had never heard of. The novel itself appeared more like a doorstop than a piece of literature. Beside her in the reclined seat lay Sidhu, with noise-canceling earplugs screwed into each ear. The most sensible of the group was already asleep, banking a few extra hours of rest before their arrival.

With a soft tap on his arm, he woke Sidhu, then proceeded to the Bluetooth speaker, switching it off, and plunging the cabin into silence. The eyeballs of the others gawked at him.

"Okay, the party's over," he said. "We've got some work to go over before we land."

Though the group could be loud and unruly, they understood when to rein it in. After all, at some point in their lives, they had all been soldiers. Lynch and Watts were ex-Army. Middleton was one of the first women to have graduated from Ranger School in the mid-2000s. And Sidhu, before he had come to America, served in the Sikh Regiment back home in India. His stories of stints serving on the Kashmir border in the cold were enough to curl one's toes.

Lynch and Watts pocketed their phones, Middleton stowed her book, and Sidhu put his seat in the upright position, getting rid of his earplugs. Winter stood between them and found the remote control to the monitor. With a press of the red button, a screen unfolded from the ceiling, giving everyone a clear view.

"We'll be landing in two hours. Once we've got our supplies and had some grub, we're going to head out to Gilberto Sanchez's home." Winter tapped the remote control, and the floor plan of the house Dawson had supplied him appeared on the monitor. Whistles of envy sounded from his comrades.

"Looks like someone's got some money," Middleton said.

"One would hope," Lynch added. "They've gotta pay for you somehow, don't they?"

She sneered playfully at him while Sidhu pointed at the screen.

"How many stories?" he asked.

Winter revealed more images. "Two, and a wine cellar in the basement."

"That cellar is almost as big as your place," Lynch told Watts.

"If only mine was filled with that much wine."

Everyone laughed and Winter held his hands up to settle the crowd. "Sanchez's home is surrounded by security fences. There's a gate at the front and one at the back for the staff. Sidhu, you'll be stationed at the rear."

Sidhu nodded.

"Watts, you're at the front gate," Winter continued.

"Why him?" Middleton asked in faux outrage. "Don't you want someone with a little personality to greet the guests?"

Winter smiled. "I've got something much better planned for you. You'll be inside with Lynch mingling with said guests."

Watts's jaw dropped. "Does that mean she'll have to wear a dress?"

"Hey! Hey! I can wear dresses." She clicked her fingers at him. "You just wait and see. I'll knock your socks off."

The cabin erupted with laughter. As it subsided, Winter returned his focus to the floor plan. "The colonel is providing us with twelve locals from the Mexican branch of Redwind. Once I do a physical inspection at Sanchez's house, I'll divvy them among us accordingly."

Lynch raised his hand as if he were an elementary school kid. "Uh, can we trust these guys?"

"They're Redwind employees, so I hope so. But if you find they look at you the wrong way, feel free to shoot them."

Lynch chuckled. "Roger that."

"Now, the event's kicking off at 1700. From the information I've received, it's likely to go until at least midnight."

"How many guests are we expecting?" Sidhu asked.

"There are over two hundred invitees. It'll be busy, and even though Sanchez has a nice big house, with the large number of people there, it's going to be tight."

"What's your gut say?" It was Middleton's turn to speak, the humor in her tone gone. "What's the likelihood we might have to deal with some heavies from the cartel?"

Winter took pause and pressed the remote, the screen sliding into the ceiling behind him. "Like any job we do, there are risks. Gilberto Sanchez obviously has his concerns. That's why he hired us. Let's just keep our eyes and ears open, okay? By tomorrow morning, I plan to be back on this plane bound for home. In and out in under twenty-four hours."

A hush fell over the cabin, everyone's gaze finding one another. Winter pushed his thumb into the Bluetooth speakers and resumed the music. Now was not the time to dwell on the ifs, buts, and maybes. It was time to prepare in the only way the group knew how.

5

The airstair door unfolded and settled onto the tarmac. Middleton stepped down first, followed by Watts, Lynch, and Sidhu. Winter hung back to give the pilots his thanks and joined his colleagues at the bottom.

The sun blazed overhead, the heat heavier than the desert air of Nevada. Winter removed his Ray-Ban Wayfarers from his top pocket and placed them on to shield his eyes. The others did the same. They walked into the building and moved through customs, the process an easy one with no queues.

Beyond the gates, the terminal unfurled before them. Winter tried to remember a smaller airport in his travels. He had been through countless over the years, including a tiny one in Montana he once thought could not be topped. San Yetaxa's, however, might have just claimed the title.

The foot traffic was light, only a handful of passengers wandering about, vastly outnumbering the idle staff. And then there were the dining options. Only a single outlet appeared open —a coffee shop with an all-day breakfast menu which looked unappealing to say the least. Winter and the others agreed they would hold off from getting food until they reached town. Coffees, though, could not wait.

With their hot drinks in hand, they walked to the exit and made their way to the undercover parking lot. Amongst the scattered assortment of vehicles sat a pair of new gleaming black Toyota Tundras. One of the doors swung open and a young man, no older than twenty-five, in a gray tank top and green cargo pants appeared, his skin golden from the San Yetaxan sun.

"Dane Winter?"

"That's me." Winter shook his hand. "I assume you're our friendly Redwind rep?"

"I'm Fuentes." He handed over the keys. "As requested, two vehicles loaded with your supplies."

Winter went to the cargo bed and opened the hard cover, revealing the crates of weaponry required for their protection assignment at the fundraiser. "I plan to be at Gilberto Sanchez's house at thirteen hundred hours."

"My people are already on site, getting a lay of the land."

"Good." Winter closed the rear and locked it, glancing over at his colleagues sipping on their coffees. "Where can I get a decent feed in town, Fuentes?"

He considered the question for a moment. "You can't go past Hector's. It's a diner on the corner of Main and Palermo. They do breakfast and lunch. Got everything you could want. They even do gringo food."

Winter chuckled. "Sounds perfect. I'll see you when we arrive at Sanchez's place."

Fuentes walked to a waiting sedan a few parking spots over. Winter gave the signal for the others to hop in their Tundras, tossing Lynch the other set of keys.

"Hey, they didn't leave a baby seat for Watts!" Middleton said, hopping into the passenger side next to Winter with a smirk.

"Shut up, will ya?" Watts glared at her and climbed into the back, strapping himself in.

Winter started the ignition and got underway, leading the other Tundra out of the parking lot and onto the highway. The full glare of the sun greeted them, along with the ruthless heat. Winter pressed a button on his armrest, gliding the window shut as he cranked up the AC.

Desert surrounded them on all sides, the weathered-beaten and pothole-filled road into San Yetaxa a lonely and desolate one. Dust kicked up from the asphalt and swirled around them, covering the windshield in a powdery film. Cars passed them heading in the other direction. Some were more recent models. Most, however, were battered old wrecks in serious need of TLC.

In the distance, a range of rolling hills appeared, and in the foreground the silhouette of high-rise buildings. From afar, it looked almost picturesque, but as they moved closer, more of the city took shape, revealing darker elements. They passed by a sunbaked sign welcoming them to San Yetaxa, the traffic congesting with each mile they drove.

The outskirts appeared to be the roughest area, the urban sprawl of dilapidated homes requiring full restorations, or at the very least some fresh paint. More signs directed them to the center of town through the inner-city suburbs. Winter expected the scene to be a prettier one, but the state of disrepair was just as depressing. Most were old buildings. Others were new structures left unfinished, the weather destroying what little had been built.

Winter weaved his way through the traffic, monitoring the rearview mirror to ensure he did not leave Lynch or Sidhu behind. As they turned the corner at a major intersection, the heart of San Yetaxa became clear. The roads were nicer and the buildings larger. The hardship, though, was still apparent.

Graffiti-littered walls along with faded commercial hoardings.

Most of them were old advertisements for local and American products. Some were political, bursting with color, plastered with the grinning faces of candidates like Gilberto Sanchez vying for the Tlapetla governorship.

Having observed what he had so far, Winter could understand Sanchez's wish to clean up the city. San Yetaxa was obviously a place which had seen great hardship. And like all politicians, they were eager to make their own mark. What Sanchez wanted to do, however, would take a lot of work. He would have a lot of adversaries standing in his way. Could one man really make a difference?

Middleton pointed through the windshield. "There's Main."

Winter took the turn and drove them through the middle of town, where the road cut through an old plaza. Street vendors lined the sidewalk, selling various wares, drinks, and food. The smells mingled as one and filtered through the cabin, creating an aroma that was a little overwhelming to the out-of-towners.

They reached the corner which connected with Palermo Avenue and approached Hector's Diner, finding it exactly where Fuentes had promised it would be. Winter parked the Tundra in the last of two remaining spaces, and Lynch drove in beside him. The team hopped out of the cars and entered.

It was a nice establishment. And busy. So much so, there was only one table left, covered in trays and litter from earlier feeds.

"Don't worry, I'll clean that for you."

They turned to a server hurrying over to them to scoop up the piles of rubbish stacked up. Winter stepped to the opposite side of the table and reached for some of the trash.

"Let me help you with that," he said.

"No, you really don't have to—" She stopped and their gazes locked. The woman had brown eyes, her dark hair knitted in a bun, and her skin radiant.

Winter grinned and looked down at her name badge. "It's no bother, Maria."

She returned the smile. "As long as I don't get in any trouble from my boss."

"I'm sure he won't mind." Winter took half the stack and walked with her to the trashcan in the corner, throwing his garbage in after hers.

"Thanks."

Winter shrugged, and they strolled back to the others, who simply stood watching the interaction, smirks painted across their faces. Maria took a cloth from her belt and wiped down the table, finding some spare menus sitting in a plastic holder at the nearby wall. Everyone pulled out a chair and sat, their stares still plastered on Winter.

"Now, I don't know whether you've been here before." Maria handed them their menus. "By the looks of you, probably not. We have a daily special…"

Winter got lost in her words, the sound of her voice filtering into silence as he watched her speak. By the time she had finished, it took a nudge from Middleton's bony elbow to snap him out of it.

"Sorry, what?" he stammered.

"Would you like a coffee?" Maria asked.

"Uh, yeah. That one from the airport was horrible."

"Okay, I'll come back with your drinks. Then if you're ready to order, we can take care of your food."

Everyone smiled at her and she walked off. Once she was out of sight, the other four turned on Winter once again.

"I know that look," Middleton said.

"I have no idea what you're talking about."

"She's nice."

"So are you. When you want to be."

"You've never looked at me that way, though. I think she liked you."

"She's just working for tips."

"I wouldn't be so sure."

Winter rolled his eyes.

"We're only here for twenty-four hours, remember?" Middleton smoothed out her crinkled menu. "Don't let the chance slip away."

Winter shook his head and picked up his own menu, ignoring the banter. But as he scanned the options, his gaze drifted past the top of the page to Maria, standing at the coffee machine, making their drinks, their eyes once again meeting in the silence.

6

The road leading to Gilberto Sanchez's house took them past many fine homes. Since leaving the main part of the city, Winter had climbed a steady incline into the scenic hills. With each gentle rise, the houses only got larger and more modern. The elegantly designed residences would not have looked out of place gracing the glossy pages of a high-end real estate magazine.

"You're an idiot," Middleton said, sitting in the passenger seat beside him.

Winter shook his head at the remark. "Are you going to keep harping on about this?"

"She was gorgeous."

"I realize that."

"Then why didn't you make a move?"

"At a diner?"

"Why not?"

"Because we've got a job to do. Besides, what would I have said? 'Look, I'm only in San Yetaxa for a day. How about we go have dinner sometime.' Oh, wait, I can't say that, because I'm never coming back here."

"He just knows he couldn't have pulled her," Watts added.

Winter glanced at the back seat. "I could've pulled her."

Watts shrugged. "I don't see any proof of that."

Winter ignored the two babbling on at him. As he steered the black pickup truck through the streets, more of the area's wealth revealed itself, its residents not afraid to flout their money, the luxury European cars in the driveways only confirming the show of affluence.

"I think we're coming up to it." Middleton held her phone aloft with the maps application opened. "Should be around the next corner."

Winter took the turn and entered the crescent. He had not thought it possible to be more impressed than he already was. That was until he saw the front of Gilberto Sanchez's house. Everything else had looked like a slum in comparison.

"Wow..." Watts muttered in the back seat.

"No kidding," Winter said.

Behind the polished gray Bentley Bentayga SUV sitting in the driveway beyond the security gate appeared the home of the man who would be governor of Tlapetla. Its angles were sharp, the walls built of a magnificent light stone. The windows went from floor to ceiling and looked out on an artificial water feature weaving like a creek from the front of the house to the back. As indicated from the floor plan, it was two stories high, but it seemed so much taller, the sheer size of the structure dwarfing everything around it.

Middleton placed her phone in her pocket. "I don't think I'm good enough for this place."

"You're not," came the brisk comment from the back seat. Middleton instantly slapped Watts for the smart-ass remark.

Winter nodded toward the gate creaking open. "Looks like the welcoming committee."

On either side of it waited a guard dressed in black. They gave Winter a wave as they entered, allowing the two Tundras through. Winter parked near the Bentley where Fuentes stood with another of his men. Winter killed the ignition, threw open the door and stepped out into the warmth of the early afternoon.

"Hello, Fuentes."

"Mr. Winter."

Winter turned to find the gate closing behind Lynch and Sidhu on their arrival. "What can you tell me?"

"We're in luck," Fuentes said. "The site's a secure one. We should have no issue keeping everything under control tonight."

"Have you looked at my initial plans?"

Fuentes nodded. "There'll be no problem implementing any of it."

"Good, but I don't want to be complacent. Give me the tour, so I can see the rest of the house."

Fuentes gestured ahead and the team entered through the front door. The lavish beauty of the palatial home hit them the moment they stepped inside, the dazzling display one of affluence and grandeur. High ceilings loomed overhead, adorned with breathtaking chandeliers that guided the way into the grand living area.

The floor-to-ceiling windows produced a view of the artificial creek and the meticulously tended garden. Continuing through the house, Winter noted the furniture. None of it was meant for comfort. Every piece existed as a statement. And even though he was impressed by it all, he could not help but feel the place was stuffy. He wondered how often Sanchez lived here. Was it one of many homes? Did he travel a lot?

He brushed aside the questions and took in the rest of the tour. The remainder of the level contained the kitchen and bedrooms, while upstairs opened out into another living space, which connected to a balcony and a view of the city. The outdoor setting was substantial, with a pool, a large sitting area, and a bar.

A pair of house staff were getting the water clean, while a third stood behind the bar serving a figure before it.

Fuentes ushered Winter and his team toward him. "Come."

The bartender slid across a clear drink, the ice cubes inside it clinking as it went.

Fuentes cleared his throat. "Mr. Sanchez."

The man turned with the glass in hand, the images matching up with the one Dawson had shown Winter during his briefing. He even wore the same black suit, his thin hair slicked back, attempting to mask the encroaching baldness. "You must be Dane Winter."

"Yes, sir."

"I'm Gilberto Sanchez." He extended his hand. "Welcome to San Yetaxa."

"You have a magnificent home."

"Thank you. Many years of hard work has paid off for me."

Winter smiled politely.

"I appreciate you coming, Mr. Winter. I know it had to have been difficult at such short notice."

"Redwind Security aims to please."

"Indeed." Sanchez turned to Fuentes. "Would you mind giving us a moment to speak?"

Fuentes took a step backward, extending both his hands. Winter nodded to his people with a wink, his silent instructions loud and clear. Without hesitation, the others withdrew, leaving him and Sanchez alone.

"Would you like a drink?" Sanchez asked.

Winter stared at the glass and then the bartender. "I don't think that would be appropriate."

"No, I suppose not." Sanchez ushered him to the pool and

they sat down at the table nearest to it. "I want to thank you again for being here. These last few days have been an unhappy affair."

"I was sorry to hear about your campaign manager."

"Vargas won't be an easy man to replace. But it's his family I feel for the most." Sanchez frowned. "He had a wife and a young daughter."

"Have you confirmed it was the cartel?"

"I don't need to. It was them. I've been climbing in the polls for months. My closest rival, Ciro Lugo, and I are now neck and neck. The cartel wanted to make a statement."

"Has Lugo had these problems?"

"Not to my knowledge."

"Even though he holds the same view of the cartel as you?"

"Lugo's a career politician. I'm a man who built an empire in retail." Sanchez threw up his hands. "Perhaps they see me as a target because they're aware I'll do what I say, while Lugo's just another in a long line of empty suits. I don't know for sure."

"What do you plan to do when and if you get elected?"

"Whatever it takes, Mr. Winter. Men like Alfonso Berrera have no place in San Yetaxa. And the people here deserve better."

"That might be difficult. By your own account, you won't have the support of the local police."

"Support comes from money. I'm someone who knows its value. I can create it and make it disappear in the blink of an eye. Once it stops flowing through San Yetaxa, I'll cut the cartel off at their knees in Tlapetla. Those who once gave them their allegiance will no longer get paid. They'll have nowhere else to turn."

Winter nodded. "So you chase Berrera out of town. What about El Maestro?"

Sanchez paused. "I see you've been studying up."

"I like to know what I'm getting myself into."

"Very wise." Sanchez sipped his drink and nestled it back on the table. "El Maestro is a coward. He remains in the shadows allowing those around him to do his dirty work. I don't deny that it won't be difficult, Mr. Winter. But if I have my way, Alfonso Berrera, the police force, they'll be just the first dominoes. My plan is to draw El Maestro into the light. Once I've done that, then I can finally stop the cartel once and for all."

7

Winter emerged from one of the many lavish bathrooms in Sanchez's estate, dressed in his tailored black tuxedo. While not unaccustomed to wearing such formal wear, it was never his preference. He found suits constraining. And if at any point he needed to draw his firearm during the evening, he would have preferred to do so unshackled.

"Damn, you look almost as good as me."

Winter turned to find Lynch walking from a bedroom on the other side of the hall. He wore a near identical tuxedo, though because of the snugger fit, it was much easier to spot the shoulder holster underneath.

Winter went over to him and adjusted the jacket, fixing his collar. "Shouldn't you know how to dress yourself by now?"

Lynch chortled, and the pair walked out of the hallway into the large living area on the first story. House staff prepared the space which was to act as one of the main areas for guests to mingle. Some did last-minute cleaning, others lugged in chairs, while the rest rigged up the sound system.

"This is gonna be a hell of a shindig," Lynch said.

Winter strolled to the center of the room. "I want you to take charge here tonight. I'll give you three of the local security staff." He pointed to the top of the stairs. "Post two up there. You and one other are to patrol the floor."

"What if we have some guests who decide to get rowdy?"

"With the amount of booze up for grabs, I expect to have a few bad eggs. With that said, Sanchez has invited them here so that they'll give him their money. Just keep a close eye on anyone that steps over the edge." Winter tapped his ear. "If you end up with a major problem, I'll be a call away."

"Roger that."

"Think of yourself as lucky. At least I haven't put you on pool party duty."

"Where is Middleton, anyway?" Lynch asked.

Winter shrugged. "Not sure."

"Did someone say my name?"

Both men turned toward the staircase as Middleton descended.

"Fret not boys, the queen is here!" She wore a deep midnight-blue evening gown, its stylish cut exposing her neckline and arms, revealing the sum of the tattoos running down her alabaster skin. Her hair, usually long and wavy, had been straight-ened into a more graceful arrangement, the style exuding sophis-tication suited for such an occasion. It was an uncharacteristic look, but striking nonetheless.

"Lynch, close your mouth," Winter said. "You're drooling."

"You first," he shot back.

Middleton reached the end of the stairs and glided toward them. "Well, what do you think?"

Winter and Lynch glanced at one another, both mumbling incoherently, until finally Lynch pieced something together.

"You scrub up good as a lady."

She slapped him across the arm and jabbed her finger into Winter's chest. "I hope you know the sacrifices I'm making for this little job of yours."

"Why? I think you look lovely, Middleton."

"All the nice words in the world won't get you out of this."

Winter chuckled. "Are you all set up on the balcony?"

She nodded, her demeanor becoming more serious. "I've already talked to the local security. We'll have everything locked down up there."

"Good. I better go see how Watts is faring. I'll leave you two to prepare." Winter walked across the living area and back out to the entrance of the house. Sanchez's Bentley had been moved into the garage, while the black Tundras had been placed to the side of the driveway, allowing a space for the guests to enter the property.

Watts stood about fifteen feet from the door with Fuentes, where they had set up a walk-through metal detector. One of the items Winter had requested for the event.

"How are we looking?" Winter asked.

"We're just going through the guest list now," Watts said, tapping his clipboard. "Also, got the metal detector hooked up and running. Not that Sanchez was too pleased."

"Oh?"

"Mr. Sanchez would have preferred that we spare his guests the inconvenience," Fuentes informed Winter.

"I hope you told him it was a non-negotiable—"

"He understands. I smoothed everything over. There won't be any issues."

"Thanks, Fuentes."

He nodded. "If you'll excuse me, sir?"

"Of course."

Fuentes walked inside the house and Winter turned to Watts, whose expression portrayed concern.

"Okay, spit it out."

Watts frowned, placing the clipboard under his arm. "I wouldn't mind a few M4 carbines, if you get my drift."

Winter stared up at the two local security guards stationed on each side of the driveway at their elevated positions, both holding Remington 870 Police Magnums by their sides. "You know how it is, pistols and shotguns only. We're lucky to be carrying those. If it weren't for Redwind's agreement with the Mexican government, we might be here with little more than baseball bats."

"I'm just saying if things get hot—"

"I know."

Watts nodded. "Well, I should get ready. Still gotta throw on my suit and tie. Good thing there was a kid's section at the shop."

Winter laughed at Watts's self-deprecating humor and walked around the side of the estate via the artificial creek and the surrounding garden. At the back of the property was Sidhu. The rear gate was open, and a small SUV was making its way through. Sidhu checked the driver's credentials and got them to hop out of the vehicle to do a metal detection check. A pair from Redwind's Mexican contingent did a thorough bomb exam of their car, which appeared to pass with flying colors. Sidhu allowed them to park and head into the house.

"How's it looking, Sidhu?"

He glanced at Winter on approach, ticking off a box on his clipboard. "We've got a few more staff to arrive and another catering truck. Once they're taken care of, we'll be able to lock down the gate for the evening."

"Very good. Any issues?"

"None. There is, however, someone who arrived about ten minutes ago I think you should be aware of."

Sidhu invited him to take the clipboard. He grasped it and checked the bottom of the list.

"Maria? Maria from the diner?"

Sidhu nodded, taking back the clipboard. "Maria Pineda."

"Isn't that interesting?" Winter did his best to play down his happiness. "Small world, huh?"

"Small world."

"Where, uh, would one find her? If, uh, they should want to—"

"The kitchen. She's a caterer."

"Hmm. Well, if I pass by there, maybe I'll say hello."

"Of course."

Winter slapped him on the shoulder. "Keep up the good work."

He left Sidhu as another vehicle approached the rear gate. Winter walked inside through the back door of the house and weaved around the ever-growing swell of house staff preparing the estate for the arrival of the first guests.

He took a slight detour to the kitchen to find the workforce in the vast galley getting the catering efforts underway. There among them stood Maria. The mellow-yellow diner uniform from Hector's was gone, replaced by a crisp black top and skirt accented with a neatly tied white apron.

Winter leaned his arm on the empty servery and peered inside. Maria glanced up from the kitchen counter, her eyebrows arching upward. She put some cling wrap over the tray in front of her and placed it in the industrial-sized refrigerator.

"Are you following me?" she asked.

"Not at all. I had no idea you worked anywhere but Hector's."

"A girl can't say no to extra cash on the side."

"I understand. It's good to see you."

She walked closer to him. "And what are you doing here, exactly?"

"Well—"

"Let me guess: you're protecting Mr. Sanchez?"

"How'd you know?"

"A group of Americans roll into town" —she lifted his jacket ever so slightly to reveal his shoulder holster— "loaded with guns. Kind of obvious, isn't it?"

"Guilty as charged." Winter grinned. "A boy can't say no to extra cash on the side."

"Please don't keep Mr. Sanchez waiting on my account." She smiled, the curl of her lips accentuating the sharp lines of her face. "Besides, I've got work to do too."

Winter put up both his hands in surrender and stepped backward. "It's good to see you."

"I think you already said that."

He tapped his fingers on the servery. "By the way, my name's Dane. Dane Winter."

She smiled, her radiant eyes seeming to brighten the entire kitchen. As he walked away, leaving her to her job, his insides fluttered. It was a familiar sensation, but one he had not felt for a very long time.

8

The guests began arriving at seventeen-hundred hours as scheduled. What started as a trickle, just a handful of visitors entering the gates of Gilberto Sanchez's estate, soon surged into a flood. Within minutes, the growing throng at the entrance filled the driveway, overwhelming Watts and his team.

Winter redeployed three more of the Mexican Redwind guards from inside to assist with the formalities. They, along with Fuentes, managed to herd the crowd into some semblance of control, while Winter helped Watts at the walk-through metal detector. Luckily for everyone involved, the people understood the constraints of such a party and followed the instructions asked of them.

Before long, the attendees were inside. Winter walked the length of the driveway and exited the gate to take in a view of the surrounding street. While some guests were chauffeured to the event, many drove themselves, the road now resembling a fancy car show. Every luxury brand imaginable was on display. Aston Martins and Bentleys. Lamborghinis and Ferraris. BMWs and

Mercedes. Each gleamed under the setting sun like trophies. Sanchez's invitees were not just wealthy, they were power players.

Winter returned to the house. "Have we got everyone?"

Watts checked his clipboard. "A few guests are running late, but we'll accommodate them as they arrive."

"Good."

Watts gestured to the guards to take their stations on the top side of the driveway and close the gate. "Any chance you could get me a coffee? I hear they make them here like they do at Hector's."

Winter frowned, the news of Maria's appearance at the party now widely known. "I'll see what I can do."

Watts laughed and resumed his post, noticing the shimmering of headlights heading their way. Winter left him to his work and entered the house. Inside, the murmur of voices had swelled into a cacophony alongside the classical music playing over the speakers.

He shuffled through clusters of stylishly dressed guests, their suits and gowns as dazzling as their cars. As he went by them, he took in their faces. None were familiar to him, their lives and influence exclusive to the Tlapetla region. One individual, however, stood out.

Maria.

She, along with her colleagues, flowed through the crowd with a practiced ease, offering the attendees the first trays of hors d'oeuvres and champagne.

Winter peeled his stare away from her and walked halfway up the steps where Lynch had positioned himself. The man had his hands behind his back, his eyes darting throughout the living area. "Quite the crowd."

Lynch nodded. "Looks like an even spread of people between here and the balcony."

"Everybody behaving themselves?"

"For the moment."

Winter lifted his sleeve to his mouth. "Zone leader to Zone Three."

"Receiving," came the response from Middleton in his earpiece.

"Everything under control up there?"

"So far, so good."

"Have you got eyes on Sanchez?"

"Affirmative."

"And his bodyguards?"

"On him like white on rice."

"Thanks, Middleton."

"Zone leader to Zone Four."

"Receiving." Sidhu's voice crackled across the line.

"All quiet on the Western Front?"

"Affirmative. The rear gate's locked down. No further staff expected to arrive."

"Thank you, Sidhu."

"Relaxed yet?" Lynch asked.

Winter placed his arm by his side. "I won't be relaxed until we're back in the air."

"You want to leave?" Lynch continued staring out into the crowd, their conversation not impeding his job. "So soon?"

Winter followed his gaze to Maria, who offered a pair of guests some champagne. "Not you too."

"I'm just saying, what's the harm in hanging around? The colonel owes you more leave time, right?"

"For all you know, she might be married."

"I didn't see any wedding ring, did you?"

He hadn't.

He left Lynch to his own musings and went on with his job, counting down the hours until the evening was over. He visited his colleagues every hour and roamed, watching for any trouble.

He checked his watch, after what must have been the sixth tour around the house. It was closing in on twenty-two hundred. He returned to Leach inside the living area.

"Zone Three to Zone leader."

Winter brought his sleeve cuff to his lips. "Receiving."

"Sanchez is on the move," Middleton advised. "He's heading back into the house. Looks like he's going to make his speech."

"Roger that."

Lynch gestured to the two men he had stationed at the top of the stairs. They shuffled sideways, ready for the influx of guests who were about to enter. Winter hurried down the steps and inched closer to the door, taking his station from the highest vantage point he could find.

Sanchez appeared from the balcony, and Lynch, along with the bodyguards, made a path for him. They traipsed down into the large living area, the crowd shifting out of his way as if he were parting the Red Sea. More of the attendees arrived from outside and found somewhere to stand.

The music slowly faded into the background, filling the home with the sound of hushed voices and clinking champagne flutes. All eyes drifted to the man that everyone had come to see as he presented himself near the windows overlooking his garden. A member of the house staff handed Sanchez a microphone, and the prospective governor turned to his guests.

"Ladies and gentlemen. I'd like to thank you all for joining me this evening. It's because of you I'm standing here. Without your support, I'm nothing. It's because of you I'll have the opportunity to bring genuine change to the great state of Tlapetla."

A polite round of applause permeated throughout the crowd.

"You know, when I decided to put up my hand and run for the

governorship, I had to ask myself: was I the right person for the job?"

He paused while everyone looked at him expectantly. Even Winter found himself enamored with the man. He exuded strength and was naturally suited for the stage. In another life, he could have been one of the many TV or film stars who stood in his captive audience. Instead, he had decided to make a difference.

"I was born in San Yetaxa," Sanchez continued. "My parents had barely two pesos to rub together. We lived in the inner-west of the city…"

As he spoke, a crackle filtered through Winter's earpiece.

"Zone One to Zone leader."

Winter held up his sleeve. "What is it, Watts?"

"You might want to get out here."

Winter glanced over at Lynch, who gave him a knowing look. He then proceeded to the door, marching outside to find Watts at the gate, staring onto the street. Winter hurried past the walk-through metal detector and joined his side.

"What's going on?" he asked.

"See for yourself."

Winter peered beyond their position, the night having set in to wrap the estate in shadows. There blocking the road sat a crumpled Hummer, having t-boned a parked Porsche 911. Fuentes stood with two of the Redwind guards near the large SUV, helping the driver, who appeared a little dazed from the crash.

"Someone's going to be pissed when they return to their car." Winter frowned. "Have you called the police?"

Watts nodded. "They told me they'd be awhile. They've got too many jobs to put aside for a minor accident."

"I suppose we are in San Yetaxa, aren't we?"

Suddenly, the gate started to move on its hinges. Winter

grabbed Watts by the shoulder and drew him backward, the pair watching until it closed, sealing them inside the estate.

"How did that just happen?" Winter asked.

"I'm not sure." Watts walked over to the controls, prodding at the buttons. "I can't seem to reopen the gate."

"Is there another panel in the house?"

"There is, but this one's in active mode."

"Zone Four to Zone Leader," boomed Sidhu's voice in Winter's ear.

"Receiving."

"We've got a problem back here. The rear gate's opening and I've been locked out of the controls."

A gunshot cracked. Follow by another. Then another.

"Winter!"

He spun around to Watts's call. Winter rushed to his side, drawing his Glock 17. The scene on the street had unfolded in a grisly tableau—Fuentes and his two guards laid sprawled on the road with bullet holes in their heads.

They had become little more than obstacles, as four men with black masks, embossed with white skulls, carrying AK-74U assault rifles, climbed from the Hummer. They stepped over their corpses and turned their attention to the gate, with Winter and Watts directly in their sights.

9

Watts fired his sidearm first, his shot cutting an attacker down. The dead man's three comrades scattered, using the nearest cars for cover, one of them peppering his position before disappearing to the rear of a parked BMW.

Winter grabbed Watts, who had avoided being struck, and dragged him behind the stone gate pier to the right-hand side of the closed gate.

"Son of a bitch!" Winter cursed, drawing his sleeve to his mouth. "Zone One is under attack. I repeat, Zone One is under attack. We have three men down and three assailants converging on—"

"Zone Four to all positions!" Sidhu's voice filtered through his earpiece. "Zone Four is under attack! Four vehicles are on approach! We can't close the gate! I repeat—"

An unholy boom sounded on the opposite side of the property, cutting the transmission short. Winter turned to the towering pillar of flames beyond the house, launching high into the night.

"If I didn't know any better, I'd say someone just fired an

RPG!" Watts said over the clatter of bullets homing in on their position.

"Sidhu, can you hear me?" Winter tapped his earpiece. "Sidhu?"

Winter slid out from behind the gate pier and rattled off a spray of gunfire into the street with his pistol. He returned to Watts's side, pressing his back against their stone barricade. "Lynch! Middleton! Respond!"

"This is Lynch!" he relayed over the comm. "We've got people panicking in here!"

"They're all making a break for the exits!" Middleton added.

Winter played out the scene in his mind, the shouts and cries of the guests spilling through the windows and doors, their terror echoing into the night. The sound was interlaced by the burst of automatic fire carrying not just from past the front gate, but from Sidhu's position.

"You need to prepare to evacuate the attendees via the front entrance," Winter instructed them. "They cannot, I repeat, cannot exit through the rear."

Under normal circumstances, he would have expected a few wisecracks in response to his orders. Instead, both Lynch and Middleton acknowledged his directives like the true professionals they were.

"Has anyone got eyes on Sanchez?" Winter asked.

"I do," said Middleton. "His bodyguards have him surrounded."

"Make certain he comes out with the other guests."

"Roger that!"

Watts popped off a series of shots past the gate pier. "Are you sure it's a good idea evacuating through here?"

Winter risked a glance from behind their cover, jerking back to safety as a bullet fizzed by. "There's only three of them out there. The cartel's forces are concentrated on the rear of the house because they know it's easier to access. They plan to funnel everyone either here or on the obstructed street. It'll be like fish in a barrel."

Watts furrowed his brow. "So tell me again why we're bringing the fish to the barrel? With that gate closed and the Hummer out there, we're blocked in."

"Then we unblock it, don't we?" Winter gazed back at one of the parked Tundras. "Have you got the keys?"

Watts glanced warily at him, yanking the set from his pocket and palming them into Winter's hand. "I'll cover you."

Winter stepped backward, ready to make a run for the car. Watts eased himself away from the gate pier and fired a burst at the trio, continuing to converge on them. The assailants shielded themselves to the rear of the luxury cars, giving Winter the signal to hoof it.

He bolted for the black pickup truck, wrenching the door open and hopping into the driver's seat. With the key in his pocket, he prodded the push-button ignition and shifted the car into reverse, taking the pickup all the way back to the garage, to give himself a fifty-yard head start.

He revved the engine, glancing at the shotgun sitting in the passenger side. Watts nodded to him, and Winter planted his foot on the gas. The new Toyota picked up speed rapidly. The attackers quickly realized their predicament. They leveled their rifles on him and fired, shredding the hood and denting the grille. He ducked to avoid the rounds shattering the windshield and continued on course, plowing through the gate.

The steel barrier buckled from the force of the huge vehicle, what remained of the bars flinging through the air. Keeping his head low, Winter homed in on the combatant firing ahead. The man stood behind a stationary Maserati, his eyes ballooning at the sight of the Tundra heading his way.

Winter crashed the nose of the Toyota into the fancy Italian car, sending it into a spin. The car clipped the assailant and Winter finished the job, collecting him on the way through, his body launching over the hood and sliding down the side of the pickup truck with a thud.

He veered toward his next target: the crashed Hummer obstructing the evacuation. Not letting up on the gas, he rammed it at just the right angle to dislodge it, propelling the SUV down the hill. The jolt of the impact rattled his bones, and the airbag deployed into his face.

Shaking off the momentary effects of the collision, he attempted to get the car moving. The engine sputtered, but nothing came. Winter stared into the rearview mirror. The two remaining combatants had split up. Watts continued his feud with one at the gate, while the other peeled away from the fight, hurrying in Winter's direction.

Winter punched out what remained of the windshield and grabbed the loaded shotgun. As he did, the rear windshield exploded from automatic fire, showering him in shards of glass. Winter waited for the assault to pause and dived through the front of the car, sliding down the bullet-ridden hood and onto the road.

He pressed his stomach on the asphalt and peered under the pickup at the closing attacker. Winter aimed the shotgun from his horizontal position and fired.

The spray made contact, and his stalker fell with a crash, taking the shot to his legs. Winter returned to his feet and rushed out from the cover of the car to find the man tearing his mask off. He clenched his disguise in one hand and his ankles with the other, his cries of agony bellowing into the night.

"*Bastardo!*" he screamed.

Winter wasted no time putting him out of his misery, pointing the shotgun at him and squeezing the trigger to silence his wails.

Winter tore his focus past the blood-spattered remains, directing his attention to the last standing attacker, still locked in a fight with Watts. The Mexican noticed his approach and backed up behind another car, not wishing to get caught in the crossfire. Winter moved in quickly and pulled his sidearm from his waistband, catching the man in his shoulder. Watts came to the party and settled the score, driving two more rounds into his chest.

"The front entrance is clear!" Watts said into the mic on his sleeve. "Commence the evacuation!"

Within seconds, the guests streamed from the front door of the estate, led by Sanchez and his bodyguards. The surge of bodies was seismic, a human tidal wave crashing forward as if a dam had burst. Beyond the hysterical shrieks accompanying the men and women alike was the persistent crack of automatic gunfire sounding from the rear of the home.

Winter picked up the fallen assault rifles on the road and approached Watts, tossing one into his grasp. "You're on evac duty. Stay here until every single person has left this property."

He gave his colleague no chance to countermand him and ambled toward the house, passing Sanchez as he went. Their eyes met for the briefest of moments before his bodyguards thrust him forward, sweeping him away with the deluge of terrified souls. Winter shoved his way through the panicked attendees, heading in the other direction, eventually reaching the door.

"How many more?" he asked Middleton, who stood ushering everyone onto the driveway.

"Still quite a few guests," she said. "And house staff."

"Lynch? Sidhu?"

"Lynch took the rest of the Redwind guards to the back of the estate to hold off the attack with Sidhu."

Winter nodded. "Make sure every single person gets out of here."

"I will."

He brushed past her and sprinted through the living area, weaving around the remaining civilians until he reached the hallway. The lights flickered overhead, before finally extinguishing, leaving him in darkness. He followed the staccato bursts of gunfire, arriving at the back door to find Lynch and his team of guards dug in behind cinderblock garden beds, their weapons trained on the attackers beyond.

The heavily armed cartel members had taken cover to the rear of their four parked SUVs, firing on their position, shredding the plants and carving away at the concrete.

Winter threw himself onto the ground and crawled over to Lynch. "The evac's almost complete! Once Watts gives us the signal, we'll pull back and get the hell out of here!"

Lynch bobbed up to fire off a round.

"Where's Sidhu?" Winter asked.

Lynch ducked behind the cinderblocks, his face unreadable as he cast a quick glance to his opposite side. Winter went over to the motionless form next to Lynch and tugged at the blood-soaked shirt covering its face. Beneath, riddled with shrapnel wounds, lay Sidhu.

10

Winter put the shirt back over Sidhu's face, covering the remains of a man he had called a friend. He placed a hand on his chest and bowed his head in respectful silence.

"Get down, everybody!" Lynch shouted.

Before Winter could take stock of what was happening, a deafening blast wailed above, an enemy RPG smashing into the house, rattling the ground beneath his feet. Stone tumbled from the well-built facades and cascaded down the wall of the home. The shattered fragments crashed on top of the group of guards on the opposite side of the door, burying them under the weight of the avalanche.

Winter sprang up from his cover and unleashed a torrent of gunfire with his pilfered rifle, seizing the moment to assess the battlefield. He obtained a target and took them down, quickly returning behind his cinderblock refuge.

"There's at least fifteen out there!"

"And we just lost three men!" Lynch held up his sidearm. "We might as well be shooting at them with B.B. guns!"

As the remaining guards attempted to hold back the cartel's

forces on the flanks, Winter raised his mic. "Zone leader to Zone One. How's the evac going?"

"We're nearly there!" Middleton advised through his earpiece. "The last of the house staff are heading through the front door now!"

"That's good enough for me." Winter tapped Lynch on the shoulder. "Let's pull back!"

His friend nodded, signaling to the other guards to retreat inside. They laid down covering fire and moved as quickly as they could through the entrance. Winter crouched by the door, counting everyone through. He rattled off some suppressive fire of his own as the last of his Redwind operators, along with Lynch, disappeared.

That was when he saw him.

The enemy combatant with the RPG...

He emerged from behind the parked SUV near the back gate, the weapon poised on his shoulder. Time seemed to stretch around Winter, incoming bullets thudding into the stone wall at his back, missing him by mere inches. He raised his gun into the open and aimed at the faceless figure beneath the black mask, his dark clothes painting him like a phantom in the night.

Winter squeezed the trigger.

Click.

He was out of ammunition.

The RPG fired and streaked through the air, shattering the window above the door. An explosion erupted from the upper story, the flames spewing outward in a torrent of destruction. More of the stone façade cracked and broke free of the wall, plummeting over the outdoor area. Winter took the opportunity as a diversion and hurried inside.

The hallway lay in ruins and collapsed beams scattered the wreckage, while drywall debris drifted through the air like falling snow. Through the carnage, a figure materialized on the floor, a broken beam from the wall across their back. Winter fell to their side and heaved the piece of timber off them, flipping the body over.

"Lynch!"

His eyes were open, a haunted finality etched across his features. Winter placed his fingers against his carotid artery. No pulse. He wanted to curse, but the approaching sound of footsteps from outside kicked him into action. He regained his balance and pushed on through the storm of flaking wreckage, leaving another of his friends behind.

A pair of apparitions appeared through the debris. One was tall, the other short.

"Winter!" someone called out.

"Is that you?" shouted the other.

Winter recognized the voices. "Middleton! Watts!"

He moved toward them, stumbling over the bodies of the guards who had got caught up in the RPG attack with Lynch. At the end of the gauntlet, a pair of hands reached for him, and he dove into the arms of Middleton in the empty living area.

"Where are the others?" Watts asked.

"Gone." Winter closed his eyes for a moment. "Both dead."

A gaze lingered between Watts and Middleton, while Winter pulled himself from her grasp.

"We have to keep going," he said.

Suddenly, the exterior windows looking out onto Sanchez's garden shattered. The trio turned to find more of the masked intruders stepping through the broken glass. Middleton pivoted and discharged her shotgun, launching her victim to the ground. She got off a second shot and peppered another in the arm, throwing them off their feet.

But they kept coming.

Winter ushered his team up the staircase, the cartel's forces converging from all angles. He and Watts fired a burst from their sidearms. None hit their targets, the attackers taking cover behind chairs and other furniture wherever they could.

Middleton reached the top of the stairs first, pulling out her sidearm and giving the others suppressive fire, allowing Winter and Watts to reach her side. With a firm hand around her waist, Winter dragged her from the edge. What remained of his team sprinted for the balcony, the footfalls of those on their tail getting heavier with each passing second.

"I think I want to go home now!"

Middleton's quip got lost in the gunfire screaming from the rear. Winter dashed for cover behind a large potted plant, pulling her along with him, the enemy rounds shredding the greenery growing from them.

"Watts!"

Winter dragged himself upward, spotting the cause for Middleton's distraught tone. Watts stood before the swimming pool in the open, holding on to his chest, a spray of bullet wounds tattered across his back. Blood covered him, the crimson cascade trickling down his legs, creating a puddle of death at his feet.

Somehow, he remained standing, staggering closer to the poolside. His head turned to his friends, and he smiled at them with bloodstained teeth.

Then his eyes rolled back.

His body pitched forward, and he crashed into the water. A single powerful splash shattered the surface, the clear blue now stained with red.

Time slowed again, and all the battles Winter had previously waged returned to him in a tsunami. The people he had lost under his command. The friends he'd had to bury.

"There!"

Middleton's cry pulled him back to the present. He followed her pointed finger to the edge of the balcony.

"There's a car parked under there!"

The pair rose, the masked forces appearing on the pool deck. Without so much as a glance downward, he and Middleton threw their legs over the railing and jumped, the duo landing like cats on the roof of the vehicle below.

They hopped onto the ground, and Winter recalled the map of the estate in his mind. To their left would be their avenue of escape, the narrow path taking them to the driveway and onward to freedom.

"This way!" He led Middleton onward and they made a dash for it, only to be stopped in their tracks by shadows appearing from around the corner.

The hurried footsteps of the assailants pounded in their direction. Winter glanced backward for another route of escape. None existed.

"What now?" Middleton asked.

Winter pointed the other way and stripped back an overgrown hedge to reveal a green door. He heaved it open and they entered, slamming it shut behind them. Darkness greeted the duo, the moonlight from the small windows on the other side of the enormous space the only semblance of illumination lighting their way.

"Where the hell are we?" Middleton whispered.

Through the gloom, Winter took in the shapes of their temporary refuge. The arched ceiling, carved from the same weathered stone as the estate's exterior, loomed overhead. Along the walls, hidden alcoves concealed rows of wooden storage racks, each cradling dozens of dust-covered bottles.

"The wine cellar." He hurried her through the shadowed confines. "There should be an exit on the other side. How are you for ammo?"

"One mag left. You?"

"I'm out."

As he spoke the words, the door they had entered swung open. Winter and Middleton turned to find the skulls on the masks of their attackers glowing in the moonlight, transforming the underground chamber into a haunted house.

Their assailants said nothing, instead launching a barrage of automatic gunfire into the dark, hoping to hit their mark. Stone dissolved into dust. The wooden racks splintered into deadly shrapnel. And the wine bottles exploded into glass fragments.

Winter and Middleton threw themselves to the floor, the violent maelstrom raging around them. Winter gazed to the end of the cellar where the avenue of their escape presented itself.

"Middleton," he whispered. "There it is. The door. Our way out."

She did not respond.

Winter rolled closer to her, shifting just enough for the moonlight to illuminate her form. Her face remained pressed against the cold concrete. He reached out with his fingers and brushed her back.

Blood. Warm and sticky.

"Oh, Middleton..."

A knot formed in his gut as the footsteps of the attackers drew nearer. They had silenced their rifles, now moving like sharks in the deep, circling their prey, waiting for the perfect moment to strike and make their final kill.

Winter had only one option left if he was to have any chance of survival.

He took the gun from Middleton's grasp and stayed prone for a moment longer, luring in his predators. Counting to five, he pulled himself to his feet, firing into the darkness at the closing ghosts, uncertain if his shots were making their mark.

He edged backward, his fingers fumbling for the door, eventually finding the handle and flinging it open. He stumbled into the night, his gun exhausted of ammo. But before he could pull the door shut, a crack sounded, the earsplitting noise echoing inside the cellar.

Winter did not feel the bullet at first.

Within seconds, though, the shock wore off, the searing pain surging through his side as if he had been stabbed with a hot knife. He stumbled beyond the cellar, his footsteps unraveling from under him. He caught the edge of some steps and his world tilted around him. Gravity took hold and sent him spiraling. His body slammed against the unforgiving stones. One after another, he landed on them, his head striking the surface hard.

A burst of pain flared.

Then everything went black.

11

Inspector Sergio Alvarez stood at the gate, sipping the coffee he had bought from Hector's Diner. The long black had gone cold. As usual, he had not drunk it quick enough. He never did when he knew a big job was waiting for him.

And what a job it was.

The morning had started like any other. He met his partner, Inspector Martinez, at the station house, arriving before the younger man. The pair collected their radios and sidearms, then signed out a vehicle. They followed a conga line of police cruisers into the hills and reached Gilberto Sanchez's estate just on the cusp of sunrise.

The fire department was in attendance when they arrived, hosing down the last embers still smoldering. The scene before Alvarez had not done the rumors justice. Sanchez's home had been reduced to a crisp, leaving what remained of the lavish stone architecture a crumpled wreck.

The local media crews had gotten wind of the blaze and had set up their cameras along the road. The reporters beamed pictures from the site to the morning news shows, all speculating on what had taken place. Initially, they ran with the story that it had been a simple house fire. The narrative had not lasted long when those who had been on the scene began talking.

Gilberto Sanchez's home had, in fact, been attacked.

"Get a load of what one of the examiners have found."

Alvarez glanced over his shoulder as his partner approached from the driveway with a plastic evidence bag. Within, a black fabric mask stared back at him, the surface painted with a crude white skull.

"It was nice of the cartel to leave their calling card," Martinez said, his brown mop of hair shimmering in the morning sun.

Alvarez harrumphed. "Everyone knows they did it. This just proves it."

"It's pretty brazen."

"So's Gilberto Sanchez. Ever since he started running for the governorship, he knew the only way to cause a dent in Lugo's campaign was to call out the Tlapetla cartel. El Maestro was always going to fight fire with fire."

"This is some serious destruction, though. The examiners have already found some RPG fragments at the rear of the house."

Alvarez's partner had earned his shield twelve months earlier. He was young, but filled with determination and highly skilled at his job. Sometimes, however, he could be a touch naïve. "El Maestro wanted to make a statement."

"Do you think Sanchez will pull out of the race?"

It was a question Alvarez had pondered since he arrived on the scene. He had never met the retail magnate. What he did know, however, was that he was strong-willed. But no time in his life would someone have tried to kill him and two hundred other people just to make a point. "He's got two options: step away and let Lugo win. Or..."

"Or?"

Sanchez stared at the camera crews on the sidewalk. "Or double-down and..."

The sound of a small convoy of vehicles speeding up the hill disturbed his train of thought, its red and blue flashing lights cutting across the rising sun. The trio of police cruisers came to a halt at the gate, and the passenger door of the center car hurled open.

Martinez clasped Sanchez on the shoulder. "I'll let you take care of this."

Before Alvarez could fire off a sarcastic "thank you", Martinez was already on the move back to the scorched estate. The door of the cruiser thudded shut and the bulk of San Yetaxa's police chief heaved into view. He removed his hat and placed it at his side, ambling toward Alvarez.

"Chief," he greeted him.

There was barely a grunt from Espinosa as he trudged to the top of the driveway to take in the devastation. He shook his head and returned to Alvarez, pointing at the evidence bag.

"What've you got there?" he asked through his bushy mustache.

Alvarez held it aloft. "Sanchez's attackers left a note behind."

Espinosa took the bag and examined the contents. "I've just been talking with Gilberto Sanchez's representatives. He's alive and well."

"Good for him, I suppose. What about everyone else? He had two hundred guests here last night, not to mention dozens of staff."

"Our people back at the station house are making phone calls, doing a final head count. So far, it would seem that everyone got out with their lives intact."

"That's impressive." Alvarez glanced at the ruins. "I hate to be the bearer of bad news, but the examiners have already started digging bodies out of the ruins."

"Likely some of the cartel hit squad that got caught up in the firefight with the Redwind security force."

"Redwind?"

"Sanchez suspected the cartel might come after him."

"I wonder what would have given him that idea?"

The chief ignored the jest. "He hired a security firm from the States to help him during the fundraiser. Five Americans were brought down here to coordinate with a dozen locals. He's claimed if it wasn't for them, no one would have got out safely."

Alvarez rubbed the stubble of his unshaved chin. "I'm going to need a full list of names."

"You'll have them."

"Did any of them get out?"

Espinosa shrugged. "We don't believe any of the Mexican contingent did. As for the Americans, they haven't checked in with their employers in Nevada. So, we doubt they did either. You'll be the first person to find out. I hope you brought a shovel with you."

It was Alvarez's turn to ignore the chief's attempt at humor, instead focusing on the media crews. "This isn't going to look good for us."

"We weren't on Sanchez's protection detail."

"We should've been."

"He didn't ask us."

"Why would he?"

The two men stared at one another. Espinosa took a step closer to him, his giant stature blocking out the sun and covering him in a daunting shadow. "I'll pretend I didn't hear that insinuation."

Alvarez held firm. He was too old to fret over his career like

Martinez. He'd be retired soon and would no longer have to worry about the dirty streets of San Yetaxa. "I wasn't implying anything of you, sir. But you have to admit, if the man running for governor can't trust the local police force, because some of its members might be in bed with the cartel, it isn't a great look."

The reporters closed in like vultures, hungry for a headline, their microphones thrust out before them. Espinosa held up a waiting hand to keep them at bay and prodded Alvarez's chest. "I'll worry about the department's reputation. You just do your job. Don't forget your place, Inspector."

The chief glared down at him one final time and spun to face the eager reporters, his expression shifting to one more polished for the cameras. Alvarez let out a breath and mock-saluted his superior behind his back.

He mused a shovel right about now would have been quite handy—if only to bury his frustrations along with a certain someone's ego.

12

Captain Winter sat inside the tactical tent, his ringing ears still rattling his skull. His head throbbed, the memories of the mission raw and unprocessed.

But they had been processed.

He had been debriefing with Colonel Dawson for three hours.

Winter had seen several battles during his time with the Marine Corps, forging a path through many deployments. It all started with Operation Enduring Freedom as a green rifleman. Not long after, he left the bleak terrain of Afghanistan behind to fight in Operation Iraqi Freedom. He ping-ponged between the two countries for most of his career, playing the good soldier.

Winter had been through hell and back more times than he could remember. He had lost comrades, lost men under his command. So, what was it about the Taktur Mountains that had rattled him so much?

Perhaps he had simply had enough...

The flap to the tent brushed open and Dawson entered with a mug in each hand. He placed one in front of Winter, the steam rising out of the coffee like a smoldering IED having just been detonated.

The colonel sat behind his makeshift desk, his gigantic frame causing the chair's upholstery to groan under his weight. He slid his coffee to the side of the open folder. "Captain?"

Winter did not answer, Dawson's voice lost in the ringing permeating his ears.

"Captain Winter!"

The sharper tone yanked him to his days at MCRD San Diego, where his drill instructor's commands had been as unrelenting as the Reaper hike. He shook off the haze and turned his attention to the colonel. "Sorry, sir."

Winter wrapped his fingers around the mug and drew in the aroma of the awful coffee through his nostrils. He then took a sip. It was just as bad as it smelled.

"Are you good now?" Dawson asked.

"Yes, sir."

The colonel closed his folder. "Well, I don't think there's anything more we can go over. The enemy strongholds were taken out of commission and we have the ISIS fighters in the region now on the run. The brass will be very pleased with this result. Expect another medal for this. Maybe even a Bronze Star."

Winter had lost count of how many commendations he had collected during his time in the service. None were earned without bloodshed. Reality warped around him once more and his decades in the Marine Corps merged as one. The faces that had come and gone. Those who had served years, and those who had served mere weeks to never return home. They coalesced into a field of red, the blood of the dead soldiers forming a crimson river of the damned.

Winter pushed the nightmarish images deep within, finding the gaze of Dawson upon him. The colonel's stern demeanor was not what it had once been. Whether that was because of age or his familiarity with Winter, he could not say.

"Sir?" he said.

"Yes, Captain?"

"Sergeant Hicks and Corporal Collins. I trust both men will receive similar commendations?"

"You can count on it."

Winter nodded. "I'd also like to make a request."

"Of course."

"I know under operations of this size, you like to write the letters to their families. In this instance, I'd prefer to do that, if I may?"

"Are you sure?"

"They were my men. I should be the one to do it."

Dawson steepled his fingers on the desk, craning his neck. "Very well."

"Thank you, sir."

Winter had already started forming the sentences required in his mind. He was no wordsmith and nothing he could say would convey the hurt he felt for losing such fine men. Nor could anything express how sorry he was to their parents and wives for not bringing them home alive. Dawson would have been able to pen a far better message to them. He'd had much more practice. But Winter would not shirk his last duty to Hicks and Collins.

Dawson stood and walked over to the filing cabinet. He slid open the drawer and withdrew another drab cream folder. He tossed it onto the other side of the desk, landing it next to Winter's coffee.

"What's this, sir?"

"Your golden ticket."

Winter opened the folder to find his discharge papers.

"You knew this was coming, didn't you?" the colonel asked, retaking his seat.

"My men haven't let me forget all week." Winter stared at the DD 214 form. Once he filled it out, his life, as he had known it for the past twenty years, would be over. "It's ironic, isn't it? I've served for longer than I've been a civilian."

"You joined when you were eighteen, didn't you?"

"Ten months before 9/11."

"Then you've seen and done it all." Dawson arched his brow. *"I suppose I can't convince you to stay on board..."*

"To become a major and rot behind a desk? No, sir. That's not the life for me. Besides, the plan was always to finish after twenty." Winter touched his pocket, feeling the edges of the photograph within. *"It's time to settle down. Maybe even start a family."*

The colonel's harsh exterior cracked further, the hint of a smile appearing. *"I'm proud of you, Dane. To have arrived a recruit, survived this mess and come out the other side an officer... You've done a hell of a job."*

"Thank you, sir."

"You're going to be missed."

* * *

Winter's eyes snapped open, his dream evaporating into a kaleidoscope of colors. His head pounded, and his limbs ached. But it was nothing compared to the pain in his side.

It all returned to him.

Gilberto Sanchez's house. The attack.

He howled out, his hand grabbing something soft. "Where am I?"

There was a pillow, sheets and a mattress. He was on a bed.

"Hello!" he yelled out.

No reply came. He rubbed his eyes, attempting to filter the haze, but the agony bit into him, the hellfire of the wound pulsing throughout his body.

He had been shot.

In the cellar.

More memories surfaced. Middleton. Watts. Lynch. Sidhu. His friends... All dead.

Winter touched his side. Someone had bandaged him.

"Where am I?"

Some footfalls sounded in the distance, followed by the slamming of a door.

"Hey?" he called.

More footsteps approached until he felt as if a dark shadow had fallen over him.

"You're awake," the person said to him. He spoke English, his accent distinctly Mexican. Winter could not discern the face, the lack of light and his grogginess making it difficult to decipher any shapes.

He recoiled, sensing the man nearing, but there was nowhere to go. He was in no condition to run or fight back. "Who are you?"

The question went unanswered. Instead, a sharp prick stung his arm, followed by the cool rush of whatever was contained within the needle. Before he knew it, the swirling colors vanished once again, enveloping him in darkness.

13

Alvarez was buried. Not beneath the rubble of Gilberto Sanchez's home, but under the weight of the paperwork it had produced. Of course, as an inspector, it came with the territory. On the bright side, the administrative element of the role was cleaner. Much less blood, unlike that found on the streets of San Yetaxa.

The attack on Sanchez's estate was just another such incident to have befallen the region. The shameless nature of the cartel who ran business through Tlapetla was common knowledge. It was ironic, considering their ambiguousness. Despite being the face of the crime alliance, Alfonso Berrera was known as Teflon to law enforcement. When crimes were committed, which had obvious connections to the cartel, his influence on such offenses could never be traced back to him. Authorities often hauled him in for questioning, even taking him to court when evidence surfaced. But nothing ever stuck.

There were reasons for that, of course. One: he excelled at what he did. Two: he had help on the force and in the local judicial system. For many years, Alvarez suspected judges and senior police officers assisted the cartel. He would not have been surprised to find Chief Espinosa among them. And three: Alfonso Berrera was but a front who served as a decoy. Yes, he was the man everyone knew, but there were darker forces in charge.

El Maestro was the true power.

He was the link that brought everything together, ensuring the drug trade flowed through Tlapetla without issue. Alvarez, and other colleagues not tainted by the cartel, had been hunting for him for decades. Most believed it a futile endeavor, some believing he may not even exist. Alvarez, however, was certain he was out there somewhere.

"Alvarez."

He looked up from the paperwork, slipping off his glasses. "What is it, Martinez?"

"The Americans are here."

"Okay, bring them up."

Martinez nodded and rushed back down the rickety old timber stairs. A few moments later, he returned with a pair of men. One was large, but muscular, pushing mid-sixties. The other was short, ten years younger, skinnier.

"Gentlemen, this is Inspector Alvarez," Martinez said, gesturing toward him. "And these are Mr. Dawson and Mr. Bridges from Redwind Security."

Alvarez shook their hands. "I'm the lead investigator on this case. I'm sorry we couldn't meet under better circumstances."

Dawson cleared his throat, his demeanor stern and forthright. "I've been told there's been some developments since this morning."

"Yes." Alvarez motioned them down the hallway. "If you'll come with me."

They followed him through to one of the interview rooms which he had commandeered for his investigation. He opened the old door, its rusty hinges groaning under the stress, and invited them inside. At the center of the space, two small tables sat side by side, with envelopes laying on top.

"I'll get you up to speed as quickly as I can. With the timeline we've been able to put together, it's believed the initial assault on the estate took place at the front gate at 10 p.m. last night." Alvarez opened one of the envelopes and placed three photos on the table, a trio of males lying dead on the road with gunshot wounds to the head. "Three Redwind security guards were gunned down in the street."

Bridges pointed at the image in the center. "That's Fuentes."

Alvarez slipped out four more photographs from the second envelope. "These are their attackers. Two were shot with conventional sidearms. One took a shotgun to the legs and face, and the other was run down with a pickup truck." He tried to discern some semblance of emotion in Dawson's expression, but the man remained unreadable. "Other bodies have been found in the remnants of the house. Naturally, they're not in the same pristine condition. So far, the tally has reached fourteen, but I expect our examiners will find more as the days roll on."

He laid out the snaps of the bodies from another of the envelopes. The fire had charred the remains, reducing them to a blackened, unrecognizable mess.

"Have you been able to make out an ID on any of them yet?" Dawson asked.

"We're waiting on the DNA results. However, many of the deceased had identifiers which we've been able to match to your list of names." Alvarez reached for the fourth envelope and tipped the contents into the space between the photos.

Dawson collected the dog tags, shuffling them between his thick fingers. He gave them to the other American, who examined them with the same sharp scrutiny.

"Lynch and Watts," Bridges said. "They still wore these in civilian life?"

Dawson nodded. "Both were pretty sentimental."

Alvarez picked up a ring shaped like a dragon and handed it to Dawson. "Our examiners believe this was from the lone female body excavated."

"That's Middleton's. Not sure what value it held, but she'd worn it as long as I'd ever known her."

Bridges scooped up the final item. "A dagger?"

"It's a kirpan. A ceremonial blade. Sidhu was a Sikh." Dawson stared at Alvarez. "Anything else?"

"We've matched other items to some of the guards employed by the Mexican branch of Redwind Security. Considering none of them went home last night, we expect to find the rest of them under the rubble."

"What about Dane Winter?" The query came from Bridges, though Alvarez could tell the question was on the tip of Dawson's tongue. "Were you able to uncover anything that might ID him?"

Alvarez had memorized the list Redwind Security had sent through to the office that morning. Dane Winter was at the top of it, employed as the chief operations officer for the protection job on Gilberto Sanchez. "Not yet. Is there something we should be looking for? Was he ex-military? Dog tags perhaps?"

Dawson plucked the dog tags from Bridges' hand. "Winter didn't wear them. But he did have a chain."

"A chain?"

"Silver with a ring looped through it."

"What kind of ring?"

"A white gold engagement ring. Three diamonds."

Alvarez nodded, glancing at Martinez, who had last talked to the examiners thirty minutes prior. The younger inspector shook his head. "Nothing like that's been found. As I stressed earlier, we anticipate discovering more corpses."

Dawson glanced at Bridges. "I'd like to speak with the inspector alone."

Bridges backed toward the exit and departed. Alvarez gave a subtle nod to Martinez, who walked out too, leaving the pair by themselves.

Dawson closed the door and turned. "I'm about to ask you a candid question, Inspector Alvarez."

"Please do."

"We're adults here. We know the cartel's behind what happened last night. There's not a lot to this investigation. What I want you to tell me is, once the case is wrapped up, what are you going to do about it."

Alvarez sat on the edge of the table and crossed his arms. "I assure you, I'll follow every clue. If they can lead me to individuals within the cartel, I'll go after them. However, you have to understand how things run in this town."

"I understand perfectly well. They own this city. If they have the balls to kill a politician, what would they do to a simple inspector?"

"This simple inspector might be the best ally you have in San Yetaxa. Trust me when I say I would love nothing more than to give the cartel a bloody nose. And if I can, I will."

Dawson looked intensely at Alvarez. He was undoubtedly once a soldier, his countenance equally as powerful as his physical stature. "I hope you get that chance. Because after last night's events, the cartel is bound to have more trouble than they bargained for if justice isn't served."

"Is that supposed to be a threat, Mr. Dawson?"

"Not at all. It's the reality of the situation."

Alvarez stood, a chuckle rumbling in his chest. He refused to let the American intimidate him. "What do you plan to do? Bring an army of Redwind assets down here to avenge your people's deaths?"

Dawson took a step closer to him, his size daunting in such dim light. "So far, you've found no trace of Dane Winter. Knowing him as well as I do, there's every chance he survived that encounter last night. Take my word for it, if he's alive, I won't need an army to avenge those I lost. All it will take is one man."

14

An intense pressure clutched at Winter, wrapping around him like a vise. He fought against it, but his body was too weak to obey his commands. His eyelids flickered open, and he exhaled with ragged breaths, a dark shadow shrouding him.

"What... the... hell?" he stammered.

His distorted vision twisted into a series of shapes, the colors eventually amalgamating into a form that was familiar to him. He lay on a bed, the sheets a muted gray. There was a lamp on the nightstand, and next to it his chain and the three-diamond ring looped through it.

A man stood over him, his hands binding fresh bandages around his midsection. "Don't worry," he said to Winter. "I've just got to put some new—"

Winter did not let him finish the sentence, instead reaching out and clasping his throat. A sharp pain throbbed at his side. He gritted his teeth, refusing to relinquish his grip. "Who are you?"

The other man dropped the spool, attempting to break free from Winter's lock. Even under such duress, Winter managed to hold on. Uneasy gasps percolated from the person's mouth, his words amounting to nothing but a babble. Winter finally let go, and the man recoiled, staggering backward into the wall, his fingers brushing the raw marks left behind.

Winter looked down at his torso. He wore no shirt, a bandage semi-wrapped at his side.

The memory returned to him. "In the cellar."

The room around him was small, filled with faded photographs hung on the peeling wallpaper. It was a rustic setting. The quaint double bed he found himself on was made of stained timber, the springs creaking beneath him at the slightest of movements. Black curtains draped the room's sole window, while the lamp on the nightstand produced a dull yellow glow throughout.

He glanced up at the man he had attempted to strangle. He was young, with short but wavy dark hair. He was not that much shorter than Winter himself, but lacked the size and raw strength of someone who did his line of work.

"Who the hell are you?" Winter asked.

The man stretched his neck, dabbing his reddened skin. "My name's Ruben. I'm a doctor."

"A doctor?"

"That's right."

"What happened to me?"

"You were shot."

"No kidding." Winter pressed a hand to his temple, steadying himself from the pain coursing through his body. "I remember running from the wine cellar when I got clipped. I think I fell down a set of steps..."

"You did."

Winter darted his eyes from side to side, paranoia sparking within. "Who are you?"

"I told you, I'm Ruben." He hesitated, no doubt noticing Winter's increasing wariness. "You believe I'm with the cartel?"

Winter nodded. "I was captured."

"No."

"Then where the hell am I?"

"I can explain it all. Just allow me to finish tightening that bandage."

Winter held up his hand. "You'll tell me now, or so help me, I'll strangle the life out of you if you come a step closer."

"Let's make a deal then. I'll provide you with all the information you want. Then you let me do my job? Agreed?"

Winter nodded.

Ruben remained rooted to the spot at the end of the bed. "I'm not with the cartel. And this isn't some cartel compound, if that's what you're thinking."

"So you say."

"If I was with them, wouldn't you be dead right now?"

The images of Winter's friends flashed before him, their deaths seared into his memory. Sidhu beneath the bloody shirt. Lynch under the rubble from the RPG blast. Watts's haunting smile before nosediving into Sanchez's swimming pool. And Middleton, sprawled on the cold wine cellar floor, floating on a lake of crimson.

He closed his eyes for a moment, the anguish consuming him, his stomach twisting in a knot, a plum-sized lump of guilt rising in his throat. "If you're not with the cartel, where am I?"

Ruben took a cautious step forward. "You're at a house on the other side of the hills."

"Other side?"

"Gilberto Sanchez's estate is—or should I say *was*—located within one of the wealthier areas of San Yetaxa. We're about a twenty-minute drive away, in the less fortunate part."

"Whose house is this?"

"This is my sister's home. Well, half-sister actually. We shared the same dad, but—"

"Doc, cut to the chase."

"Sorry. I wasn't there. She told me she got caught up in Sanchez's estate after the cartel began their attack. She remained behind to help some of the staff evacuate. That's when she saw you."

Winter furrowed his brow.

"She heard a gunshot from the door of the wine cellar and watched you tumble to the bottom of the steps in the garden," Ruben continued. "She and some others dragged you out of there before the cartel could finish the job. I was already on my way to the party after she called me to come and get her. When I arrived, you'd lost a lot of blood. In my free time, I help the locals with anything they might need, so I always have ample supplies on hand here at the house."

"So, you saved me?"

"I did what any medical professional would do." Ruben gestured to the wound. "I would've preferred taking you to the hospital, but I didn't want to move you, so I kept you here. I've done a few runs back and forth to get some blood—"

"The bullet?" Winter brushed the bandage. "Has—"

"I removed it. You're all stitched up. Now it's a matter of managing you with painkillers."

"I guess that explains why I'm feeling like I do."

"It's been less than forty-eight hours since you sustained your injury. You're healing well. With any luck, you'll be on your feet within the next couple of days."

"Days? I can't afford to—"

"Since I've told you everything, you owe me," Ruben said. "The bandage. I have to wrap it."

Winter relented and allowed him to lean over the bed to finish the task, the firm compress making him wince.

Ruben walked over to a small plastic medical kit he had sitting on the dressing table and removed a syringe. "Now, I'm going to give you some more painkillers—"

"No."

"I strongly recommend—"

"No more painkillers, Doc."

"I know you're hurting. There's no point being a hero, you..."

Winter glared at him, and Ruben put his hands up in surrender.

"Fine." He tossed the needle back in the kit and fished out a pill bottle. "At least have these."

He placed it in Winter's grasp, and Winter stared at the label.

"They're nowhere near as strong as what I was about to give you. It'll take the edge off though." Ruben slid a glass to the side of the nightstand. "I've refilled your water. If you want more, just let me know."

Winter put the container by its side. "Thanks."

"And I meant what I said before. For the next two days, you can't move. You mustn't risk opening those stitches. I didn't fill you with all that blood to have it come gushing out."

"I'll take that under advisement." Winter stared beyond him at the photographs on the wall. He narrowed his eyes at the one at the end of his bed, the weathered image sparking a flicker of curiosity within. "Doc, can I have a look at that?"

Ruben turned, likely interested in what had caught his attention, until he too noticed the photo. He went to it and carefully removed it, bringing it closer. "There's a blast from the past. This was on one of our family vacations to Playa Azul at my cousins' beach house. We always had tons of fun there."

Winter grasped it and studied the haze of history captured

inside the frame. Ruben would have been a teenager, no more than sixteen years old. Next to him stood a girl, perhaps thirteen. "Is that your half-sister?"

"Sure is."

Winter arched his brow. Though she was younger, she shared all her features. "The sister that saved me?"

Ruben nodded.

"Doc, what's her name?"

Ruben took back the photo, his fingers tapping the edges. "Maria."

15

Maria bundled the trays from the table with one arm, balancing the stacked cartons and paper cups, determined to reach the trashcan before gravity had other plans. It was the first of many tables that she would have to tidy. Advertised as an all-day diner, Hector's was known as the place that never slept. There were busy times and lulls. She found herself in the latter, the dinner crowd having departed, leaving the restaurant looking like a hurricane had swept through.

She, along with the other waitstaff, had to prepare for the late evening crowds who would stumble from the local nightclubs and strip joints in search of greasy food and sugary drinks to ease their weary heads.

Maria stopped at the trashcan and threw the garbage inside, slapping the trays in the pile above. Her addition filled the plastic bag. As the unwritten rule went, whoever stuffed it had the honor of replacing it. She hauled it out and twisted the top with a bunny-ear knot, before yanking out a fresh liner from the hidden compartment.

On her way out the back, she walked past Juliana, who smiled at her, their tired but knowing looks confirming what a busy shift it had been. She went by the kitchen, the cooks' stares lingering on her as she passed. Their leers were nothing new. She smirked and shook her head. They were harmless and all knew if she were going to entertain dating someone, it would not have been one of them.

When would she have had the time, anyway?

She opened the roller door at the back dock and climbed down the steps to the dumpster, flipping open the lid and tossing the bag of trash inside it. Her mind filled with the image of Dane Winter. The man she had met in the diner only two days earlier. A foreigner, but handsome. He radiated sophistication, yet there was also an undeniable ruggedness about him. He spoke quietly, but with a power that exuded the strength of his muscular body.

"You okay down there?"

Maria looked up at one of the cooks peering out at her. "Uh, yeah, I'm fine."

She scaled the tiny ladder and closed the roller door, the picture of the American persisting in her mind. He had appeared different the last time she saw him. His strength had been stripped, his guard removed. Thank God for Ruben. If it were not for her brother, Dane Winter would be dead.

Her hands trembled from the horrors which had been seared into her soul from the evening at Gilberto Sanchez's estate. When she rescued Winter, the house was already ablaze, the flames engulfing the magnificent house. She attempted to push the memory deep into the recesses of her mind.

Growing up in San Yetaxa had given her many stories to tell. She understood darkness and those who could wield it. Maria had become accustomed to the terror. But that night was one she would never, no matter how hard she tried, be able to forget.

She traipsed by the barrels of cooking oil and returned to the restaurant floor. Her shoulders slumped at the sight before her, dozens more tables still scattered with dishes, her ever-present boss watching over the waitstaff from the cash register.

Maria's phone buzzed loudly, and she glanced sideways at Hector, his attention focused on the money in the till. He had not heard it. She sidestepped to the bathroom and entered a stall, closing the door behind her. Lowering the lid on the toilet, she sat and trawled the cell from her pocket, its pink protective case reassuring her she could never misplace it.

She swiped the screen, immediately recognizing the caller ID. "Hello, Ruben."

"Maria."

"How's Dane?"

"Awake."

Her eyebrows rose, and she smiled. "That's great to hear. Is he okay?"

"He's doing well. He had a lot of questions."

"That's to be expected. The last thing he probably remembers is people shooting at him."

"I think I've convinced him we're friends."

"Should we keep him at my place until he recovers?"

"He'll be up and about in two days. There's little point in moving him now. Once he's recuperated, it wouldn't hurt bringing him to the hospital, for a thorough check-up."

"He can stay for as much time as he wants."

"I'm sure you'd like that."

Maria blushed, her half-brother likely noticing the concern she held for Winter, despite barely knowing him. "I didn't mean it that way."

"Yes, you did." Ruben chuckled on the other end of the line. "With that said, I don't know how long he'll want to stay."

"Do you think he'll try to make a run for it?"

"Now that he's cognizant of his surroundings, he might. I'd hate for his stitches to tear. Then he'd really need to go to the hospital. He needs to see a familiar face to talk some sense into him."

"Me?"

"You're about as familiar a face as he's going to see. He hasn't said much, but as far as I can tell, the people he came down here with all died in the attack."

Maria recalled the group who had entered the diner two mornings prior, the same faces that had gathered at Sanchez's. They appeared a hodge-podge. Part reckless and juvenile, part seasoned professionals. Their demise was tragic, a testament to the grip on power the cartel held in Tlapetla.

"If you can come home soon, that would be great."

"I have to work until ten o'clock, Ruben. I promise I'll be back before you have to head to the hospital for your shift. Do everything in your power to make sure he doesn't leave."

"That's—"

The door to the bathroom opened, and Maria swiped the call to an end, putting the phone on her lap. Heavy footsteps echoed beyond the stall and stopped on the other side of the door.

"Maria!"

The voice was deep and hoarse. One her ears had become attuned to since beginning work at the diner. She rose from the toilet and flushed, placing the cell in her pocket and swinging open the door.

Hector stood before her, his thick arms planted on his wide hips, his presence filling the space in a way that made everything else shrink.

"What are you doing in here?" She brushed past him to wash her hands. "This is the women's!"

He trailed her to the basin, staring her down through the

cracked mirror. "You realize I'm going to dock you for this time, don't you?"

"What? I can't go to the toilet now?"

"We both know you weren't in there to pee. You're lucky I don't throw that stupid pink phone in the trash."

Maria lathered her hands in soap and held them under the tap. Hector closed on her, his breath warm against her ear, sending a shiver down her spine.

"Do that again, and you'll be looking somewhere else for work."

The man stormed out of the bathroom, leaving her lost in thought. If she could, she would quit. The reality was, she needed Hector's. In San Yetaxa, not having a job was like signing your own death warrant.

16

The door to the cramped bedroom opened, the golden rays of morning light spilling inside. Winter had been drifting in and out of sleep. For how long, he could not be certain. From his back, he rolled onto his good side, the pain in the other still tender from the gunshot wound.

Framed in the doorway, with the rising sun bathing her from behind, stood Maria. For a moment, Winter wondered if he were dreaming. Maria closed the door halfway, snuffing out much of the brightness, and kneeled by his side. She placed a hand on his arm, her warmth radiating through him. Winter was not dreaming, or in heaven, but for all he knew, he was looking at an angel.

"Maria?"

She nodded.

"The doc said you'd visit last night."

"You were asleep when I got home." She smiled. "I didn't want to disturb you."

Winter glanced at the pill bottle next to the extinguished lamp on the nightstand. "They had more kick than I expected."

"Ruben just wants to make sure you feel as little pain as possible. Has it helped?"

"I'm better." The agony had diminished physically. But no amount of pills would cure his mental anguish. "It would seem I've got you to thank for that."

Maria appeared to brush off the compliment and grabbed the old wooden chair from the corner of the room, dragging it to his side. He stared at her, caught in the depth of her caring brown eyes. "I'm sorry about your friends."

A tightness seized his throat, and he turned away, unwilling to let her see his weakness.

"You're all being hailed as heroes—"

"Heroes..."

She took his hand and squeezed it tight. "You and the rest of Redwind ensured every single one of the guests got out of there with their lives."

The horrific images of the evening flashed before him. "My friends didn't deserve to die."

"No, they didn't."

"I should've perished with them."

"Don't say that." The warmth Maria had exuded disappeared, replaced by a fire from deep within. She pulled her hand away.

Winter immediately recognized what he had said and turned to her. "I'm sorry. That's not what I meant. I can't thank you enough—"

"You don't have to thank me." She shook her head, the softness in her features returning.

"But I do. If it wasn't for you, I'd be..." Winter's voice faltered. "Can you tell me what happened?"

She closed her eyes as if revisiting the event, the images she was recalling as difficult for her as they were for him. "Two of the other caterers got caught in the storeroom at the back of the house during the attack. When the evacuation began, they'd got forgotten. I had to find them."

"The RPG?"

"When the cartel smashed the rear wall with that rocket launcher of theirs, the caterers got trapped behind the door. I managed to free them and we made a run for it through the garden. Then we saw you..."

The crack of the bullet that struck Winter echoed in his thoughts. In that instant, he was thrown back into the past again. He'd staggered from the wine cellar door and stumbled at the top of the steps, the world around him fading to black.

"You went flying down those stairs," Maria continued. "You were unconscious by the time you tumbled to the bottom. But we were able to get to you before the cartel came looking."

"How did we leave the estate?" he asked.

"A hidden track."

"A hidden track?"

"I've worked at Gilberto Sanchez's before. A couple of years ago, he threw a big party for some of his investors. It was one of my first catering jobs. In between handing out food and drinks, I got to see a lot of his estate. I remembered an old path which I found. It led off the property past the fence line. The trail still exists, even though the gate's now gone. My car was parked at the back of the house and likely destroyed, so I called Ruben. He met us at the bottom of the track. I'm glad he did. You'd lost a hell of a lot of blood."

"Yes, he mentioned that."

"Knowing that my place was closer than San Yetaxa General Hospital, Ruben brought you here. He did some home surgery and here you are."

Winter nodded slowly and grasped her hand. "You did good, Maria."

She blushed, evading his gaze. "I guess I was just in the right place at the right time."

Winter stared past her, lost in a cascade of thoughts. Perhaps it was the painkillers wearing off. Perhaps his brain was finally starting to work again.

"What really happened that night, Dane?"

"Hmm?" His gaze settled on her concerned expression. It was a good question. The details had blurred, swallowed by everything that had taken place after the fact. "The cartel did exactly as Sanchez feared..."

"But they failed to kill him."

"Sanchez got lucky."

"Because of you."

"Perhaps. At the end of the day he didn't have to die. What happened would have scared the hardest of men. If he pulls out of the race, then they'll have achieved their objective."

Maria went quiet, her own gaze drifting.

"What is it?" Winter asked.

"I don't think it's possible to scare Sanchez."

"What do you mean?"

Maria took her phone from her pocket, the hot pink combination glimmering in the sunlight escaping the door. She swiped the screen and scrolled to a video from a local news report. She pressed the play button and an image of Sanchez appeared on the steps of San Yetaxa's city hall. A mass of reporters surrounded him, thrusting the microphone at his solemn face.

"I am incredibly grateful to Redwind Security for their actions. I've already spoken to Joseph Dawson, their CEO, and conveyed my deepest sympathies to the families of those who were lost. The sacrifices they made so that more than two hundred people could live is a testament to their training and their humanity."

"What are the implications for your campaign, Mr. Sanchez?" a reporter asked him.

Sanchez peered out at those before him, as if trying to connect with them individually. "What happened at my estate highlights the real problems we have in this great state of ours. The cartel are running wild in San Yetaxa. They killed many innocents and would have murdered many more if they'd had the chance. We the people have got them scared. They're frightened by what a Sanchez governorship could look like for Tlapetla."

"So does this mean you're not pulling out of the race?" another reporter questioned.

Sanchez straightened and looked directly down the lens of the camera. "No, I will not be pulling out of the race. Come election day, I plan to be here on these steps, casting my vote for a Sanchez government."

Maria paused the video. "He's got bigger *cajones* than I gave him credit for."

Winter stared at the man's frozen image. "No kidding."

"Well, I should let you get more rest. Doctor's orders. Is there anything you need?"

"Yes." He smiled. "That phone and a packet of cigarettes."

17

Winter inhaled the cigarette, the smoke filtering deep into his lungs. In that moment, it felt like nothing else mattered. He flicked the ash onto the ground and peered out into the morning hush. The surrounding forest stretched out before him in a blanket of green, the trees swaying ever so slightly in the breeze and the birds tweeting a serene soundtrack.

He winced, attempting to keep himself upright against the wall of Maria's log cabin home. Reality flooded back to him. He had mistaken the tranquil scene for paradise. Beneath it hid dark forces. Ones that had taken his friends. Winter had somehow avoided them. He had got lucky.

It was the same on the battlefield. No matter the training, no matter all the drills, when the moment of truth arrived, the person on the other side was still trying to kill you. They were desperate and would not shirk from making the kill. To get out alive, one always required luck.

Winter slipped out Maria's pink cell from his pocket and swiped it to reveal the home screen. He opened the call menu and dialed in a number burned into his memory. It began ringing, and he brought the device to his ear.

"This is Joseph Dawson."

"Hello, Colonel."

There was a faint pause at the other end of the line. "Dane, is that you?"

Winter closed his eyes. The man's booming voice was music to his ears. "Yeah, it's me."

"Where are you?"

Winter once again gazed out at his tranquil surroundings, the warmth of the sun radiating across his skin. "I don't know. Somewhere in the San Yetaxa hills. But that doesn't matter right now."

"You have no idea how good it is to hear your voice."

"Thank you, sir."

"What happened, Dane?"

"We were ambushed." Winter drew back another drag of his smoke. "They knew exactly what they were doing."

"What do you mean?"

"The cartel had Sanchez's entire estate scoped out. They realized they wouldn't be able to launch a frontal assault because of all the guests' cars, so they concentrated their forces at the rear. Then they figured out how to hack into the security system. They gained access through the back gate without issue, while closing the front on us. If they'd got away with what they were planning, we'd have been looking at over two hundred people dead."

Dawson paused. "You did a bang-up job down there, Dane."

"But at what cost? The—"

"I know. I've been in contact with the San Yetaxa Police Department. They're all over the scene, digging up the bodies of those left behind. We've so far got matches on Middleton, Watts, Lynch and Sidhu. When no sign of you turned up, I..."

Winter finished off his cigarette, tossing it to the ground and stamping his foot on the last of its deadly glow. "Colonel, the cartel must pay for what they did."

"And they will. The police have assured—"

"Dammit, you know as well as I do that even if the cops wanted to do something about it, they couldn't. San Yetaxa is the Wild West. The outlaws reign down here. There won't be justice. Not the justice we're after."

"Dane, I understand your frustration. I'm mourning our people too. They—you—are like children to me. Losing them..." Dawson's voice softened. "Look, as much as there's part of me that would find satisfaction from the cartel getting what's coming to them, I can't have you tearing up half of Mexico on some kind of vendetta. Where would you even start?"

"Alfonso Berrera."

"Alfonso Berrera? The police have already talked to him."

"And?"

"They obtained nothing that'll pin him to the attack."

"Maybe I'll have more luck."

"You know, it's a hell of a lot more complex than that. Berrera understands how to stay out of trouble."

"Then I'll go after El Maestro instead."

"No one knows if El Maestro even exists." Dawson sighed. "And I doubt after so many years some gringo is going to flush him out."

"You forget who you're talking to, Colonel. I'm—"

"Listen, Dane, you remain employed by Redwind Security," Dawson interjected. "I'm instructing you to lie low. Wherever you are, get better, then return to the United States and report back to Camp Redwind."

"Colonel—"

"This discussion is over. You'll follow your orders. Let's allow the local law enforcement to do their job. If we're not satisfied..."

Dawson drifted off, his reasoning loud and clear.

Winter understood. "Very well."

The line went dead and Winter held the phone by his side, the frustration inside him bubbling over.

The door to the house opened and Maria appeared. "Are you done?"

Winter smiled and walked toward her, handing her the pink cell and returning the smokes to his pocket. "Not by a long shot."

"Come on. I don't like you being out of bed this long. Let's get you settled. Ruben will be here soon to check you over. I'd hate for him to tell me I've been a terrible nurse."

Winter obeyed, the injury forcing his obedience. When it came to Dawson's directive, however, that was a different story. When he was healed, following it would be a much tougher challenge.

18

Alfonso Berrera sat at his fine walnut desk, the pitch of his home perfectly allowing the afternoon sun to bathe his office through the floor-to-ceiling windows. The man was a creature of the warmth.

He looked up from his laptop and gazed at the horizon. There, beyond the arid valley, were the scenic San Yetaxa hills and the opulent estates perched upon them. Berrera's house should have been among them. He was, after all, worth more than most of those who called it home combined. But he was never one to get too close to others. He valued his solitude. And in his line of work, a professional distance was required.

Fortunately, he loved the desert. The imposing hills on the opposite side of the valley provided him with the seclusion he craved. The estate had been purpose-built for his needs and constructed to withstand the relentless elements the harsh Tlapetla climate threw at it.

As he continued to stare across the valley, he paid special attention to the property which had once been home to Gilberto Sanchez. The spiraling wisps of smoke had subsided, the remnants of his estate now nothing more than a blackened blemish upon the landscape. It had been a magnificent estate. Its destruction meant Berrera and his business partners could continue their work undeterred.

In instances such as these, sacrifices had to be made. If that meant the occasional visit to the station house of the San Yetaxa Police Department, then so be it. He never feared his run-ins with the law. Caution was paramount, and influence a safeguard. He had the right friends in the right places, and if they dared betray him, their fate would serve as a warning to others who might think about going against him.

Berrera returned his attention to the computer and the various numbers contained on the screen. What stared up at him was his bread and butter. To the people of Tlapetla, he was a ruthless taskmaster who built the cartel through violence and bloodshed. The truth was, the business thrived from the calculations in his spreadsheets.

To some, the ledgers might have appeared complex. There were, after all, a lot of moving parts. His organization not only shipped various drugs, such as cocaine and marijuana, through the state; it also manufactured its own. Producing methamphetamine had been a turning point, the quantities created rivaling all others throughout Mexico. When those around him said entering the meth game would be a pointless endeavor, he pressed his case. Luckily, they listened, and he proved everyone how wrong they were. Berrera took great pride in the construction of the facility, which had turned Tlapetla into a national powerhouse.

A phone rang, and he opened the drawer to his left, revealing dozens of various handsets. He reached for the one with the lit screen and removed it, nestling it next to his laptop and placing it on speakerphone.

"Good afternoon, El Maestro," he said.

"Berrera."

"What can I do for you, sir?"

"We need to discuss the operation on the Sanchez estate."

Berrera glanced over again at the San Yetaxa hills and at the scorched earth which had once been Sanchez's home. "Of course."

"There's a loose end which needs to be taken care of."

"Sir?"

"The Redwind operators. One remains alive."

"How do you know?" Berrera straightened in his seat. "The last I talked with my police contacts, they claimed the examiners were still digging up bodies and that the fifth Redwind operative might yet be among the ruins."

"I have other sources."

An email appeared in Berrera's inbox with two attachments. He clicked on the photo file and an image filled the screen of a man standing by a door. He had dark hair and eyes, a well-built physique, and skin much too pale for the Mexican sun.

"This is Dane Winter," El Maestro said. "He was the head of operations on the Sanchez protection detail."

"And you're telling me he survived?"

"I've provided his last known whereabouts."

Berrera clicked on the next file, examining the information. "Very well, I'll put my best man on it. Winter will be eliminated by nightfall."

The line went dead without so much as a thank you. Berrera tossed the phone into the drawer and closed it. With one hand he printed the files, and with the other he reached for the intercom.

"Cruz, get in here."

He stood and walked to the printer in the corner next to the large window. The door to his office opened and Roberto Cruz entered. He was tall and imposing, and his expression remained unreadable. There was not a single hair out of place in his methodically tied ponytail. Even Berrera found his demeanor unsettling. And he was not intimidated easily. Perhaps it was the dark tattoos painted down the left side of Cruz's face that made him look more phantom than man.

Berrera took the inked pages from the printer and returned to his desk, handing them over to Cruz. "His name is Dane Winter. It appears he survived the attack on Sanchez's estate."

Cruz examined the documents with his dull eyes. "He wouldn't have if you'd put me in charge of the operation."

"Be that as it may, I need him removed asap."

"I'll see to it."

"That'll be all." He waved off the assassin and Cruz marched from the office, slamming the door shut behind him. It jolted Berrera back to his seat.

With a shake of his head, he refocused on his computer. Cruz could revel in all the blood and brutality he wanted. Berrera preferred the quietude of his spreadsheets, where true power was measured in profits.

"And what kind of chicken is this?"

Winter jabbed his fork at the meal before him while, across the dining table, Maria watched him with a knowing smile.

"It's Mole Poblano," she said, taking a bite of the food on her plate. "Chilies, spices, nuts, and even some chocolate. Nothing groundbreaking. Do you like it?"

Winter scooped a portion of the chicken and rice, the sauce oozing throughout. He placed it on his tongue and gave it a hearty chew. "Delicious."

"Are you certain there's not too much spice? I made sure not to—"

"It's good." Winter shoveled another serving into his mouth. "Really. Thank you."

Maria glanced at the window, the dusk giving way to night, the last traces of the sun fading into the darkness. She got up and flipped a switch on the wall, bathing the kitchen and dining area in soft light.

Winter ate more of the chicken, shuffling to get settled in the rustic wooden chair. Maria had provided a pillow for him to sit on, but he remained uncomfortable, the throb at his side still permeating through his torso.

"Are you sure I can't help you more?" she asked, returning to her seat.

He brushed off her concern with a wave of his fork. "It's fine."

"Perhaps you should go back to bed. I could bring your dinner—"

"Trust me, Maria." Winter chuckled. "I've spent enough time in that room to last a lifetime. Anyway, when the doc came to check me out earlier, he said I was doing well and that I could start to move a little more."

She nodded, likely resigned to the fact that Winter was a stubborn man, and that she would have to pick her battles with him wisely. "How about a drink?"

"That'd be good."

Maria stood again and went to the kitchen. "Would you like water, or something a bit stronger?" She opened a cupboard and held up some tequila. "Did Ruben say anything about drinking alcohol?"

Winter ogled at the half-empty bottle in her hands, his throat tightening. "Uh, yeah, I seem to remember him saying I should lay off the booze until I'm healed," he lied.

"Of course. What was I thinking?" She stowed the tequila away and poured two glasses of water, coming back to the table and putting one next to each of their plates.

"Thank you." Winter took a sip, enjoying the chilled drink. "So, what's Ruben's story, anyway? Was it the San Yetaxa General Hospital he's based at?"

"Yep." Maria skewered more chicken. "He's a smart boy. Much smarter than me. Our dad desperately wanted to get him into medical school. He worked three jobs to make it happen. Eventually, his wish came true."

"And you're half-siblings? You share the same father?"

"That's right. Ruben's mom died of cancer when he was two. A couple of years later, Dad met another woman, my mother, and they got married. Not long after that, I was born. Ruben and I might be half-siblings on paper, but he's always been there for me. He's always protected me. He's my brother, plain and simple."

Winter had more of the meal. "And your parents? Where are they now?"

The quick back and forth slipped into an awkward silence.

Maria finished a bite, chewing her food before washing it down with a large gulp of water. "They died three years ago."

"I'm so sorry." Winter frowned. "What happened?"

"An accident on the Camino Sin Vuelta Astras."

A lump formed in Winter's throat, recognizing the name of the treacherous road.

"They were returning from Playa Azul and had a flat. The car went over the embankment. Neither survived the impact at the bottom." Maria stared past him. "It was a long way down. I suppose it would've been a quick death."

Winter stayed silent, the words he longed to say difficult to form.

Maria gestured to her surroundings. "They left the place to me and Ruben."

"But Ruben doesn't live here?"

"No, he's got a place in the city. He prefers to be close to the hospital at the center of town."

"So, you're all by yourself out here?"

She nodded.

"Have you ever thought of moving to be closer to him?"

"No. I grew up in this house. I like it out here."

"I don't blame you."

"And if we're being honest, San Yetaxa's a dump."

Winter chuckled.

"It's true. If it wasn't for this place, and the fact I have no money, I probably would've left by now."

Winter finished his dinner and drained the rest of his drink. "Do you mind if I go for a smoke?"

"Not at all."

Winter propped himself to his feet, gripping the sturdy timber table for support. He lumbered through the front door to be greeted by the night, the stars having fully claimed the sky. The tweets of the birds had evaporated, replaced by the hooting and hollering of small primates. He stepped into the shadows past the edge of the window and removed a cigarette from the packet. He lit it up and inhaled a deep puff, staring at the woman inside the house. The more he had got to know her, the more he reveled in unraveling her inner beauty. A warmth stirred within, a giddiness he could not quite shake.

He took the cigarette from his mouth, his thoughts swirling in uneasiness. Guilt twisted his gut, the kind he had not felt for years. He knew he should not have been ashamed of the feelings. It had been a long time, after all.

He frowned and returned his focus to the forest, drawing back more of his smoke. He understood why Maria would hesitate to leave such a spot. It was not just an anchor to her past. Her home was inherently peaceful. And in a place like San Yetaxa, where chaos often simmered, to find a pocket of calm was a rare and precious thing.

The distant tranquility took a turn. The familiar chatter of the monkeys faded, drowned out by something less natural. The buzz of an engine. It got louder, becoming more obvious. A motorcycle.

Winter craned his ear to the void. The bike neared and continued to close, its headlight off. He remembered during one of the many chats he'd had with Maria earlier in the day that she mentioned her house was largely secluded, her nearest neighbor several hectares away.

He dropped the cigarette at his feet and extinguished it with his sole. The motorbike's engine cut out and silence returned to the forest. Winter narrowed his eyes, peering into the distance, his form remaining hidden in the shadows. While the stillness hung heavy, a sudden tingle crawled up his arm. Not from the wound, but something else. He had always wondered if he possessed a sixth sense. Perhaps an awareness of dangers unseen.

As if to confirm his suspicion, a laser appeared from the night. A red dot sight. It swept over the house and settled on the window, aiming directly at Maria's head.

Winter made a dash for the door.

"Maria! Get down!"

The sniper rifle cracked, the clap of the bullet echoing through the forest.

20

The window shattered, the glass dusting the kitchen like exploding snowflakes. Each fragment shone in the light, splintering into a thousand pieces. Winter hurled himself through the front door to find Maria sprawled under the dining table.

His heart sank at the sight, the air thick with more bullets homing in on the house. The rounds thumped into the drywall, while others ricocheted off the pots and pans dangling from the hooks affixed to the kitchen ceiling. He ignored the shooting pain coursing down his body and hurled himself to the floor, sliding to Maria's side.

"Maria!" Winter grabbed her by the arm and flipped her onto her back. He could not see any entry wounds. "Have you been hit?"

She cupped her hands over her ears, the approaching chaos deafening her. "I don't think so!"

A breath of relief escaped Winter, his warning for her to take cover coming just in time.

"Who is it?" she asked.

"I'm not sure. But they aren't in the mood for talking. Do you have any weapons? Any guns?"

Maria shook her head, flinching from another bullet thudding into the light fixture above the table. The impact sent it crashing, their only source of illumination disappearing and immersing them in darkness. The shooting ceased, their attacker, whoever they were, appearing to believe they had done their job.

"That's our cue." Winter got to his feet and offered Maria a hand. She took it and they dashed toward the hallway.

Winter stopped by a door, noting the series of switches beside it. "Do any of these control the exterior lights?"

Maria pointed to the two at the top. "Those do."

Winter flipped them and nudged Maria into the adjacent room, protecting her from sight. As hoped, the outdoor lights flickered on, revealing a figure slowly walking in their direction from the forest. His face matched that of the merciless assailants who had unleashed hell upon Gilberto Sanchez's estate, obscured by a black mask adorned with a white skull. His body was slender but powerful, his gait more of a swagger than a walk. He held a bastardized Remington 700 sniper rifle with a modified red dot sight in one hand, and in the other, an AK-74U matching those used at the fundraiser.

The shooter ditched the long-range gun on the ground and brought the assault rifle to bear. Maria stepped out of the room to get a look. A scream threatened to escape her lips. Winter noticed, putting a hand over her mouth and motioning her to the back of the house.

She acknowledged his instruction with a slight nod and they edged down the hallway, past the bedrooms and the bathroom, all the way to the door. Winter felt for the handle just as the automatic gunfire erupted, tearing into the front of the dwelling and shredding everything in its path.

Winter shoved their exit ajar, and the pair burst out, the sounds of wood splintering, glass shattering, and metal ringing creating a destructive symphony. With their hands intertwined together, he and Maria ran up the side of the hill. Winter kept an eye behind them to ensure they were not being pursued.

The assassin appeared focused on the house. He placed a magazine in his rifle and launched another attack on the façade of the poor old log cabin.

Winter pointed to a nearby tree and a collection of shrubs. They slid to a stop and crouched low behind the cover. Maria's hands trembled, her body quaking under his touch. Winter put an arm over her shoulder and pulled her in, nuzzling her head against his chest.

"It's okay," he said. "We got away."

The assassin stopped firing and entered the house, hurling what was left of the front door from its hinges.

"What does the cartel want with me?" Maria asked.

Winter had the same question. "Have you ever been involved with them?"

"What! Never!" she shot back, releasing herself from his grasp. "Believe me, if I'd had anything to do with the cartel, I wouldn't be working at Hector's..."

She trailed off. Winter noticed.

"What is it?" he asked.

"Nothing."

"Are you sure?"

"I don't know."

"This is important, Maria."

She pondered for a moment. "The diner."

"What about it?"

"I've always wondered if everything was on the level there."

"What do you mean?"

"The barrels."

"The barrels?"

"I've worked in my fair share of restaurants and diners," Maria went on. "Some busier than Hector's. None of them disposed of the grease as much as he did."

"What's that got to do—"

"Hector has a barrel of grease taken away every single day. For a place of that size, it should take at least two weeks before the deep fryers need emptying."

Winter brushed his chin. "You think Hector's linked with the cartel? Using the transport of his grease in their supply chain?"

She shrugged. "It wouldn't surprise me."

"That's thin reasoning, Maria. Have you let anyone else know you suspected foul play?"

She shook her head. "It was just an observation. I've never told a soul."

"Then I doubt the cartel's after you. They can't read your mind." Winter attempted to put the puzzle pieces together. "What about Ruben? Could he have connections?"

"No way. He's as clean as they come."

The assassin emerged from the front of the house, stopping by the door and tossing something back inside. A match. Flames vented from the interior, crawling the walls and spreading to the ceiling, engulfing everything in a fiery blaze. Tears streamed down Maria's cheeks, the last link to her parents going up in smoke.

Winter took her hands again and wrenched them both upright. "We have to keep moving."

Maria dragged her feet until an explosion discharged from the kitchen, sending blistering sparks into the sky. They hurried farther up the hill and over the crest until the glow of the fire disappeared into the abyss.

"I'm sorry, Maria," Winter said. "I think they might've been after me."

She wiped her eyes of the remaining tears. "You?"

"I don't know why, but it can't be a coincidence, right? I was at Gilberto Sanchez's."

"You were hired to protect him. Three days ago, you hadn't even set foot in San Yetaxa. To them, you're a nobody. It doesn't make any sense."

"I realize that." Winter brought them to a halt, and they collected their breath in the heart of the forest. "But if neither you nor Ruben have gotten in their bad books, it has to be me."

"If that's the case, how did they find you?" Maria put her hands on her hips. "I haven't told anyone you were at my house. I can guarantee you Ruben hasn't either. The hospital board frown on those who perform at-home medical procedures."

Winter peered beyond their position, the silence enveloping them. "However they've done it, we can bank they won't stop looking for me. We need to keep going. Any idea where we could hunker down for a while?"

Maria paused, her mind racing for a solution. "I may know a place."

She took his hand and led him further into the wilderness.

21

Inspector Alvarez gripped the steering wheel, weaving around the jagged potholes ahead. With the smooth tarmac of the road from San Yetaxa behind them, he navigated the rugged hillside with razor-sharp focus, aware that one wrong move would send them sliding into the bog.

"I think we should've signed out the SUV." Martinez smirked in the passenger seat. "Are you sure you wouldn't prefer me to drive?"

Alvarez ignored the youthful wit and aimed the car down the narrowing trail where a rickety old wooden fence appeared on their right. He drove for an additional two hundred yards to the entrance of the driveway, framed by weathered timber posts. He veered onto the property, slamming over another treacherous section of road and scraping the underside of the vehicle, a heavy thump reverberating through their seats.

They cruised to the house at the end of the long driveway, each side enclosed by tall mahogany trees matching those dotted throughout the rest of the hills. While the trail leveled out compared to the steep street leading to the home, several tire tracks crisscrossed the surface, creating a less than comfortable ride.

Alvarez tapped the brake on approach to the house and came to a stop. Surrounded by two fire trucks still on the site, and the van belonging to the medical examiners, were the remnants of the dwelling. Unlike the blaze which had claimed Gilberto Sanchez's stone-built home, this much humbler abode was constructed of lumber. Little was left to show for it, the fire having devoured everything in its path.

Alvarez threw his door open and stepped out of the cruiser. Martinez followed, the pair taking extra care to step around the tracks imprinted in the driveway. They made their way to the house, passing by the firefighters who were packing their gear.

The examiners stepped throughout the ruins, scouring the site with a methodical touch. Alvarez noticed Trevino among them, the lead on the Sanchez crime scene. Normally, investigators of Alvarez and Martinez's ilk would not have been called out for what seemed at first glance to be a simple house fire caused by a faulty gas cooker.

Trevino had seen it differently.

He waved at the two inspectors and moved through the charred vestiges of the home, stepping through what once was likely the front door. "We keep meeting like this, Alvarez."

"I think you just enjoy your job too much. What have you found?"

Trevino produced a small plastic evidence bag and handed it to Alvarez. "That's a few of what we've discovered so far. The ashes are riddled with them."

Alvarez examined the spent bullets and shell casings inside. "Two different rounds."

Trevino nodded. "You've got five-four-fives and .308 Winchesters."

Alvarez turned to his partner. "What do we think?"

The younger man pondered, glancing around the property. "The .308s could've come from a sniper rifle."

"And the five-four-fives?"

"An assault rifle. An AK74U."

"A Krinkov? A cartel weapon?"

Martinez nodded. "The attacker probably fired from distance on the house with the sniper rifle and finished at close range with the AK."

"Very good, Martinez. We might make an inspector of you yet." Alvarez gave the bag back to Trevino. "What about the fire?"

"It appears our assailant cranked the gas," the examiner said. "All it would've taken was a match and whoosh, up she went."

"And you've found no bodies?"

"None."

"Do you expect to?"

"With a scene of this size, we should've seen something by now."

"Whoever was here must've got away."

Alvarez raised an eyebrow at Martinez. "Why do you say that?"

"Well, the attacker was shooting at someone, weren't they? It's unlikely you fire a sniper rifle unless you have a target. Looks like our guy missed and closed in with his Krinkov."

"And whoever his intended victims were, they were smart enough to flee. Makes sense, I suppose."

"Have you been able to determine who owns this place?" Trevino asked.

"The residence goes under the names of Luis and Rosario Pineda. Both died in a car accident three years ago. The guys at the station house are checking in on who their next of kin was."

Alvarez turned to Martinez. "Give them a call and see if they've had any luck."

"Will do." His partner pulled out his phone and walked off, leaving Alvarez to focus his attention on Trevino.

"I won't get in the way of your work. Let me know if you find anything that might help."

"Of course." Trevino whistled. "The cartel, eh?"

"They keep us busy, I'll give them that."

The examiner frowned and returned to the house. Alvarez interlaced his hands behind his back and did a circuit of the rubble, returning to the parked car where Martinez remained on the phone. Alvarez furrowed his brow at the tire tracks at his feet and continued down the driveway. He noted the deep prints left by the fire trucks and the shallower ones produced by Trevino's van and the unmarked police cruiser.

Most of the grooves had been fashioned by another vehicle. Likely the owner of the residence. A car that did not appear on site. Alvarez scratched his chin. Then he spotted something. More tracks. Fresh ones. They were skinnier than the others. He crouched down and brushed his fingers through the narrow trenches.

"A motorcycle," he muttered, figuring the rider of the bike had stopped about halfway down the driveway. Alvarez pivoted on the ball of his foot and pretended to hold a sniper rifle, aiming it at the house. "Hmm..." He slung the imaginary gun over his shoulder and ambled back to Martinez. "Any luck?"

"You could say that." Martinez slid his phone into his pocket. "Luis and Rosario left the place to their son and daughter. Ruben Pineda, a doctor at San Yetaxa General Hospital, and Maria Pineda, his sister."

"Maria Pineda? I know that name."

"You should. She was a caterer at Gilberto Sanchez's fundraiser."

Alvarez recalled the document sitting on his desk. He had planned to talk to everyone on it. But it was a long list and Maria Pineda was near the bottom.

"Our colleagues did some more digging," Martinez continued. "It would appear Maria put a claim in with her insurance agency."

"Her car?"

"Yep. She lost it during the assault at Sanchez's."

"That explains why it isn't here. We have to assume she escaped this little attack on foot." Alvarez placed his hands on his hips. "I wonder what the cartel wanted with her?"

"Inspector!"

The throaty shout of Trevino jolted Alvarez's thoughts. The examiner signaled them into the charred house. Alvarez edged through the ruins with Martinez, meeting the other man near the center of the remains.

"Do you remember the phone call we had the other day?" Trevino asked.

"There were several," Alvarez said.

"You told me to keep an eye out for a chain with an engagement ring at Sanchez's estate. One with three diamonds." Trevino held out a gloved hand, the blackened item of jewelry on display for the inspectors to see.

"Well, I'll be damned." Martinez clucked his tongue. "Dane Winter was here."

Alvarez took some gloves from his pocket and placed them on, taking the chain from Trevino's grasp. "Unless Maria Pineda came into its possession at the party. She could've robbed his corpse."

"I might remind both of you that there's still no positive DNA matches for Winter at Sanchez's house," Trevino added.

"So if we assume Winter was here," Martinez said, "why?"

Alvarez cleaned some of the ash from the chain between his fingers. "Her brother was a doctor, wasn't he?"

"Yeah."

"What if Winter was hurt in the assault? Maria might have brought him here and got Ruben Pineda to heal his wounds."

"I suppose that's plausible enough."

"It opens up another question." Alvarez returned the chain to Trevino. "We're assuming that the cartel went after the owner of this house. What if that's not the case? What if they were coming for Winter instead?"

"But why?"

Alvarez shrugged. "I don't know. But considering no bodies were found in this fire, it stands to reason both Pineda and Winter are alive. If we want answers, we'll have to find them."

22

"Would you like that in a bag, sir?"

Winter nodded at the attendant with the refined English accent behind the counter. The man stepped around his desk and slipped the item into a tiny plastic pouch. He returned and handed it to Winter over the counter.

"Good luck to you, sir."

Winter smiled and turned, finding himself in the heart of Heathrow Airport's main terminal. With the lavish store fading into the distance, he slipped into the crowd of excited yet weary travelers. He checked the information board above, the mass of tourists' voices getting lost in the PA announcement requiring a passenger to board their flight before it was too late.

Winter did not want to be one of the unlucky ones left behind. The screen revealed his United Airlines service to New York departing within thirty minutes. He came to a halt at a bench and pulled his heavy backpack from his shoulders, unzipping the front compartment. He took the plastic bag in his hand and squeezed it inside, refastening the zip to ensure his purchase could not escape.

As he reached for the straps, a little boy, no more than six, *approached, his back ramrod straight. He saluted Winter in the British fashion, his palm facing downward. Winter glanced at his attire, almost forgetting that he was still in uniform, having worn it since leaving the Middle East. He reciprocated the salute in the American manner. The child's mother came over and whisked him away with an apologetic wave.*

Winter's thoughts drifted to the future. One chapter of his life had closed. Another was about to open. Perhaps children of his own were on the cards.

First thing's first. He slung the backpack over his shoulders and found his bearings, resuming a beeline for his gate.

By the time he arrived, the flight staff had already begun boarding the enthusiastic travelers. He joined the queue and shuffled forward. An attendant greeted him and scanned his ticket, motioning him onto the plane. Half the passengers were still standing inside the cabin on board, the scene a chaotic one as people squeezed in their carry-on luggage and parents frantically got their kids set up on electronic devices for the trip ahead.

Winter found his seat about halfway down, receiving the aisle spot as he'd requested. He put his backpack in the compartment above his head and fell into his base of operations for the next eight hours.

A man with salt and pepper hair in the seat beside him gazed up from his newspaper. "Hello, Captain." *He spoke with a New York accent, a broad grin appearing across his seasoned features.*

Winter greeted him with a weary nod. "Sir."

"Oh, don't call me sir. I'm a sergeant. Well, I was a sergeant." *His joviality soured for a moment before he returned to his chatter.* "Where are you heading home from?"

"Iraq."

"Ah."

Considering the man appeared well-read and ex-military, Winter assumed he was aware of Hick's and Collins' death in the Taktur

Mountains. Winter, clad in his Marine uniform, would only have compounded his curiosity.

"I served in the army," he went on. "Retired after the Gulf War. Took on some jobs alongside you guys every now and then. Banter aside, I loved working with the Marines. You do a hell of a job."

The hatches sealed, and the plane got underway, rolling toward the taxiway. The flight crew recited the usual safety spiel, and the pilot's voice crackled over the PA, announcing their imminent departure.

"So, how long are you spending at home?" the passenger asked.

Winter took a breath, his thoughts already across the Atlantic. "Forever."

"End of the line, eh? Good for you. Got anyone waiting for you on the other side?"

* * *

Winter opened his eyes to the soft murmur of a gentle stream. He lifted his head from the ground where he had slept the night before and peered out of the makeshift shelter. Built from old wooden pallets, it was held together with rusty nails and worn screws. Beyond, Maria crouched at the creek's edge, filling a plastic bottle with water.

She pivoted and walked back to their temporary accommodation. "Looks like someone's awake."

Winter yawned. "Barely."

"How did you sleep?"

"About as well as I expected."

"How are your bandages?"

"I'm still a bit sore."

Maria entered the shanty and kneeled by his side, checking the wound. "There's not a lot of bleeding anymore. That's a good sign."

"Not bad, considering how far we walked last night."

She handed Winter the water.

He smiled, looking around the ramshackle structure. "A hotel with five-star views and room service. Impressive."

Maria smirked, tapping the timber supports with a closed fist. "I honestly didn't think it'd still be standing. Ruben and I built it years ago. When my cousins came to visit, the four of us would spend hours here. We even convinced our parents to let us camp out here occasionally."

She stared at the creek and beyond, her thoughts seemingly adrift in the past.

"I'm really sorry, Maria."

"You have nothing to apologize for."

Winter drank from the gnarled bottle of water which had likely been baking in the sun for years. His sips transformed into a gulp. He handed it to Maria and she enjoyed some, too.

"We should have some food," she said.

"You don't have a Mickey D's out here, do you?"

"Something better possibly." Maria crawled further into the shelter and brushed away some dirt, revealing a slab of timber. She lifted it, uncovering an underground compartment. Reaching inside, she pulled out a small portable cooker, a can of beans and a shabby old pan. "Looks like my stash is still here."

"I wonder if there's any gas in it." Winter rose to his feet and strolled from the shack into the embrace of the morning sun.

Maria followed and set up the cooker in the open air. With a turn of the knob and a press of the igniter, it hissed to life. She put the pan on top and smiled at Winter.

"This is perfect," he said with a sly grin. "Next time I get the urge to sleep in the dirt, I'll know who to call."

She chuckled and returned to the shelter to find more odds and ends in the underground treasure trove, including a can opener and a wooden spoon. As she leaned over to crack open the beans, her phone spilled from her back pocket.

Winter picked up the device. "I don't suppose you have electricity and a charger cable in that secret hideout of yours?"

"No. It wouldn't do us much good, anyway." She opened the can and tossed the beans into the pan. "There's no reception this far out."

Winter dropped to his knees and found a decent patch to sit.

She looked at him through the rising wisps of flavor curling between them. "Have you figured it out yet?"

"Hmm?"

"That assassin last night. You said he was after you."

"It's more than likely."

"But you don't know why."

"No. But I intend to find out." The beans bubbled and Winter inhaled the aroma. "That's if I survive your food."

23

Cruz sped across the desert highway on his Ducati motorcycle, the engine growling and the wind whipping against his leathers. What little breeze there was filtered through the vents of the helmet, keeping him cool in the desolate hellscape. He loved the open road. The speed. The solitude. The pleasure of escape. It was his favorite pastime.

Well, his second favorite pastime.

His job was what kept him most fulfilled. He did not consider himself a monster. Just a man who wanted to do an honest day's work. Everyone had a skill, a calling. His happened to be killing.

Growing up in San Yetaxa had not been an easy life. One was either a lamb or a lion. It was a tale everybody in the neighborhood of La Forja had known since they were a kid. You learned to hunt or allowed yourself to become prey. There was no middle ground. Lambs were led to the slaughter by those in control—the lions.

Cruz had been raised in the slums of the inner-west. His parents were both junkies. They had nothing. He had to fight for meals in the street while they got high at home. On the day of his eighth birthday, he watched his mother overdose. She was dead by the time the ambulance arrived. Cruz did not shed a tear.

She had deserved it. She had been prey.

After the funeral, his father continued destroying himself with any poison he could find. Cruz grew up quickly, understanding the workings of San Yetaxa before long. He hated the cartel.

When he was fourteen, he went with his father to his dealer, Slick Santos. After the exchange had taken place, Cruz watched the man drive away in his car, burning the make, model and license plate into his mind. For the next two months, he observed Slick Santos go about his work throughout La Forja.

Then he acted.

Cruz set up a deal inside an abandoned abattoir, prepared to pay for some gear of his own. When Slick Santos had arrived, Cruz pounced, trapping the man in the blood pit. Slick Santos stared up at him, his limbs trembling, ensnared with nowhere to go. The hunter had become the prey.

Cruz took out a revolver he had scored on the streets and aimed it at him.

Suddenly, he heard a clap. Followed by another.

On the upper level of the abattoir, a bald man stood in applause, with two goons by his side, their guns pointed at Cruz. They ambled down the steps, and the bald man introduced himself as Cueball.

He took the weapon from Cruz's hand and let the dealer out. "You've done well," Cruz remembered Cueball telling him. "It takes a lot of *cajones* to do what you've done. Would you have gone through with it? Would you have killed him?"

Cruz had hesitated at that moment before finally saying, "Yes."

Cueball gave the revolver back to him. "Prove it."

Slick Santos's eyes widened in horror. Cruz pulled the gun up and leveled it at his chest, the man's arms shooting up in surrender.

"What's going on, Cueball!" he wailed. "I—"

Cruz squeezed the trigger.

Three times.

Cueball smiled as the dealer fell to the floor, a pool of blood bursting from his seams. "You've proven yourself worthy."

Cruz turned the sidearm onto Cueball. "Worthy of what?"

To his credit, the bald man did not flinch. In fact, he doubled-down, kneeling and shoving the gun into the center of his head, egging on Cruz to shoot.

"In this world, there are lambs and lions." Cueball motioned to the corpse of Slick Santos. "He was a lamb. You... are a lion."

Cruz desperately wanted to fire. But he could not. The call of the wild was too much for him. He let the sidearm drop, and Cueball yanked it from his grasp. He wrapped an arm across Cruz's shoulders and guided him from the killing floor, the lion cub having feasted on his first prey.

Cruz's phone buzzed, transporting him back to the present, the ringtone sounding in the Bluetooth system within the bike helmet. He slowed and pulled over to the side of the dusty road, bringing the motorcycle to a stop and taking the phone from the pocket of his leathers.

"This is Cruz."

"I've just talked to my police contacts." The voice was Berrera's. "They've informed me that no bodies were found in the house."

"I know."

"You know! Why did you let Winter live?"

"Sometimes prey can be elusive. This man's an ex-Marine. It'll take more time."

"You had explicit instructions to kill him. There are those who—"

"You can assure El Maestro that Winter will be taken care of." Cruz gritted his teeth. "He's now on the run. My hunt for him continues."

"This isn't some game, Cruz."

"Life's a game, Mr. Berrera. I now have the sniff of blood. I promise you that soon I'll have his head for your mantlepiece."

There was a pause. Cruz enjoyed skirting the edge with the man. Why? Because he knew he was the best that Berrera had at his disposal.

"Very well," Berrera eventually said. "You'll be on your own this time. I have no information on his new location."

"Even better." Cruz smirked. "I prefer doing things the old-fashioned way."

24

Alvarez took the car toward the San Yetaxa General Hospital and scanned for the closest spot to the front door. Since the medical facility was the largest in the city, the parking lot was unsurprisingly full. He found a space near the back and narrowed his eyes at the entrance two hundred yards away.

"You know we could've parked in one of the disabled spots?" Martinez quipped next to him. "You qualify by now, don't you?"

Alvarez glared at him. Ever since they had partnered up, the younger inspector had slowly but surely developed into quite the joker. "You just try to keep up."

Martinez smirked at the rebuttal and hopped out of the car with Alvarez, weaving their way to the hospital's front door. Avoiding other vehicles and some incoming ambulances, they entered the lower lobby. A familiar scent hit Alvarez. The blend of sickness and antiseptic. It was a smell he had not forgotten since he was a small child, when his grandfather had been admitted to the same hospital for a routine hernia operation.

The elder statesman of the family never came out, the surgical team botching the procedure. He had loved the man so very much and had never forgiven them for what they had taken from him. He never even got to say goodbye.

"Alvarez?"

He snapped himself from the memories of the past, to find Martinez staring at him, the duo of inspectors standing in the doorway.

"Are you okay?" his partner asked.

"Yeah." Alvarez grunted. "Let's keep going."

They continued to the reception desk and waited for one of the three women behind the counter to take notice. All of them were swamped, their fingers darting across their keyboards and phones pressed to their ears. The one in the middle finally ended her call and stared up at them.

"Yes?" Her tone was clipped with fatigue. "How can I help you, gentlemen?"

"Where would we be able to find Dr. Ruben Pineda?" Alvarez asked.

"Do you have an appointment with—"

Alvarez and Martinez flipped out their inspector shields in unison, stopping her question in its tracks.

She got the hint and opened a thick leather folder. "He was on the night shift, but it doesn't look like he's signed off yet. You'll likely find him on the third floor in his office." She took out a map and circled the location with her pen. "If he's not there, you can ask the reception desk where they saw him last."

Alvarez took the map and Martinez nodded his thanks. They set off to the elevator and entered, punching in their destination.

The doors slid open on the third floor, revealing a chaotic scene. Wheelchairs went one way, gurneys the other. The hectic pace of a hospital was something Alvarez had never become accustomed to. He pulled a handkerchief from his pocket and dabbed the perspiration on his forehead as he and Martinez followed the map to the reception area. They strolled through the busy waiting area and flashed their shields at the receptionist.

"We're here to see Dr. Ruben Pineda," Martinez said.

The woman's weary eyes widened. "Try his office. Second door down. If he's not there, he's probably in the changing room at the end of the hall."

"Thank you."

Alvarez and Martinez shifted onward, reaching the doctor's inner sanctum. Alvarez rapped on the door, but there was no response.

He knocked again and nudged it ajar. "No one's home."

He motioned farther down the hallway and he and Martinez entered the men's changing room. There, standing by an open locker, stood a man with his shirt off, his dark blue scrubs at his feet. He glanced sideways at those who had intruded.

"Who are you?" he asked.

Alvarez ambled in his direction with his shield held out, the space flanked by metal lockers and furnished with wooden benches in the center. "My name's Inspector Alvarez from the San Yetaxa Police Department. This is my partner, Inspector Martinez. Are you Dr. Ruben Pineda?"

"Uh... I... yep, that's right," he stammered.

"Is there anyone else in here, Doctor?"

Ruben looked farther down, the artificial glow of fluorescent lights revealing showers and toilets. "I don't think so."

"Good." Alvarez motioned to the door and Martinez locked them inside. "Put your shirt on, Doctor, and take a seat."

Ruben did so, his fingers fumbling with the buttons. "What's this about?"

Alvarez tucked away his shield, and the pair sat. "It's about your sister Maria."

"What about her?" Ruben blurted.

"There's been an incident at her house."

"An incident? What happened?"

"We were called to her home this morning to investigate a house fire. I regret to inform you that the blaze destroyed it."

Ruben's jaw dropped. "Is she—"

"Her body wasn't found in the debris. However, there was a very concerning detail discovered."

"Which was?"

"There were bullets unearthed in the ashes. A lot of them. We believe it was the work of the cartel."

"What! Did they take her?"

Alvarez glanced at Martinez, who had remained near the door at a generous distance for Alvarez to conduct the informal interview. "We don't believe so. This has all the markings of a hit job, which means the objective was to kill those in the house."

Ruben allowed himself a heavy sigh of relief. "So she got away."

"It's a distinct possibility. Now, Doctor, we have to understand what's going on here. We suspect that the attack took place between seven and eight o'clock last night. When did you last see her?"

"Yesterday afternoon. I'd say about two."

"At her house?"

Ruben nodded.

"Have you talked to her since?" Alvarez asked.

The doctor pondered. "Again, at about six on the phone."

"So, to be clear, you've had no contact with her following that?"

"No, I've been on the night shift. Are you insinuating something here, Inspector?"

Alvarez shook his head. "No, just trying to lay a foundation for the case. We want to do everything in our power to protect her. If the cartel realizes she escaped the blaze, they'll continue going after her."

"But she didn't do anything."

"She's had no dealings with the cartel?"

"No!" Ruben shot back. "Maria's not like that."

"Like what?"

"Like someone who gets involved with the cartel."

"Do you know that for certain?" Alvarez pursed his lips, attempting to be as diplomatic as possible. "She's a minimum wage waitress and caterer. People who need money—"

"I guarantee you, Maria has done nothing wrong."

"Very well, Doctor." Alvarez nodded. "What about you?"

Ruben chuckled dryly. "If you're asking me if I've ever worked for the cartel, I can confidently say no. They might be among my patients, but I'd never know it if they were."

"That's good. The question is: why would they have tried to kill Maria? Any ideas?"

Ruben considered for a moment, his eyes evading Alvarez's, a finger tracing a line around his lips. Alvarez reached into his pocket and took out the chain and ring salvaged from the ashes of the house fire.

He placed the item on the bench between the two men. "As you consider what I'm asking, I'd like you to keep in mind, I'm only posing these questions for your sister's sake. Anything you may have done at the residence regarding off the books medical procedures is irrelevant to me."

Ruben stared at the jewelry, seemingly unwilling to touch the blackened remains. "You know that the American was there."

"What was his name, Doctor?"

He took a breath. "Dane Winter. Maria rescued him from Gilberto Sanchez's estate. He had a gunshot wound. I managed to save him."

Alvarez again looked over at Martinez, their suspicions confirmed.

"Was he who the cartel was after?" Ruben asked.

"If neither you nor Maria have gotten on their wrong side, it's logical to conclude this Winter character was on their radar." Alvarez scratched the back of his neck. "Why, that is, I can't be certain yet. But his body wasn't found either. We can only assume both he and Maria escaped and are currently in hiding. What we do know is, because of the American, Maria is now involved."

Ruben rubbed his temples, closing his eyes as the weight of the conversation took its toll.

Martinez stepped toward him. "We need to find them before the cartel does, Dr. Pineda. If you were her, where would you go?"

Ruben remained slouched, until suddenly his shoulders perked up and his eyes cracked open. "There might be somewhere..."

25

Cruz tore into the parking lot of the San Yetaxa General Hospital, the powerful Ducati howling as he screamed around a slow-moving SUV. He gunned it for the entrance, riding onto the pavement and skidding to a stop next to a trashcan.

He stretched out the muscles in his neck and upper back, his bones cracking one by one. A slovenly security guard barged from the door and ambled in his direction. By the time he reached Cruz, he was gasping for air, his legs threatening to buckle beneath him.

"Hey, you can't park that here!" he said.

Cruz lifted the visor of his helmet and fixed on him with a cold, unblinking stare. The menace in his eyes and the intimidating tattoo inked on the side of his face was all that was needed to keep the fat man silent. He turned and shuffled back inside without so much as a whimper.

In the opposite direction, a middle-aged son helped his elderly mother out of the door. He grasped a handle of her wheelchair with one hand and her oxygen tank with another. They went over to one of the many wooden benches designed for visitors. The son took a seat, while his old lady lit up a cigarette. Cruz shook his head at the woman—some people just won't help themselves.

He flicked down the kickstand and prepared to dismount, ready to make his next move. Since his phone call with Berrera, he had to come up with a Plan B. Dane Winter, as he had explained to his employer, would not be an easy kill. Cruz investigated what other information was out there about the man. Winter had fought in Iraq and Afghanistan for twenty years, amassing more commendations than most soldiers could dream of.

Cruz was not a soldier. He was not forged by the juggernaut of the US war machine, but he was battle-hardened and every bit as lethal. Not because he had sought it out, but because it was a necessity in San Yetaxa if one wanted to survive. And Winter was on his turf. Cruz's biggest advantage of all. Yet he still had to find him.

That was where Dr. Ruben Pineda came in. Prior to Cruz launching his assault on Winter, he did his due diligence, uncovering the person who had been harboring him. The burned home belonged to a pair long dead. His contacts at the Tlapetla Ministry of Mobility and Transportation, however, confirmed one individual, very much alive, was using the address. Maria Pineda. He discovered the same name on Gilberto Sanchez's list of caterers. She must have brought Winter back to her house after the cartel attack. Why? He could not be sure. Regardless, her brother held the key to his questions. Including their whereabouts.

The automatic doors at the entrance of the hospital opened and three figures walked out. One he recognized. Dr. Ruben Pineda. To his left was a man of a similar age; to his right, an older guy with a short-brimmed hat, around sixty. While Cruz did not know them personally, it was obvious who they were. The way they dressed, the way they carried themselves. They were cops. Probably inspectors, given the lack of uniforms.

Cruz dropped his visor and cursed silently in his helmet. The San Yetaxa Police Department were surprisingly efficient this morning. And if neither of the inspectors were paid for by the cartel, it would be a problem. But perhaps they could do his job for him.

The trio walked past him and marched to their car at the far end of the parking lot. Cruz flipped up the kickstand and fired up the engine. The unmarked police vehicle lurched out of the exit and Cruz followed, keeping a safe distance on the roadway. It did not take him long to figure out their destination. They were going straight to Maria's house. Were they simply taking Ruben there to survey the wreckage, or was it something more?

They exited the outskirts of the city and climbed the hills, the traffic thinning until Cruz could no longer blend in with the flow of cars. If they were inspectors, as he assumed, they would smell a tail miles away. At the fork in the road, the cops took the right for Maria's residence. Cruz went to the left. It would take him longer the more indirect way around, but it would mask his approach.

The trail beneath shifted from asphalt to gravel, the Ducati's tires threatening to throw him off balance. Cruz would have preferred his dirt bike, but his more expensive ride would have to do. He rocketed up the incline as fast as the surface would allow and sped down the opposite road, slowing at the tree line near Maria's fence. The police had already arrived, the three men standing in front of the house. The doctor, visibly shaken at the wreckage of his childhood home, could do little to hide his sadness.

"At least you had somewhere to live," Cruz muttered.

Ruben and the cops moved off, leaving the ashes in their wake, and walked into the wilderness beyond. Cruz smiled. Just as he had hoped, they were not here to play sightseers. He switched off the bike and nestled it behind a tree. Removing his helmet, he set off on foot and resumed the hunt, maintaining the perfect distance to stay out of sight. They were the skills he had learned on the street. The skills of a hunter chasing its prey.

The stroll through the forest reached the half-hour mark when Ruben's legs began to slow. He led the cops down a steep decline toward a fast-flowing creek and a structure by the water. Cruz got as close as he dared and pressed himself against a nearby tree. The construction appeared to have been built out of a random arrangement of timber, large enough to hold three adults should the need require.

Ruben and the inspectors stopped before it, finding some items on the ground between it and the creek. Cruz narrowed his eyes. The older cop picked up a portable gas cooker and an opened can of beans.

Cruz smirked. All his Christmases had come at once. Winter and Maria Pineda must have fled there after he attacked the house. Considering they had left evidence of their meal, they were likely still nearby.

Unfortunately, the forest was not where Cruz excelled. He preferred the chaos of urban neighborhoods. And the police getting in his way would only worsen matters. He would have to wait until Winter and Maria entered civilization. Until then, he would keep a close eye on Ruben.

26

Maria lowered the binoculars from her eyes and passed them to Winter, who lay beside her in the dirt, their stomachs flat against the forest floor. "That's definitely Ruben."

Winter scanned for himself with the crude old binoculars, which Maria had found in the secret compartment of the shelter. He got the focus right and zeroed in on the three men standing around the old shanty. She was correct. One was the doc.

"I wonder who the other two are?" Maria said.

Winter swung his sight to the left, centering on the oldest with a short-brimmed hat and graying hair poking from the sides. The man slipped a hand into his pants pocket, tugging at his jacket to reveal something metallic tucked in his breast pocket. "Cops. They've got inspector shields."

"They must have gone to see Ruben at the end of his shift at the hospital. If they'd asked him where I might be, it makes sense he brought them here." Maria snatched the binoculars from him to take another look. "He's probably worried sick about me."

"He'll know you're alive."

"How?"

Winter gestured for the binoculars, discovering the eldest inspector picking up the portable cooker and can of beans. "Because nothing says 'we totally weren't here' like a steaming can of beans."

He would have preferred to leave no evidence of their stay at the shelter, but the sound of the movements in their direction had forced them into a quick retreat. They could not have risked it if it had been the assassin from the night before. "Would Ruben know any other places you would go?"

"No. We didn't venture too far beyond this part of the woods. If we follow the creek, the forest gets quite dense."

"Where does it lead?"

"It loops around to the road on the other side of the hills."

"Which means we might be able to stay ahead of them."

"What do you mean?" Maria craned her neck at him. "They're the police. They've asked Ruben to come out here so they can find us. We should go down there."

Winter put a hand on the arch of her back to stop her from taking matters into her own hands. "That would be unwise."

"Why? We haven't done anything wrong. The villain here is the psychopath who tried to kill us last night."

"Do you have any idea who those guys are?" Winter returned the binoculars, and she looked through them to double-check. She shook her head.

"Well, that's a problem, isn't it?" he said. "We don't know if they're good cops or bad cops. If they're paid for by the cartel, we'll be walking straight into their trap. There'd be nothing stopping them pulling out their guns and shooting you, me, and Ruben right here in the woods where no one would be any the wiser."

Maria's lips parted, but no words came out. The cogs in her

head turned as she grappled with the weight of what she had gotten herself into. "What do we do then?"

"If I were smart, I'd go back to the States and forget this whole thing ever happened. Unfortunately, that won't solve anything." Winter let out a breath. "They'd still come after you, because you're their only lead to get to me. And even if I went home, nothing would stop them from crossing the border to finish the job."

Maria stared at him expectantly.

"I need to stay in Mexico to find out why they want me so badly. I also have to remain here to protect you from them. And..."

Maria raised her brow. "And?"

"And I need to teach them a lesson."

"I don't understand."

"They killed four of my friends. They can't get away with that."

"What do you intend to do, take on the cartel all by yourself?"

Winter chuckled. "You sound like my boss."

"Maybe he's right. You won't defeat the cartel." Maria shook her head. "You think it'll be as simple as taking out Alfonso Berrera? Everyone knows that there's someone behind his power—"

"El Maestro."

"Just because you know his name doesn't mean you can beat him."

"Maybe. Maybe not. I have to try."

Maria sighed, glancing at her half-brother. "What do you plan to do?"

"To begin with, we need to get you somewhere safe. Preferably not in San Yetaxa. What about your cousins' beach house? Playa Azul, was it? Any chance they still have it?"

Maria nodded. "They do."

"Good."

"What about Ruben? You talk about my safety, but what about his?"

The doc and the inspectors left the shack and began their trek back to the remains of Maria's house.

"He'll be fine."

"You can't guarantee that."

"If they're good cops, they'll protect him. If not, they won't kill the only person who has the ability to help track either of us down."

"And I'm supposed to just take your word on all of that?"

"Yes, you are."

Maria rolled her eyes and wriggled closer to Winter. "I won't flee San Yetaxa without my brother. I can't leave him behind. Do you understand?"

Winter bit his bottom lip and pulled himself to his feet, offering Maria a helping hand. He led her in the opposite direction to Ruben and the cops.

"Did you hear what I said?" she asked.

"Loud and clear."

"Then what are you going to do about it?"

"I'm thinking."

They trudged down another crest and found themselves in some thicker underbrush, needing to wade through it carefully so they did not cut their ankles and legs.

"Ruben will have eyes on him everywhere now. If we try to get to him, there's every chance we'll be discovered."

"That's a risk I'm willing to take, Dane."

Winter attempted to formulate a plan that might keep them alive. He owed it to her. If it had not been for Maria, he would have died at the hands of the cartel. If it had not been for Ruben, he would have bled out in a pool of his own blood. "How long until we reach the road beyond the hill?"

"Six or seven hours, I'd say."

"And your brother? When does he return to the hospital for work?"

"He's on the night shift. So after dinner tonight." She placed her hand on his shoulder to stop him. "What are we going to do?"

Winter kicked away a large branch in their path. "I'm not sure yet, but I'll think of something."

27

The trek through the woods was every bit as arduous as Maria had promised. Winter, though mostly recovered, could tell from the speckles of blood down his shirt that he had aggravated the wound. That, along with the pain in his legs and lower back, had punctuated their journey.

Maria was the first to emerge from the tree line, the hum of traffic greeting them beyond the wilderness. The mid-afternoon sun revealed itself too, breaking free from the canopies of towering mahogany trees, which had kept it at bay during their hike.

Winter stepped to Maria's side, planting himself to the spot to rest his weary feet. "Do you know where we are?"

Maria glanced up and down the road, which appeared to stretch endlessly, a smattering of cars traveling in both directions, the lack of signage offering no clues. She hesitated for a moment, before pointing left. "If we go that way, we should swing back south to San Yetaxa."

"You're sure about that?"

"I've lived here for thirty-four years. How long have you been here for?"

Winter suppressed a smirk and put his hands up in submission. "I'll surrender to your better judgment."

Maria took the lead. Though she lacked his training, her stamina was formidable. Winter lagged slightly, but refused to let it show. He wondered what was weighing him down the most. The pain of his wound? Or the faces of those who had perished? Never on a mission had he lost so many. Not even when he'd served. He pictured Colonel Dawson back at Camp Redwind, delivering the news to their next of kins. More letters to grieving families. More loved ones that would never return home.

It should have been Winter writing them. At least while he remained in San Yetaxa, he could make it up to them. Or so he told himself.

"Hey, look over there!" Maria pointed ahead. "A gas station!"

Winter caught up to her and they shoved on for another half mile, the tiny speck of their oasis taking shape into a small-time business with a pair of pumps up front and a humble service center at the rear. Winter's throat was raspy, his soul dying of thirst. Maria's was too, the cracks of dehydration etched onto her lips.

"I don't suppose you have any money on you?" she asked.

Winter put a hand in his pocket, quickly realizing his wallet would have been consumed in the blaze. He then reached for his chain, only to find the familiar weight of the dangling jewelry missing from around his neck. It was the first time he noticed it was gone.

He stopped at the front door to the service center and pondered, visualizing the chain on the nightstand. The doc must have removed it from his neck when he was taking out the slug in Winter's side.

"Dane?"

"Uh." He shook his head. "I've got no cash on me."

"Neither do I." Maria bit her bottom lip. "Don't worry, I'll see what I can do. You stay out here."

She entered the store and Winter turned, walking to the pumps where an older man with long silvery hair was fueling his banged-up 1980s Ford pickup truck. Winter eyed the bucket of water next to him, a squeegee resting inside, hoping that the contents within were fresh enough to quench his thirst. Unfortunately, it resembled a murky shade between brown and black.

Winter glanced back at the service center. Off to the side near what was likely once a car wash station, a pipe protruded from the concrete with a tap affixed to the end. He hurried over and crouched down, twisting it on. A splash of water burst from the spout. He held out his hands and cupped them together. What flowed into them was far from the clean, sparkling refreshment he had expected. Instead, it mirrored the cloudy liquid he had found in the bucket. Disappointed, he let the dark stream slip through his fingers and rubbed his hands down his pants to scrub away the grime.

"Dane? Please tell me you didn't drink that."

Winter looked up to find Maria pulling out two bottles of water from beneath her shirt. He turned off the tap and stood up with a raised brow. "Of course not. I was just admiring the color."

She handed him one of the stolen bottles.

Winter twisted the cap and guzzled the drink, the water relieving his parched throat. "How long until town?"

"On foot? Still a while."

"I think my feet have done enough walking for today." Winter peered past Maria at the man in the old pickup, who had finished paying at the counter and returned to his car. "There's our ride."

He took Maria by the hand and they rushed over before he

could put his key in the ignition. "Excuse me, sir. Are you heading into San Yetaxa, by any chance?"

"I am," he said.

"Could we get a lift?"

The man looked at Winter and then at Maria. "I only have one seat in here. If I take you, the lovely lady will be sitting up here with me."

Winter turned to Maria and leaned into her ear. "I'll have a tire iron in the back," he whispered. "If he makes a move, I'll make sure I knock his lights out for you."

"Not if I do it first." She brushed past him and got into the passenger seat. "Thanks for helping us. I'm Maria."

"No problem. I'm Jorge."

Winter threw his leg over the side of the tray, a stab of pain coursing up his torso as he did. He settled into the sun-soaked cargo bed and rested against the window of the cab, ignoring the ache in his body. Jorge hit the gas, swinging them out onto the road, forcing Winter to grip tightly. The scenery flew by considerably faster than it had for the day, the breeze a welcome relief in the oppressive conditions.

They crossed into the city limits of San Yetaxa, the traffic picking up with every mile they drove. Jorge ended up being a total gentleman, not so much as making a single pass at Maria. He even stopped at his favorite fast-food outlet, buying everyone dinner.

By the time they finished, night had descended. They returned to the road and Jorge dropped them near the hospital. With a wave, he set off, the taillights of his truck disappearing into the evening.

"Well, wasn't that nice?" Winter said.

Maria smiled and the pair turned their attention to the hospital, the red and white neon signage lighting up the night. They crossed the road, and Winter ushered her behind the rear of a parked car.

"Have you still got those binoculars?" he asked.

She crouched beside him and removed them from her pocket. Winter held them aloft and leaned over the vehicle, scanning the vast parking lot. He homed in on a sedan not too far away from the entrance. There were a pair of men inside it. He dropped the binoculars around his neck.

Maria placed her hand on his shoulder. "What is it?"

"The two cops from this morning. Looks like they're doing some overtime."

"Are they watching Ruben?"

"They know that there's every chance you'll try to make contact with him. I'd be surprised if there aren't others inside the hospital."

"Are you sure it wouldn't be a better idea to see him at his house tomorrow?"

Winter shook his head. "You can bet if he's under surveillance here, he will be at home, too. At the hospital, we might get lost in the crowd."

"How are we going to do that?"

Winter peeked through the binoculars again, sweeping his sight across the parking lot. He focused on an elderly man in a dark brown jacket and ratty old hat, gently pushing his frail wife, wrapped in a long shawl, toward their car. "I think I have an idea."

28

Winter guided Maria over the crossing in her wheelchair and toward the entrance of the hospital. Dressed in the brown jacket and drab hat, lent by the kindly couple, he hunched his shoulders to complete his disguise. Maria sat with a stoop that matched his, a shawl draped over her to conceal her face. So far, the deception had held.

Winter fought the urge to glance back at the car with the two inspectors sitting within. He knew the slightest movement or shift in posture could betray them. He continued on slowly, taking on the advanced years of his masquerade and pushing Maria to the entrance. The automatic doors opened and invited them inside.

The muffled announcements over the PA, an occasional cough, and patients' chatter filled the air. Winter eyed the direction boards dangling from the ceiling in front of the reception desk.

"Where's your brother's office?" he whispered, careful not to break character, should there be other undercover police officers amidst the gentle flow of people.

"Third floor."

"Is there a back way?"

Maria contemplated for a moment and gestured to the left. "Take that elevator."

Winter veered, keeping the same pace of movement. They entered the elevator and Maria poked at the button with the number three on it. Their ride jolted into action, and shot them to the second floor. A trio of nurses entered. Winter and Maria averted their gazes, attempting to hide their younger features. It was nearly impossible in such close quarters. The nurses, however, were polite enough not to gawk and went about their duties, chatting about their shifts.

At the third floor, Winter steered Maria forward and into the open.

"Take a right," Maria instructed him.

Winter complied and tugged the wheelchair away from the busiest section of the hallway where patients and medical staff filled the way. Maria directed him past various closed doors and a junction which split off into another wing. They went left, then left again, coming out into a corridor with a locker room at one end.

"There," she said. "Three doors down."

They carried on until they reached the office. The nameplate —Dr. Ruben Pineda—was boldly plastered on the center of the door. At the far end of the hallway stood the reception desk they had luckily avoided. A uniformed police officer was stationed next to it, chatting with the receptionist, both appearing in a flirty mood.

Maria turned the handle and Winter pushed her inside, avoiding detection. Ruben looked up from behind his desk, his jaw dropping at the sight of Maria throwing off her shawl and leaping from the wheelchair. He hopped out of his own seat and rounded the desk, flinging his arms around his sister in a warm embrace.

"I can't believe you're here!"

Winter moved the wheelchair into the corner next to a life-size plastic skeleton and closed the door.

Maria let out a sigh of relief. "It wasn't easy."

"I've been so worried about you," he said. "Are you all right? Where have you been?"

Maria explained everything to him. From the moment the first bullet shattered the kitchen window at her house, all the way to how they had slipped past everyone to reach his office.

Ruben shook his head in disbelief. He turned his attention to Winter, who had taken a seat. Ever the healer, Ruben went to his side and lifted his shirt to check on the bandage. "What's this all about?"

"The blood?" Winter asked.

"The blood I can understand. You pushed too hard and popped some stitching." Ruben walked over to a cabinet and retrieved some antiseptic, a needle, and thread. He returned, peeling away the remnants of the old bandages, his eyes narrowing as he examined the injury. "I mean the cartel. Why did they burn down Maria's house?"

"Because they're after me."

Ruben cleaned Winter's wound of dry blood. "That's what Inspector Alvarez thinks. What did you do to them?"

"Apart from protecting Sanchez, nothing. I don't understand it anymore than you. I just wish neither of you had gotten involved."

Ruben chuckled. "Don't worry about me. I've never felt so safe in my life. There's a police officer out at the desk and inspectors scattered through the parking lot. If the cartel comes for me, at least I know they won't get very far."

"Unless they're dirty cops."

Ruben turned to Maria as she spoke. "Is that why you won't go to them?"

"We can't risk it." Winter grimaced as a stitch went in. "They may well be the genuine article. If they're not, they'll deliver us to Berrera. We all understand what that'd entail."

"It might mean Maria and I would be safe." Ruben's statement lingered in the silence. "If it's you they want, they wouldn't—"

"Ruben, do you hear yourself!" Maria snapped at him. "Are you saying we give him up to save our own skin?"

Ruben stopped mid-stitch, his face flushing red. "No, of course not. Sorry, Mr. Winter. I guess I spoke—"

"I understand." Winter waved away the apology. "And you know what, I wouldn't think any less of you if you handed me over to them—"

"That's not going to happen, Dane." Maria went to her brother and clamped a hand on his shoulder. "Is it, Ruben?"

"No." He shook his head vigorously, affixing a new bandage. "I, uh, didn't remove that bullet so that they could put another one in."

"I appreciate that, Doc." Winter placed his shirt back on. "But until I take care of the problem, it means you'll have to leave town."

"What exactly do you mean by 'take care of the problem'?"

"The less you know, the better."

Ruben glanced at Maria with a nervous smile. "I, uh—"

"We don't have time to discuss this." Winter stood. "Both of you have to get out of here and head to that beach house. Once it's safe, you can return to San Yetaxa."

"How though?" Maria asked. "Ruben won't be able to leave the hospital without the police knowing about it."

"I'll be the decoy." Winter pulled at Ruben's navy scrubs. "I'm going to need to borrow those."

"Uh, okay."

"Maria, pick up the shawl," Winter said, undressing. "Doc, I assume there's a back door you can use to get to the ambulance bay."

"There is."

"Take Maria with you in one of the paramedic vehicles. Your car? Is it the red Lexus in the underground parking garage?"

"Yeah. How'd you know?"

"Maria told me. Give me the keys."

Ruben did so and Winter rifled through them. "Is this the one for your house?"

Ruben nodded. "You're going to my home? How do you know where—"

"Maria told me that, too."

The men finished swapping their clothes and Winter placed the keys in his pocket.

"Leave San Yetaxa and don't look back, okay?" he said.

The brother and sister bobbed their heads. Before Winter could open the door, Maria flung her arms over his shoulders. She rose on her tiptoes and pulled him in for an unexpected, but not unwelcome, kiss. Winter responded in kind, their lips meeting, the kiss igniting something inside him. In that fleeting moment, time warped and the memories of the past flooded back to him.

Ruben cleared his throat, and the two of them separated, their eyes still firmly locked on one another. Maria brushed his chest and kissed him again on the cheek.

"This can't be the end, okay?"

He managed a faint smile. "It won't be. I've got too many mistakes left in me."

"Come on, Maria." Ruben got the wheelchair from the corner. "We have to go."

She got into the wheelchair and put the shawl over her head. Ruben shook Winter's hand with a firm grip.

"Now, two last instructions. First: you're likely going to get a phone call. If anyone asks, you're heading home because you're feeling a little sick, okay?"

The man ruffled his brow, a little uncertain at what Winter was getting at. "Okay."

"Second: after that you'll need to get rid of your phone. Yours too, Maria. The cartel know both of you now. I don't want them tracing you to Playa Azul."

The pair nodded at him.

"Good luck, Mr. Winter." Ruben wheeled Maria out and the pair gradually faded into the distance.

29

Cruz had sat in the waiting room for two hours. He had been tracking Dr. Ruben Pineda since earlier that morning. Unfortunately, so had the cops. They knew his value just as well as he did. Hence, the police officer stationed at the reception desk. And though he spent more time flirting with the attractive young receptionist than keeping his eyes peeled on the doctor's door, he was still a burden that Cruz could not ignore.

His patience was wearing thin. Not just because he craved the kill, but because the last thing he needed was Berrera on his back, questioning him on how to do his job. It was not good for his reputation.

The whole day had been one obstacle after another. First, he had trailed the inspectors to the remains of Maria's house, and then to where Ruben thought Maria and Winter may have been located. The doctor had been right on the money. They were just too late, the pair having already fled before their arrival. When he and the inspectors had left the scene, Cruz stayed behind against his better judgment for the next several hours attempting to trace Winter and Maria Pineda. It was a pointless effort in such dense forest. To track them properly, he would have needed a legion to comb through the thick underbrush.

Cruz had decided to return his attention to the brother. The cops were all over him. First, they hauled him to the police station in the city for further questioning. After that, they allowed him to go home to get some rest. But only on the condition they maintain a close watch on him. The cops surrounded his house, parking a car at each end of his street, to keep a look out should his sister and Winter establish contact. Not to mention someone like Cruz. They knew the cartel would be watching him, too.

Cruz did not make his investigation of the police stakeout obvious, changing up his angle of surveillance throughout the afternoon. He watched from the nearby park, an empty neighboring residence, and even did a few laps of the streets in his car, having ditched the Ducati. He needed intel on Ruben's home. Getting inside, he determined, was possible, just not during the daylight hours. The risk was too high.

Eventually the doctor had stirred from his slumber and began his day. He left the house and headed back to the hospital for his night shift. One of the unmarked police cruisers followed him to his workplace and took a position in the parking lot.

Cruz remained seated in the waiting room, under his black baseball cap which was pulled low, while pretending to read a boating magazine. He had witnessed a steady stream of patients come and go. More recently, an old lady in a wheelchair, escorted by her equally ancient husband, had passed through via the far end of the corridor. Not long after they had departed, Ruben left, likely to the ER or another surgical bay.

Cruz gritted his teeth. Before he could dwell on his frustration anymore, the cop's radio crackled. He yanked it from the belt, holding up a finger to the receptionist, and responded to the call.

Though Cruz was unable to hear the words exchanged, it was clear the officer was getting a dressing down. He peeled the walkie-talkie from his ear and hurried down to Ruben's office, returning to his radio for yet another conversation with his superior.

The flustered cop shook his head and returned the device to his belt, rushing from the waiting room. Cruz tossed the boating magazine onto the pile on the coffee table and stood, stepping by the scattered patients and the desk.

"Excuse me, sir, you can't go back there," the receptionist called out to him.

Cruz ignored her and kept moving, reaching the doctor's office. He flung the door open to find an empty room. He narrowed his eyes, pondering the last visual he'd had on Ruben. Was he still in the hospital? If he was, why did they pull the cop from his detail?

He turned to the receptionist, who had popped out from her desk and marched in his direction, ready to eviscerate him again. Before she could say a word, he locked eyes with her.

"Where's Dr. Pineda?"

"I can't give you that information."

He grabbed her by her hair and hurled her inside the office. Her flailing arms crashed into the plastic skeleton and she tumbled to the floor. The terror silenced her, and she scrambled backward.

Cruz closed further. "I asked you a question."

She shuffled away from him until she bumped into Ruben's desk, the back of her head pressing against the laminated timber. She raised her trembling hands in surrender, tears welling in the corners of her eyes. "He's gone home..."

"Home?" Cruz prowled further and lifted her up by her shoulders. "His shift doesn't end for another ten hours."

"I don't know," she whimpered. "He mustn't have been feeling well."

Cruz glared at her, searching for any sign of deception. And while there was no reason for her to lie, he had to be sure. He released her onto the desk and strutted from the office, checking the male changing room, just to be certain.

Cruz closed the door to the empty space and strode down the rear stairwell, the trail ending at the underground parking garage. He took care exiting, pulling his baseball cap that little lower to hide his face from any prying eyes within the dark concrete jungle of cars.

There appeared to be no surveillance. No cops, in uniform or otherwise. As he walked to the opposite end of the lot, he spotted exactly what he had feared.

The doctor's red Lexus was gone.

30

"Is that right?"

Alvarez pressed the phone to his ear, the sergeant informing him of everything that had taken place in the hospital, each of his words more urgent than the next. "Maybe next time get him to be a little more mindful. We don't pay him to stand at that desk to stare at the ceiling."

Alvarez ended the call and shook his head in disbelief, letting the cell fall into his lap.

Martinez glanced at him from the driver's seat, conscious of the traffic around them as they continued to follow the doctor's car out of the parking lot. "What did they say?"

"He said his man wasn't aware that Dr. Pineda had left work early."

"Who did we have stationed at the reception desk?"

"Ramos."

Martinez chuckled. "He was probably chatting up the receptionist. Never put someone like him on that kind of job. His dick thinks more than his brain."

Alvarez grunted and scooped up his phone, dialing another

number. It rang for what seemed an eternity before it was answered.

"Inspector Alvarez?" the voice said on the other end of the line.

"Dr. Pineda, you've led us on a merry chase. I thought we discussed with you that if your plans changed, you needed to tell Officer Ramos."

A brief silence lingered, dispersed by the hum of the car engine in the background. "Uh, yeah, I'm sorry about that, Inspector. I'm feeling unwell. I just wanted to get home and have some sleep."

"Fair enough. Next time please realize that we're doing this not only to keep you safe, but your sister too, should she make contact."

"Of course. I completely understand."

"We've got eyes on you now, Doctor. We're in the car right behind you on the main street. I trust you won't be making any alterations to your trip?"

"Um... I... No. No, I'll be going straight home."

"Good to know. As discussed earlier today, we'll continue our surveillance of your house while you're there. If you need anything, call me on this number."

"I will. Thank you, Inspector."

"Have a nice sleep. I hope you feel better."

The line went dead and Alvarez tossed the phone into the center console.

"The guy sounded delirious," Martinez said.

Alvarez scratched his chin. "I guess once we let him go from the station earlier, it was well past midday. By the time he got home, he would've been lucky to get two or three hours of sleep. I'd probably feel like crap, too."

"At least the lieutenant will be happy." Martinez drove them off the main road into a side street. "He won't have to pay Ramos any overtime."

"He can give it to us instead. I've booked us on until midnight."

"I'll take the extra money." Martinez faux-winced. "Whether my wife talks to me when I get home, well, that's another matter."

Alvarez yawned, settling deeper into the passenger seat. As they followed Ruben, he replayed the events of the day in his mind. The fire. Their meeting with the doctor. The trip to his sister's residence and their trek through the forest, which culminated in a visit to the station house. There, they had to break the news to Ruben that they would have to keep him under twenty-four-hour surveillance. The reason was two-fold. Alvarez strongly suspected Maria would make contact with her half-brother. But he also knew the cartel would not sit idle if they had no further leads on Winter. If that were the case, Ruben would need protection.

Dane Winter—the center of everything. An American who had come to Mexico for a simple job, now caught up in something that had nothing to do with him. Or did it?

"You okay over there?" Martinez asked.

Alvarez rested his arm on the windowsill. "Just trying to figure out what the cartel wants with this Winter character. I got all the information I could get from Redwind today. Scoured the entire report. Even received his paperwork from the National Customs Agency."

"Find anything?"

"He's visited the country three times prior to this week. Once to Tijuana when he was a kid, and twice working for Redwind. Both jobs were in Mexico City. He'd never set foot in San Yetaxa until the Gilberto Sanchez op."

"Did the gigs tie him to the bad guys?"

"None were cartel related."

"Sounds like a dead end."

Alvarez tapped his fingers on the side window. "Yeah."

"How about that Sanchez?" Martinez changed the subject. "I saw him on the news again this afternoon, when I was in the break room. He was doubling down on his campaign. At least he's not messing around. The guy's got serious *cajones*."

"Those *cajones* will either get him killed before the election or assassinated after he takes office."

Martinez turned right at the next intersection, still glued on the rear of Ruben's car. "You going to vote for him?"

"I don't know. The other guy reckons he'll clean up the state, too."

"Lugo just sounds like all the others."

"So what makes Sanchez so different?"

"I dunno." Martinez shrugged. "I suppose it's because he has no fear."

"Maybe." Alvarez rolled his eyes. "Well, until the election, he's holed up in one of his other properties out of town. I hope he can make it to the vote."

They drove onto a quaint suburban street, where most of the fences were lined with either white pickets or glossy brick. Ruben aimed his car to a house surrounded by the latter, entering the driveway and turning off the ignition. His headlights dimmed, and his silhouette got out of the vehicle and disappeared into the shadows of his home. Through the window, the downstairs lights flickered on first, then upstairs.

Martinez brought them to a stop on the opposite side of the road from the doctor's house and cut the engine. Down the end of the street, the unmarked police cruiser, which had been permanently stationed there, remained in its spot, now likely manned by a new pair of officers.

Alvarez peered through the windshield in wait. The lights on the lower floor went off, followed by those upstairs. "Looks like someone's snug in bed."

Martinez reached into the back and grasped his thermos. "Would you like a coffee?"

Alvarez hesitated for a moment. "Uh—"

"Come on, it has to be better than that slop you got from the vending machine at the hospital."

Alvarez did not want to insult the man, or his wife's skill at making coffee. Angela was a lovely woman. Very attractive too. The truth was, the brew would in fact be worse than the slop from the hospital. "Sure, why not?"

Martinez grabbed two mugs and filled them, handing the first to his partner. It was hot, at least. And in the cover of darkness, Alvarez was unable to make out the unappetizing shade of brown it had turned.

Martinez screwed the cap back on the thermos and raised his mug. "Cheers."

Alvarez returned the gesture and took a sip. It was godawful, the burn of the rancid swill tingling down his throat like battery acid. He feigned a smile and set the coffee on the dash. Silence settled between them, and Alvarez yawned.

"God, this is going to be a long night."

31

Cruz deviated off the main road, coasting into the tree-lined streets of the affluent eastern inner suburbs. It was not the home of San Yetaxa's ultra elite, instead belonging to those who had clawed their way up, whether through sheer grit, intellect, or the right connections. They were lawyers, bankers, academics, entrepreneurs, even doctors. Each had carved out a slice of paradise in the apocalyptic wasteland that was San Yetaxa.

Cruz had seethed ever since he left the hospital, appalled that Ruben Pineda had slipped away, leaving him none the wiser. He found solace in the fact that the cops had been fooled too, but they had still been quicker on the uptake. When Cruz arrived, a car was stationary, opposite the doctor's house.

He passed at a deliberate pace. Slow enough to avoid drawing attention, but fast enough to slip under their radar. He recognized the faces inside. The two inspectors who had taken Ruben to his sister's home that morning. The old man and his younger partner. They sat in the front seats, enjoying a coffee. The pair were obviously burning the midnight oil.

He continued, driving by another unmarked car at the street's end. The duo inside it were unfamiliar to him, likely a new team who had signed on to the evening shift.

As expected, he would have to deal with the police presence. But under the cloak of darkness, he had an opportunity to go one on one with the doctor. The man's sudden sickness had been quite helpful, even if it had fooled Cruz. Now he just had to use it to his advantage.

He took a left at the end of the street and then another, bringing him to the road running adjacent. He parked at the curb and yanked the keys from the ignition. From the glove compartment, he retrieved his sidearm, ensuring as always that he had a complete magazine. Satisfied, he tucked it into his waistband and stepped out into the night.

He crossed the road, sliding down the driveway of the house opposite, avoiding the lit-up window. Through the curtains, a young family was watching a comedy show on the TV, oblivious to the outside world. The kids, still awake, laughed at the jokes, the sound of their joy strangely infectious.

Cruz wondered if he had ever giggled like that as a child. He snorted derisively and pushed on to the back fence through the well-trimmed yard. He was careful not to trip over the wayward bikes and random football near the net in the corner, hitching his right foot on the post and climbing over to the other property.

The yard was much more subdued. There were no toys scattered across the lawn or sports gear leaning against the small shed. If anything, the grass had grown too long, and the hedges on either side of the opposing fences stood in need of a cut. It lacked the warmth of a family residence. It was the home of a bachelor.

Cruz dashed toward the house, keeping low, quickly arriving at the back door. He went for the handle and turned it. Locked as expected. He trawled out his lock picks and inserted them into the barrel, manipulating the pins until one by one they shifted, giving way and granting him entry.

Cruz slipped inside, easing the door without making a sound. With the lock picks back in his pocket, he removed the gun from his waistband, pointing it into the darkness. The lower story of the house was filled with what Cruz would have expected. Two living areas, a kitchen, a dining room, a study space, and a laundry room with access to the driveway. He moved through each of them. All empty.

He tiptoed up the stairs, his footfalls not betraying so much as a squeak of movement. At the top, he was met with several closed doors. The lack of illumination made it difficult to get a proper layout. But from what he could guess, most led to bedrooms, with a bathroom and another small living area among them. He elbowed the door to one and checked inside.

It was bare. No furniture or pictures on the walls. Ruben was a man in his late thirties. He had no woman or any children. Just a big empty house. The other vacant bedrooms confirmed it. He had given his life to medicine at the detriment of anything else. Some might call it noble, but Cruz knew better.

It was a waste. He clenched his jaw. Vacant rooms while there were people on the streets who could barely scrounge a cardboard box for shelter.

The doctor was only meant to assist him in his investigation. He was the key to finding his sister, and through her, Dane Winter. He was not marked for death. As Cruz stood there, he thought perhaps he should have been.

He edged closer to the only space in which he was yet to check. The master bedroom. He turned the handle slowly and prodded the door ajar. On the other side was the largest room of all. Through the open window, the faint glow of the street light filtered in. There, sprawled on the king-sized bed, was the lumpy shape of a man beneath the covers. Cruz closed further and put one hand on the edge of the sheets, the other gripping his gun, the barrel aimed at the sleeping doctor.

He tore the sheet back, ready to begin his interrogation. Before he could register what was happening, a blinding flash of light from the ceiling snapped on. He went to shield his eyes, staring downward at the pillows arranged to resemble someone sleeping.

There was no one there.

Cruz pivoted, all his instincts kicking in. There, standing next to the door, was a man holding a piece of lumber. He swatted it at Cruz's head before he could raise his weapon, the force sending a shockwave through his skull. As a gloomy haze filled his vision, a face took shape.

It belonged to Dane Winter.

32

The man toppled onto the bed, his gun slipping from his hand and flinging along the floor. Winter pounced before he could regain his senses and scooped up the weapon, backing up to the closed door and leveling the pistol at his would be-assassin.

The ponytailed figure was tall, dressed in black, a dark tattoo running down the side of his face. Whether any of the markings inked on his skin held meaning was anyone's guess.

Winter tossed the two-by-four he had taken from the garden shed and used as a makeshift weapon to the floor, waiting for the other man to stand. There was a fire in his eyes; not rage, rather raw frustration. Winter could tell in his demeanor he was not accustomed to losing. It made sense. If the cartel were going to dispatch someone to take care of unfinished business, they were naturally going to send their best.

The tattooed terror heaved himself upright and glared at Winter. The patch where he had smashed him with the lumber started to transform from red to black and blue. He gave him credit. Most people would have lost consciousness from such a hit.

Winter motioned at the pillows on the bed that he had arranged deliberately to mislead someone looking for Ruben. If the cartel wanted Winter as much as he assumed, it was not only the police who had eyes on the doctor. His assumption turned out to be correct, the stunt also helping Maria and her brother to escape unharmed.

"Ruben's gone by the way. So's his sister. You can forget about them. I know it's me you want." Winter aimed the gun at his head. "Now you're going to tell me why."

The assassin offered no response.

"This is going to be a very boring conversation if I'm the only one who speaks." Winter waited, hoping for at least a quiver of the other man's lips. Nothing. "Who gave the order to waste me? Was it Alfonso Berrera?"

Silence, yet again.

"I suppose it was probably El Maestro, through Berrera." Winter silently fumed. He wanted answers. "Why were you sent to kill me?"

He stepped closer to the gangly killer. "Those who fell at the estate, I understand. We were hired to protect Gilberto Sanchez against a possible cartel reprisal. My friends and I at Redwind got in the way of that. But why still come for me? I have no connections to any of your enemies. I haven't even seen Gilberto Sanchez since the fundraiser. I'm just an out-of-towner."

Winter kicked his foot at the assassin's ankles, sending him crashing to the floor. "We can do this all night if you like?"

The man grunted on impact and quickly hauled himself up, an utterance of curses spilling from his mouth.

"What was that?" Winter asked.

"I said, I can't provide the answers to your questions."

"Why?"

"When you fought in the Middle East, did your commanding officer go over every piece of intel they had on hand?"

Winter paused at the comment. The man standing across from him was a killer. No question. But he was not just a typical thug. There was an edge of intelligence hidden within. "I see you've done your homework on me."

"It's ignorant not to study one's prey before making the kill. You have to be aware of potential surprises."

"I still fooled you, though, didn't I?"

A hint of a smirk crept into the ghastly facial features of the assassin. "I'll award you the battle. It doesn't mean you've won the war."

"I don't believe you quite grasp the situation you're in. I'm the one holding the gun."

"But you're pointing it at someone who can't tell you anything. You're just wasting your time here."

"If I kill—"

"If you kill me, another will be sent in my place. You're far from home—"

The doorbell rang, and Winter furrowed his brow. He shuffled past the closet, keeping his sidearm trained on the man. He peeled the curtain back ever so slightly to catch a glimpse of their visitor. It was not some neighborhood prankster. It was the older inspector in a hat. The one from that morning.

Before Winter could refocus his full attention on the assassin, the light blinked out, the man quick enough to get to the switch. In the brief instant of darkness, he moved with a skill and speed Winter did not anticipate. Winter aimed into the abyss and prepared to squeeze the trigger.

From the shadows, a blur streaked past the edge of his eyeline, the wiry predator striking and sending him sailing to the floor. The thud against the polished timber and the weight of his opponent rattled his bones, igniting pain up and down his side. The gun burst from his grip, disappearing into the gloom.

He turned his attention to the assassin, who pounded into him with his fists, the glow from the street light casting him in a terrifying silhouette. Winter shielded the blows as best he could with his arm, while using his other hand to search for something as a weapon. He found the wooden leg of the nightstand behind him and gave it a tug.

The lamp atop it came crashing down, and he snatched it, hoisted it high above his head with a sweeping arc. Winter made contact, the assassin grunting from the impact to his face.

Winter used the moment of weakness to extract himself from the floor, tossing his assailant aside. He lowered his center of gravity and went on the attack, grabbing the other man's throat with one hand and punching with the other. He struck him three times. On the fourth attempt, his opponent clutched his fist and flipped him with force, the twisting motion searing a jolt of agony through his arm.

The pair scuffled across the floor, rolling over each other in a chaotic tangle as they collided into the closet. But it was not the only door that made a noise.

A crash echoed from downstairs, followed by a murmur of voices. The inspector had likely heard the commotion and barged inside the house. It would be only moments before he came across the two fighting with one another. Things were complicated enough without police involvement.

He seized the assassin by the shoulder and slammed him against the closet door, but the man broke free and launched himself at Winter. They tumbled back to the center of the room next to the bed. Both scrambled to their feet and within the darkness the two shadows squared off. Parry and blow. Strike and block. Their moves mirrored each other, both men attempting to get the upper hand.

The assassin sensed Winter's weak side and targeted the wound. Winter absorbed the hits, gritting his teeth through the pain. He used it to his advantage, his opponent's momentum carrying him forward that little too much. Winter pivoted and swung him backward, driving his skull into the wall.

The sound of footsteps echoed from outside the door up the staircase, the inspector rushing to the top story, their intervention only seconds away.

The assassin recovered and ambled at Winter, his fists ready to fly once again. Winter stepped back and hoisted the side of the bed, kicking out the brake of the caster wheels and launching it in front of him. His stalker flew onto it and Winter propelled the bed into the door, placing the brake on to stop any unforced entry.

With the moment still, and his vision having adapted to the dark, he spotted the two-by-four he had initially used to incapacitate his opponent. He lunged for it and turned just at the right moment to wallop the assassin's head. This time, he dropped for good.

Fists pounded against the other side of the door, the bangs getting loud with each clobber.

"Doctor Pineda!" the inspector yelled out.

"What's going on in there!" called the other, his partner no doubt.

Winter rushed for the window and ripped the curtain aside. He slid the glass open and leaped into the darkness, vanishing into the night.

33

Alvarez narrowed his eyes through the one-way mirror at the man sitting inside the interview room. Only a few days earlier the table he was at held the photos of those who had perished at Gilberto Sanchez's estate.

The ponytailed harbinger of death painted a gruesome figure. The left side of his face was filled with a slew of black tattoos, the other scars from his melee in the bedroom from the night before.

Martinez entered the observation room with Festa. He had been one of the officers on duty the previous evening in the unmarked cruiser at the top end of Ruben Pineda's street, witnessing what Alvarez and Martinez had.

During the ensuing hour after Ruben's supposed arrival at home, Alvarez had sipped at his awful coffee in the car, his mind racing with the happenings of the night. The bedroom light had flicked on after a decent period of darkness. At the time, he thought Ruben was going to the bathroom. But it stayed on, making Alvarez more suspicious.

Nothing had added up about the doctor. He was an intelligent man. When Alvarez and Martinez had talked to him at the station that morning, about keeping watch over him until his sister was found, he was more than appreciative. So when he left the hospital without telling anyone, it rung alarm bells. Even the phone call with Ruben on the way home sounded fishy. Alvarez should have investigated further. But he didn't.

When the light had remained on, he acted. He had told Martinez he intended to check it out, and crossed the road to knock on his door. There was no answer. There was, however, a faint noise from upstairs. Crashing and banging. A scuffle?

Alvarez waved for Martinez's assistance and the pair forced their way inside and hurried up the stairs to the master bedroom, only to be halted by an obstruction on the other side. With some strength, they had heaved the door open, discovering a king-size bed in the way. They flipped the light on and found a body sprawled over it. It was not Ruben Pineda, but rather the tattooed individual who now sat in his interview room. He had been beaten and bruised, the wreckage of the bedroom telling the story of a good old-fashioned brawl.

There was also an open window.

Alvarez removed a photo from his pocket and showed it to Festa. "Was this the guy you saw climb down from the top story at Doctor Pineda's house?"

Festa nodded. "That was him. No doubt about it."

Alvarez had already read the officer's report. After the man had fled, Festa and his partner took chase from up the street, but lost him in the jungle of houses on the block. Backup was called in and the area searched. No one matching the description had turned up, their person of interest long gone.

"Thanks." He put a hand on Festa's shoulder and gestured to Martinez with a curt nod. "Let's go."

The pair exited and entered the corridor, slipping inside the interview room. The man under arrest did not so much as spare them a glance, his gaze focused on the wall. Alvarez pulled out a chair in front of him and sat directly in his line of sight.

"Hello, Mr. Cruz. How are you feeling this morning?"

Roberto Cruz's head tilted ever so slightly, checking the clock. "My lawyer will be here in five minutes."

Alvarez raised his eyebrows at Martinez, who stood by the water cooler with his arms crossed. "Got into a bit of a scrape last night, didn't you, Mr. Cruz? I wouldn't have guessed someone of Ruben Pineda's ilk could've inflicted such damage. But we both know it wasn't the doctor who did this to you, don't we?"

He took the photo provided by Redwind from the palm of his hand and slammed it in the middle of the table between them. "Dane Winter. You got your ass handed to you by this guy, didn't you?"

"My lawyer will be here in four minutes."

"I can understand your embarrassment." Alvarez sighed. "It was embarrassing for us too. Seems Ruben Pineda and Dane Winter did a little switcheroo right under our noses. The doctor's almost certainly gone now, but Winter, I'm betting, might not be too far away. There's something going on between your employers and our American friend. What is it? Why do they want him dead?"

Cruz remained silent.

"It can't be as simple as a grudge. The cartel are above that sort of drama. What business did Winter have with you that he now has a target on his back?" Alvarez stood and walked over to the refrigerator, opening it and cracking open a can of soda. He took a sip and paced in front of the table. "Did he interfere in the cartel's operations? Has it got something to do with the hit on the fundraiser?"

"He's not speaking because he doesn't know anything."

Alvarez spun around to his partner.

"You're probably right, Martinez. Cruz is just a hitman. A lousy one at that." Alvarez closed on the table. "Look at you. A sorry sight. You had the home field advantage. What's that say about you?"

Cruz gritted his teeth, but contained his fury. "My lawyer will be here in three minutes."

"I suppose only your boss would have the answers to my questions." Alvarez took another gulp and sat, setting the can down next to him. "What does Alfonso Berrera want with Winter? You're not stupid. You're not just a dumb triggerman, are you?"

Cruz continued his silent faceoff with Alvarez, slowly blinking behind his hard façade. Alvarez extended a hand and Martinez placed a folder in it. Alvarez put it down and flipped it open, the rustle of papers the only sound in the tense room.

"Then again, perhaps you are just a mindless killer. You grew up on the streets, didn't you?" Alvarez traced down the page. "Wow, La Forja. I was born there too. It was a rough place to have a childhood. You were either a lamb or a lion, weren't you?"

A subtle flicker of comprehension crossed Cruz's eyes.

"They told the same story, even back in my day." Alvarez pointed at the tattoo. "Now that we're up close, I can make it out. The lion's paw stretching over your eye. I don't know what the rest of that is, but I can recognize the king of the jungle when I see it."

"My lawyer will be here in two minutes."

"You must have seen it all. I feel like there's a shooting out in La Forja every week. About a month ago, I had to fish someone out of the sewer. He was only five years old. Imagine what he would have done to deserve a bullet at such an age." Alvarez enjoyed more of his soda. "I'm sure you remember those days. The dealers run that area. Get on the wrong side of them and bang, you're dead. Not fair to the kids though, is it? I suspect you wanted to clean up the town when you were that age. Probably thought it was possible too. You just had to get mad enough to make everyone pay. But it doesn't work out like that, does it?"

"My lawyer will be here in one minute."

Alvarez rose and drained the drink, tossing it in the trash can in the corner. "You became one of the very people you despise. Get that little taste of power and the story of the lamb and the lion fills your soul. You promise to yourself that it won't happen. But it does. To become the lion, you must slaughter the lamb. What's funny is that at the end of the day, no matter how much you try, you'll always be a lamb. There will forever be a bigger lion in the jungle. Like Alfonso Berrera."

A knock sounded at the door and Martinez answered it. He exchanged a knowing glance with Alvarez. The lawyer had arrived.

"Think about what we've discussed, kid. It's not worth protecting your boss." Alvarez stepped to the exit to follow Martinez out. "He'll just eat you up and spit you out."

"Hey, Inspector," Cruz said.

"Yeah?"

The assassin smiled. "Baa!"

Alvarez shook his head and closed the door behind him. "I thought I almost had him."

"You gave it your best shot." Martinez gestured with a nod to the man coming their way from the stairs. "Your favorite lawyer."

Alvarez made eye contact with Alvin Herrera for but a split second. It was enough to catch his smarmy grin. "Inspectors, nice to see you. I believe you have a client of mine."

"Interview room one," Martinez said.

"Much appreciated. Good to see you, Alvarez."

"Likewise," Alvarez lied.

He passed them by and entered the interview room, closing the door behind him.

Martinez slapped Alvarez on the chest lightly. "By the way, what was that about growing up in La Forja? Weren't you born on the other side of the city."

"I was. Used to be a beat cop in La Forja, though. I reckon I've heard that ridiculous lamb and lion story about a million times."

34

"*Captain...*"

The gentle shake of his shoulder and the soft words stirred Winter from his slumber. He blinked his eyes open to find himself staring at the face of the man he had been sitting next to since he left Heathrow Airport. Winter straightened in his seat, the haze subsiding.

"*How long was I out?*" *he asked.*

"*Four hours, give or take,*" *the former army sergeant informed him. "We've just landed.*"

Winter rubbed his face and raked his fingers through his untidy hair, glancing past at the tarmac through the small airplane window. "I didn't drool on your shoulder, did I?"

The man smirked with a shake of his head. Winter waited for the departing passengers to disperse from the aisle and stepped out, allowing his new-found friend the same courtesy. They collected their carry-on luggage from the overhead storage and proceeded across the air bridge, out of the gate and through customs. On the other side they clasped hands in farewell.

"*Good luck to you, Captain,*" *he said to Winter. "Trust me when I say this is the first day of the rest of your life.*"

Winter smiled, and they parted. Around him, the terminal was awash with Christmas wreaths dotting doors, garlands draping railings, and red and green lights sparkling in the night. Some passing passengers embraced the festive spirit too, donning woolen holiday sweaters. Though joyful, they were monstrosities no matter how pleasing the design.

Winter stopped at a bench and zipped open the front compartment of his bag. Inside, tucked within the plastic pouch, was the item he had purchased at Heathrow. He placed it back, nice and snug, re-zipping the bag.

Why hadn't he heard his phone? No notifications had sounded since he landed. He extracted it from his pocket and noticed it was still in airplane mode. With a quick swipe, he deactivated the setting. A plethora of messages, social media notifications, and missed calls appeared on the screen.

Most were from Jessica. And all in the last hour. He entered the menu. She had left a message, too. It read:

Call me when you land.

Winter highlighted her name and tapped the call button. The line barely rang when Jessica answered.

"Dane!" She sounded panicked.

"Jessica. I've just landed. What's going on?"

"It's Sara..."

* * *

Winter sat on the hood of the car he had "borrowed" in San Yetaxa, taking the vehicle beyond the outskirts of the city into the desolate expanse surrounding it. The landscape was barren, save for the occasional cactus-like vegetation and fidgety tumbleweed.

The warmth of the morning sun began to bite harder as it drew closer to midday. He knew that once the afternoon took hold, being out in such terrain would take its toll. A series of clouds suddenly surged overhead. They blotted the light out for mere moments, none of them so much as dispersing a drop of rain.

A current model Ford SUV approached from the north. If it were not for the dust it had collected on its journey, the shiny silver paint job would have looked immaculate under the glare. It slowed and pulled off the road, the nose of the vehicle coming to a stop five yards from Winter's position.

The windows were tinted, concealing his view inside. But as the door opened, a familiar figure emerged. Ben Colby. The man dressed in a light blue polo and tan pants, his shoes polished a shiny brown.

He removed the aviators from his eyes and walked over to him. "Dane Winter, as I live and breathe. I didn't believe it when they told me you'd called from a San Yetaxa payphone. I really wasn't sure I'd see you again."

"Then you heard?"

"That a whole Redwind team were killed at Gilberto Sanchez's fundraiser? Yeah, I heard. Some thought you'd fallen too. I'm glad they were wrong. I gotta ask though, how'd you do it?"

"Mostly luck. And some help from strangers."

Colby approached and shook Winter's hand. "What's it been, two years?"

"I remember being in Philadelphia during the baseball World Series when Redwind helped you out on that case. So yeah, two years sounds about right. I also seem to recall you owing me one for what we did."

"Really?"

Winter tapped the side of his head. "I don't forget."

"How'd you know I was working out of the DEA office in Mexico City now?"

"I have connections."

"I'm sure you do." Colby scraped the desert dust with the tips of his shoes. "Well, spit it out. What can I do for you?"

"Nothing. But I might be able to help you."

"Oh?"

"I assume the DEA's had little success stopping the flow of narcotics through Tlapetla?"

"Alfonso Berrera runs a tightknit operation."

"I could change that, but I'll require some equipment to make it happen."

"Okay, you've got my attention."

"I thought I might." Winter smirked. "I'd like some tracking equipment. With any luck, I might discover where the cartel is producing their meth in Tlapetla. If I can do that, we should have a good idea of how it flows out of San Yetaxa. Once I've got that information, I'll hand it over to you."

"I suppose that can be arranged." Colby nodded. "But what do you get out of it?"

Winter went to speak, but Colby held up a hand to stop him.

"Uh, I get it. You want to flush El Maestro out?"

"We both know Alfonso Berrera is only a front down here," Winter said. "If you wish to take the cartel out of the equation in Tlapetla, you've got to get to El Maestro."

"After all these years, what makes you think you'll be the one to do that?"

"Let's just say I'm highly motivated."

Colby moved ever closer, as if paranoid someone might hear them in the desert. "I get it. They killed your friends. But I can't sanction your vendetta."

"Who said anything about a vendetta? I'm simply asking for some tracking equipment. Off the books, I might add. If it all works out, you look like a hero back in Mexico City."

Colby scratched the thin beard on his face. "I'll get you the gear."

"You're making the right decision."

"Hmm." Colby returned to his car and got back in, firing up the engine. He hit the road, kicking up a whirlwind of dust in his wake.

Winter exhaled, left alone in the silence of the desert to plan his first move.

35

Winter sat in the car, parked behind Hector's, the afternoon ebbing and flowing around him. Traffic was sparse in the rear parking lot, most of the patrons preferring the spaces at the front door. They would pull in for a quick meal and depart before their food was digested.

Winter was not hungry. While he'd enjoyed his first feed at the diner, he had already eaten at another outlet on the road back into San Yetaxa with money Colby had given him. It was not as satisfying as he had hoped, but after going without since the night before, his stomach welcomed it all the same.

His mind drifted to Maria and her half-brother. By now, they would likely be at their cousins' beach house in Playa Azul and out of danger. It was up to him to make San Yetaxa safe enough for them to return.

Winter reached for the oversized soda that had come with his meal at the roadhouse and took a sip. He recoiled. The afternoon sun and the lack of decent AC in the stolen car had turned it into a syrupy disappointment. He dropped it in the cup holder, pushing back the urge to go into

Hector's and get another. He needed to stay incognito in San Yetaxa.

Beyond the city limits, he did not care so much. In town, though, he had to assume the cartel had eyes everywhere. Or at least paid lookouts keeping watch on the streets. Nothing would have been more obvious than a gringo returning to the diner he had met the woman he was on the run with.

That was why he wanted the tracking device. Sure, he could tail his suspected target, but sooner rather than later, he would draw suspicion. He needed a precise record of where it went and what it did. Doing so in the old-fashioned way was both impractical and dangerous.

The roller door of Hector's loading dock opened and one of Maria's colleagues appeared with a large black bag of trash. She climbed down the narrow ladder to the side and proceeded to the dumpster. She yanked open the lid and hurled it in.

With the binoculars still in his possession, he pointed them inside the diner's storeroom. It was not nearly as glamorous as the busy restaurant. The interior was darker and gloomier, the flickering lighting above begging for much-needed maintenance. Winter suspected Hector prioritized appearances, spending money on what his customers could see. He cut costs in areas his patrons never saw, letting the engine room of his operation decay, forcing his employees to endure the shoddy conditions.

Winter swept the binoculars across the storeroom, scanning for the item he had come for. Even in the dim light, it stood out. A barrel resting on a blue pallet. He hoped it would be the key to unraveling the cartel's operations. He had decided to stake everything on Maria's attention to detail, remembering their conversation when she'd said she believed Hector might be part of the pipeline running narcotics for the cartel.

She had claimed the oil in the deep fryers was changed out

daily instead of biweekly, like most restaurants. Could Hector be simply fastidious? Perhaps. However, for someone who valued every peso, there was a chance something far more unscrupulous was in play. Winter intended to find out either way.

The server went up the ladder and prepared to shut the roller door. She stopped before she got to the control panel and looked out in Winter's direction. He ducked in his seat, but quickly realized it was not him she was looking at. Something had captured her attention from behind him. Winter checked the rearview mirror, spotting a truck ambling into the parking lot and heading to the back dock.

As it passed him, he noted the large, bold text emblazoned along its side: Tlapetla Waste Services.

The truck took a wide arc and reversed into the docking area. The driver hauled himself from his seat, his belly scraping past the steering wheel as he jumped out of the cab onto the ground. The server had disappeared, replaced with a cook who stood with a pen ready to sign off the exchange of barrels.

Winter opened the glove compartment with one hand and pulled out the small black device given to him by Colby. With the other, he eased open the car door. Nobody appeared to be paying him any attention, the driver and the cook concentrating on their paperwork. Winter strolled to the front of the truck, obscuring himself with the bulk of the vehicle.

He crouched and activated the tracker, using the magnet to place it in the wheel arch of the truck. He pivoted, returning to his car and shutting himself inside. A few moments later, the driver descended the ladder, gave the cook a casual wave, and climbed into his cab, settling behind the steering wheel. As he got the engine started, the roller door slid shut, sealing the rear of Hector's dock.

The truck edged through the parking lot, past Winter's car,

and slipped out of his line of sight in the rearview mirror, down the street and onto its next job. Winter reached into the back seat and retrieved his black laptop bag. He brought it to his lap and unzipped it, removing the computer and flipping it open. He tapped in the password Colby had provided, navigating through the startup menus, before clicking the single icon sitting on the home screen.

A map of San Yetaxa materialized with a red blinking dot moving down the street, just past Hector's Diner. The tracker he had installed in the truck was operating as promised.

It was time to play the waiting game.

36

Night had descended upon San Yetaxa, the cool desert air a welcome relief to the stifling heat Winter had endured in his car during the day. The sky was clear above the outskirts of town, every star twinkling brightly, freed from the lights of the city center. He leaned on the windowsill, idly twirling his cigarette between his fingers, his gaze shifting to the opposite side of the road where the Tlapetla Waste Services plant loomed in the darkness.

The fortress was surrounded by towering fences, while within, massive utilitarian concrete buildings made up the facility. A steady flow of trucks rumbled through the entry gate and reversed into the docking bays, unloading their hauls. Most were like the one Winter had attached his tracker to at Hector's Diner. Others were tankers which were pumped free of their collected liquid waste. Once the process was complete, the drivers guided their trucks into the vast parking lot to end their shift.

The stench wafting beyond the fence line was a blend of industrial, chemical, and organic compounds. Even though Winter had parked upwind, the stink hung heavy in the swirling breeze, the foul odor still reaching him. He felt for those who lived nearby. While the facility's location was remote, some residential areas lay uncomfortably close. When the wind shifted, there would have been no escaping the smell.

A set of headlights flared in his rearview mirror, the glare of the high beams cutting through the night and flooding the inside of the car. The truck they belonged to thundered by and the glow subsided as it steered for the entry to the waste facility. Its rear was sufficiently weighed down, a sign that the driver had had a busy afternoon. As it entered and disappeared toward the dock, where workers stood ready to receive the load, Winter flipped open the laptop resting on the passenger seat.

He accessed the operating system and took another drag of his cigarette, tapping the ash out of the window. The map of the screen displayed a red line, marking the truck's every move since Winter had affixed the tracking device to it. The vehicle had completed a vast circuit of San Yetaxa, stopping at various restaurants and food outlets. It had weaved a path through the city and climbed the hills, before finishing its trip at the south end of the town and looping back to the facility.

Winter had remained glued to the real-time data streaming all afternoon. It had been slow going, but mostly, everything seemed routine. The driver was efficient. He stopped, took on the waste, and returned to the road without delay. One irregularity, however, had caught Winter's attention. He zoomed in on a section of the map and double-checked the time stamps of the abnormal movement.

He drew in the last of his cigarette and tossed it from the window, reaching with his other hand for the phone Colby had provided him. He dialed the DEA agent's number and it picked up immediately.

"Yeah."

"I've found something you might be interested in," Winter told him.

"Very well. Same place in one hour."

Winter ended the call and threw the cell and laptop on the passenger seat. He slid the key in the ignition and pulled out onto the barren road, moving further beyond the city and deeper into the desert. At night, the endless expanse seemed to stretch into the abyss, creating an eerie stillness. Winter slowed near a large cactus he had recognized from earlier in the day and parked in wait.

Colby, true to his word, appeared an hour later from the opposite direction. He drove the same Ford SUV, its headlights bright, aiming directly at Winter as it made a beeline path for him. He peeled from the road and stopped near the parked vehicle, where Winter stood with his laptop unfolded on the hood.

He glanced behind to find his friend walking over to him. "I hope I didn't interrupt your dinner."

The jest failed to get a sufficient reaction from Colby. "What have you found?"

"Something worth investigating." Winter zoomed in on the variance. "As you can see, our truck made eleven additional stops after it left Hector's Diner. The majority of the run was uneventful. The driver didn't so much as stop to scratch himself outside of his jobs. But take a look here."

Colby peered over his shoulder at the laptop. "What am I supposed to be seeing?"

"He stopped."

"So?"

"In the middle of nowhere, for four minutes and twenty-three seconds."

"And? He probably just wanted to drain the lizard."

"It doesn't match the rest of his activities. This guy knows what he's doing. He took the quickest route between every single job, except this one. Taking a truck this way would've added at least ten minutes to his trip." Winter zoomed in closer on the map, revealing a winding route through a portion of the hills. "Prior to this pit stop, he did a pickup at Amigo's, a fast-food outlet. After that, he went to a high-end restaurant at the edge of town. Why would he take the dirt track instead of the main road?"

Colby cocked an eyebrow. "Okay, you've got me curious. What do you think we're looking at?"

"I think he's loading goods that aren't on the books. This is why Hector's getting rid of his oil every day. The barrel, likely empty, is being used to ship methamphetamine from its site of production across Tlapetla for shipment to the US. If I had to put money on it, I'd say the cartel's meth lab is somewhere close to where this truck stopped for those four minutes and twenty-three seconds."

Colby paced in front of the car. "If you're right and a swap's happening, the driver and someone in the waste facility are in on it. The barrel gets signed out, it's swapped at Hector's Diner, filled with the drugs, then taken back to the facility where it's signed in."

Winter nodded. "All the paperwork would be legitimate, no one the wiser, except for the select few who are involved."

"How's it transported from the plant across the rest of Mexico?"

Winter pulled the tracking device from his pocket and palmed it to Colby. "I don't know."

"How did you get that off the truck?"

"While I noted the driver's efficiency, I wagered he'd stop for food before the end of his shift. He did. I retrieved it when he went inside a roadhouse for his dinner."

"Got an answer to everything, don't you?"

"I might even have a solution to toppling the meth trade in Tlapetla. If that's the case, you won't need to solve how it gets to the border and beyond. I'll, of course, have to investigate to confirm my theory."

Before Colby could say a word, Winter pulled a piece of paper from his pocket and unfolded it, passing it to him. Colby held it in the glow of the laptop screen and chortled.

"This is quite the shopping list," he said.

"It's the price of getting the job done. I know you have your hands tied in Mexico City. I'm down here, so use me."

"But this—"

"You were able to get me the tracking equipment."

"This is a whole different story, Winter, and you know it."

"Be creative. I imagine you have contacts outside the DEA who could hook me up."

Colby stared at the list and pondered. "Maybe."

Winter closed the laptop and handed it to him. "Then maybe make a phone call."

Colby placed the computer under his arm and folded up the paper, sliding it into his pocket. "If I do this, we need to be perfectly clear that the DEA has nothing to do with it."

"Plausible deniability? I get it. If I end up on the front of the *San Yetaxa Herald*, I'll ensure the letters D-E-A aren't written anywhere."

37

Inspector Alvarez nursed his empty beer glass, his gaze drifting through the window to the dark city outside the tavern. While it may have been quiet on the streets, it was lively inside. The usual post-dinner crowd of off-duty cops, and those who flirted with the other side of the law enjoying a drink after a hard day's work. The bar was home to an unspoken truce by all sides, the ritual a regular event.

The ceasefire among enemies rarely broke out into a fight. That was because there was no black and white in San Yetaxa. There were good cops. There were bad cops. And then there were the villains who came in all different varieties. Some were hardliners who answered to the cartel and no one else, while others were more wary of the authorities. The delicate balance was a nightly dance where everyone watched and participated, nobody truly knowing where anyone's loyalty really lay.

Alvarez remembered his early experiences out of the academy. He had been placed on the beat with a partner, not much younger than Alvarez was now. The man was as corrupt as they came. He did not hide it either. The locals, the cartel, even the head honchos in the force—they all knew it. He was one of many. In those days, everyone looked the other way. In the modern era, the regulations were harder to skirt. Those who wanted to walk the crooked path had to be shrewder.

Alvarez had seen a lot on the streets. The good, the bad, and everything in between. He could have chosen any course. But he had made a personal vow he intended to keep: he would never cross the line. The only reason anyone did was for self-gain. He had become a police officer to serve those in need. And there were so many in San Yetaxa who required someone to stand up for them.

A shuffle of footsteps filtered through the hum of conversations in the tavern, and Martinez appeared from the other side of the bar with two more beers in his hands. He set one down in front of Alvarez and sat on the worn stool beside him, the upholstery emitting a puff of air under his weight.

Alvarez pushed the empty glass aside and ran his fingers over the frost perspiring on the edge of the new one. "Thanks."

"You okay?" Martinez asked.

Alvarez took a sip, the froth of the cold beer clinging to his lips. "Just thinking."

"About Cruz?"

"Yeah."

"Thought so. I know that look."

"Hmm."

"We can't change what we can't control." Martinez shrugged. "Cruz went out the door because we couldn't pin anything on him. There was no sign of breaking and entering, and we have no way to contact the doctor to have him press charges. And let's face it, it's not like Pineda would have anyway. Herrera had us in a corner."

"You're wise beyond your years, Martinez."

"You'll learn one day." Martinez gulped his beer. "This entire case is at a dead end. We all know the cartel was responsible for what's taken place over the last few days, but they'll never let us prove it."

Alvarez tapped his fingers next to his glass. "You're probably right."

"At least the American and the Pinedas escaped. This Dane Winter guy knew exactly what he was doing when he pulled that stunt at the hospital. He got Ruben and Maria to safety, and even managed to skip town himself, giving the cartel a bloody nose on the way out."

"Did he get them to safety, though? Everything I've read up on Winter speaks to his heroism. He's a man of honor. He knows the reach of the cartel, and would understand neither Maria nor Ruben will be truly out of the cartel's sights until he's dead. I'm betting he's still here."

"In San Yetaxa? Why? If I was being hunted down by the cartel I'd get out of here as fast as possible."

"Winter realizes the cartel are after him. He also knows they'll follow him home if they have to. His work here isn't done. For his sake, and the sake of the Pinedas, he has to make things right. Look at what he did to Cruz to illustrate his point."

"By 'make things right,' you mean take on the cartel?" Martinez puffed out his cheeks, consuming more of his beer. "He might've been a decorated soldier, but that won't cut it down here. If he goes after them, they'll tear him to pieces."

Alvarez stretched for the bowl of pretzels, snatching a few and tossing them in his mouth. "He's survived this far."

Martinez ate some of his own. "Let's say you're right. He's one man against an entire organization. We've seen the horrors they're capable of."

"Winter was a US Marine, Martinez. He won't wait for them to come to him. He'll go on the offensive. I'm not saying he'll take down the cartel, but he could do a lot of damage while he has the chance."

"If that's true, we'll be the ones, as usual, who have to clean up the mess."

Alvarez nodded. As much as he liked the idea of the cartel taking a hit, he was not one for vigilante justice. Not in his town. Still, he could not shake his curiosity of Dane Winter. What he would give to sit opposite him to pick apart his mind and unravel his story. What had he done to piss off the cartel so much?

Martinez enjoyed the rest of his beer and slid the glass across to the bar. The bartender scooped it up and rested it in the rack with the other dirty dishes.

"I've got to go home," his partner said. "I promised Angela we'd watch some Netflix before bed. See you tomorrow?"

Alvarez nodded. "Bright and early."

Martinez gave Alvarez's shoulder a tight squeeze and rose from his seat, exiting through the heavy front door.

Alvarez returned to his thoughts, swirling his glass as he did. The cycle would begin in the morning like it did every day with a new case on his desk. Perhaps a homicide in the inner-west. Maybe a corpse washed up in the sewer. Or even the bloody remnants of a shootout with multiple victims. A typical day in San Yetaxa.

A shadow fell over him and another patron sat in Martinez's spot, holding out a banknote to the bartender.

"I'll have what he's having."

Alvarez recognized the lawyer's voice. The deliberate tone one would use to convince a jury that wrong was right. Alvin Herrera adjusted his unkempt wig and smiled at him.

"A surprise to see you here, Inspector Alvarez."

Alvarez was not about to play his game, instead focusing on

his half-drunk beer. The bartender returned with the lawyer's drink and sat it before him. Herrera took a hearty sip, leaning back just enough not to topple from his stool. "A nice end to another satisfying day."

Alvarez remained silent.

"I hope there's no animosity toward me because of this morning, Inspector," Herrera went on. "We deal with each other far too often to have something come between us."

"What are you doing here, Herrera?"

"Same as you. Rest and relaxation."

"And you had to sit here?"

"When I saw you, I couldn't resist. I just wanted to reiterate how much I cherish our relationship. I'd prefer it stay a fruitful one and—"

"We both know you want to make sure I don't cause you or Roberto Cruz anymore trouble."

The lawyer held his hand on his heart in mock surprise. "Don't assume I'm being disingenuous."

Alvarez grunted and had more beer.

"Besides, I quite enjoy our little sparring sessions. You keep me in business, Inspector. I'd hate to see the day you're no longer at your post, keeping me on my toes."

Alvarez clunked down the glass on the weathered old bar. "What's that supposed to mean?"

"Please don't take it as a threat. I know retirement's coming. Time waits for no man. Whether you finish up tomorrow, or in a few years down the line, I just want you to be aware I'll miss you."

Alvarez knew when he was being mocked and intimidated. Herrera was not talking about voluntary retirement, rather one forced upon him, whether by a bullet or from someone higher-up in the department who resided in the cartel's back pocket. He fought the urge to grab the man by the scruff of the neck. Any brawl in such a place would quickly turn nasty.

"It's comforting to know you care so much, Herrera." Alvarez finished his drink. "Luckily, I'm not going anywhere. Not just yet."

Without another word, he got off the stool and turned toward the door.

"A pleasure chatting, Inspector," the lawyer said with all the contrived politeness one would expect of his position, his cheeriness drifting out with Alvarez into the night.

38

Winter drove on through the night, the moon casting an unnerving glow across the road with the sharp but yellowed beams of his headlights. He had chosen the long way around, tracing his route to Colby's associate via the back of the hills, shunning San Yetaxa to avoid any complications. The temperature had dropped further since his meeting with his DEA contact, the sky above remaining devoid of clouds to trap the day's warmth.

He shivered inside the car, thinking about Middleton, Lynch, Watts, and Sidhu. Each face appeared from the gloom, their expressions frozen in their final moments of life at Gilberto Sanchez's estate. They were the best Redwind had to offer, utterly overwhelmed by the unrelenting power of the local cartel.

Their deaths were meaningless.

The smart course of action would have been to take the easy way out. All he needed to do was phone Colonel Dawson again and arrange for his private jet to return him to Camp Redwind. But what would that solve? The cartel would still come, emboldened by what had gone down at the fundraiser. Winter would remain no closer to understanding how he fit into the deadly game, while leaving Dawson and Redwind in the lurch. Then there was the matter of the tattooed assassin who had come after him. He suspected the man would want payback of his own for the touch up Winter had given him.

No, he had to go it alone.

He swept down the western side and over the hills—the same road he and Maria had found themselves on after their hike from her house and the shelter they had called home just two nights prior. He thought about the woman, hoping she was okay. And her brother too, of course. The whole situation had been unfair on both of them. They were innocent bystanders, caught up in something they never saw coming.

The cartel had to understand that, didn't they? But then what did they understand? There was every chance they could still go after them. While their cousins' beach house in Playa Azul was far from San Yetaxa, he feared what lengths the cartel would go to. He gritted his teeth, his gut churning with the thought of what might happen to them.

A junction appeared, the sign near it matching the street given to him by Colby. He turned right, the smooth asphalt giving way to rough gravel. The rear of the vehicle slipped for a moment, threatening to send him spinning. He took his foot off the gas and adjusted to the shifting track, passing several properties. They were similar to Maria's. Vast spaces of land with small shack-like houses set far from the road.

Winter continued, reaching a gate on the left, where the number twelve was emblazoned on a rusty sign, creaking in the wind. He entered the property, bumping over the wonky terrain and down the long driveway. At its end lay a beaten-up old El Camino and Chevelle, both semi-covered in tarpaulin, while beyond sat the home he had been invited to visit.

Winter turned the key, switching off the engine, and nudged the door ajar. He tiptoed over the tire-rutted driveway and up onto the sparse area of grass which led to the house. He reached the door and knocked on the wobbly screen. The light inside shimmered, casting a shadow of someone on approach. The silhouette of the man emerged, his shape becoming clear through the worn wire mesh.

He was an older individual, closer to seventy than sixty. There was a spryness about him. His eyes, however, betrayed deep paranoia. They darted one way and then the other, finally falling upon Winter. "Yes?"

"A mutual associate of ours sent me. I'm here for—"

The man with no name held up a hand. "Just speak the words."

Winter exhaled with a smirk. "Mary had a little lamb. Its fleece was white as snow. And everywhere that Mary went, her lamb was sure to go."

The elder Mexican nodded and ushered him inside. Winter entered, immediately hit with the chaos of the residence. Old car parts littered the floor, newspapers were strewn over chairs and tables, and various electronics, including TVs and radios, lay scattered in different stages of repair.

They passed through what once might have been a living area, then the kitchen, making their way to one of the bedrooms. It was a little more organized, with less clutter, the stain-covered double bed backed against a wall with a pastel painting hanging from it.

His crotchety host put an arm out to stop him from stepping over the threshold. With a twist of his hand, he removed a panel from a nearby cabinet, revealing a rope. He tugged it, and with a groan of shifting metal, the bed slid into the wall, exposing a hidden compartment in the floor. The secret cache was a sight to behold. The rows of assorted weaponry were enough to make even Winter take pause, rivaling the stashes he had smoked out in the infamous Taliban caves of Afghanistan.

The first section contained all kinds of sidearms, including pistols and revolvers. Shotguns lined the next rack, alongside semi-automatic and automatic rifles of various makes and models. Grenades were stacked neatly nearby with plastic explosives, detonators, timers, and wires. There was even an assortment of knives and camouflage gear.

Winter whistled, taking a step into the room. "I can see I came to the right place." He balanced his feet on the joists, crouching low and examining everything on show. The arms were in immaculate condition, most of them new or barely used. "Where did you get all of this?"

"I don't ask what you're going to do with them. You don't ask me where I got them," the man replied, his tone firm and final.

"I suppose that's fair enough." Winter took the list of weapons required and handed them to him. "I'll need everything you see on this."

The dealer retrieved his reading glasses from the breast pocket of his woolen shirt and glanced down his nose at the inventory. "And how will you be paying?"

"Our mutual associate said he'd handle the financials."

"I'll add it to his tab." He folded up the paper and returned it to Winter. "The guns don't come delivered. You'll have to take what you want to the car yourself."

"I'll live, I suppose." Winter chuckled, calculating the weight. "Can't say the same for those who are gonna be on the receiving end of all this."

39

Winter steered the car with one hand, his other ensuring the cell phone remained secured on the cradle affixed to the dashboard. The map on the screen displayed a pin that he had dropped at the set of the coordinates where the waste services truck had stopped for four minutes and twenty-three seconds. It was quite the anomaly, considering the efficient run from the facility, through the city, and back again.

The sun was yet to rise, the time reading 0535 hours. His weather app confirmed that dawn would break at 0614. Just under forty minutes to get to where he needed to be and prepare before daylight swept over the forest.

He yawned from the restless night. After leaving the arms dealer's house, he got a bite to eat at a gas station. The attendant had been nice enough to nuke some microwave burritos for him. They were a flavorless imitation of the real thing, but they did the job. Purchasing a large bottle of water, some packets of chips and candy, he hit the road again, back into the hills to find a secluded hideaway for the evening.

Winter had set his alarm for 0500 and attempted to get as

much rest as possible before the new day. The combination of the cramped space in the back seat and a multitude of thoughts swirling around his mind made slumber elusive. If he had to guess how many hours he had snoozed, it would have been a grand total of two, the sleep resembling several disjointed naps. With any luck, it would be all the fuel he would need for the day ahead.

Winter narrowed his eyes at the road as it forked at the next junction. One path would carry him to San Yetaxa's city center around the hills; the other led him to a craggy track through the greener stretches. He double-checked the map and took the turn onto the trail that would lead him to the coordinates.

He had already scoped out the area with his app. It was lush, the tight road, weaving a path barely wide enough for two vehicles to pass. It was yet another reason. Winter had been so suspicious of the truck's unscheduled stop in the first place.

He negotiated the corners as they came, sliding from one side of the road to the other, the tires skimming the edges of the dirt. It got him wondering how the truck driver had done so well to navigate the route. Then again, if he did it daily, he would have mastered it by now.

Winter considered the overall supply line in his mind. If his suspicions about the entire operation were correct, the cartel was paying the driver, and likely several of the personnel at the waste facility. It was a canny scheme. Ship the product over dozens of kilometers under the cover of legitimate business in plain sight. It guaranteed no cop would think twice about pulling over such a truck. Winter suspected after it reached the facility, the drugs were offloaded in a different manner and funneled north toward the US border.

If it was a daily occurrence, which it surely was, given the routine swap of barrels at Hector's Diner, then the sheer volume of product being moved equated to a staggering amount of money. It was no wonder Berrera's organization had such a stranglehold on Tlapetla. He had the cash and the resources to operate freely, silencing any opposition without question.

At least for now.

If Winter got his way, he would bring it all crashing down. First, he needed to prove his suspicions. He had to get evidence of their operations.

He gripped the steering wheel that little tighter, the car edging closer to his dropped pin. He took the next crest, swerving sideways briefly down the dip, until he found himself within a hundred yards of the coordinates. A quick pump of the brakes slowed the vehicle, the dust behind him swirling before finally settling.

There, in the soft beams of his headlights, lay an innocuous stretch of road. One thing, however, distinguished it from the surrounding tracks. The terrain was flat.

The perfect place for an exchange.

Winter brought the car to a halt and scanned the area. The vegetation on each side of him was even denser than the original photos, the images likely several years old. He required a secure space to stake out his target. Back on the move, he approached a slight incline, the dense scrub thinning enough to permit him access.

He craned his neck and peered through the rear windshield, trying to make out a line of sight to the exchange point. He angled the nose of the car into the shrubs and moved forward through the brush, wary not to get bogged down or snag a dropped branch.

The scrub gave way to thicker undergrowth. Winter eased a little further onward, parking behind the trunk of a wide mahogany tree. Flicking the headlights off and killing the engine, he got out of the vehicle and surveyed the area around it. He could not risk being spotted. The car had to be in a place where it would not be discovered.

Winter returned, satisfied he had hidden it as best he could. He popped the trunk, revealing the goodies he had purchased from the arms dealer on Colby's credit card. Firearms lined one side and explosives on the other. Tucked in behind them were jungle camouflage gear and similarly decorated supplies.

Winter got dressed first, pulling on the green fatigues, fitting himself in the combat wear from head to toe. The color was not the sandy hue he was used to in Afghanistan or Iraq, but it was perfectly suited for the wilderness. He threw on a hat and smeared camo paint over his face to blend in with his surroundings. He then went for the new set of binoculars he had procured, draping the strap over his neck.

Then came the weapons. He wrapped a tactical belt around his waist, securing a combat knife and Beretta 92FS 9mm sidearm. Next, he removed the SIG-Sauer MCX Rattler automatic rifle from the trunk and tossed extra ammunition into his backpack, along with several pouches of plastic explosives and the various trimmings for their use. From the passenger seat, he added his gas station snacks and bottle of water to the pack, ready for what lay ahead.

Winter hauled the camouflage tarpaulin out and unwrapped it on the ground. He reached for the steel tent stakes and the hammer he had packed. With a few solid strikes, he drove them into the earth, securing each corner of the tarp through the eyelets, spreading it wide over the car to ensure it produced sufficient coverage. It may have been overkill, but if anyone happened to glance in the vehicle's direction, he wanted to make sure it was invisible.

In the distance, the first hint of dawn snuck over the horizon, the faint rays of the morning glimmering through the trees to the east. Winter had no more time to waste. He collected his gear, throwing his backpack over his shoulders, and set off through the brush. He trundled down the incline and toward a position that would give him the best view of the road.

Winter found a location that would keep him out of sight. If the truck followed its pattern, stopping in the same spot at the same time, Winter calculated he would be there for the better part of nine to ten hours. Luckily, not only was the space concealed but also comfortable enough for him to see the day through.

He went to the ground and lifted his binoculars. Satisfied with his post, he grabbed a packet of chips, tearing open the bag, ready to take his first bite. The familiar rhythm of warfare washed over him as he prepared for the wait ahead.

40

Martinez maneuvered his car into the underground parking garage of the station house, the glint of the rising sun blazing through his rearview mirror before he disappeared into the cavernous shadows below. He navigated the sharp corner, passing uniformed officers exchanging spots, the area bustling with the changeover of shifts. At another hairpin he spiraled to the next level reserved for inspectors and those in other senior positions.

As usual, his spot awaited. Something, however, was off. Alvarez's car was missing, his sloppy old 1990s Nissan usually located four spaces over nowhere to be found. Martinez furrowed his brow and reversed into his space. He got out and took a step past the front of his Toyota, wondering if Alvarez had parked somewhere else.

He had not.

Martinez rubbed his chin, recalling Alvarez complaining that his engine was giving him trouble. Perhaps it had finally broken down, forcing him to take a cab to work. Or maybe Martinez had got to the station before him. He checked his watch. He was on time. Not the usual half-hour early that Alvarez prided himself on.

Shaking his head, he grabbed his lunch pail from the passenger seat and locked his car. He made his way to the stairs and climbed to the booking area. The night appeared to have been a busy one, the benches crowded with many undesirables, and others wearily waiting to spring friends and loved ones from the overnight lockup.

Martinez passed the sergeant at the desk, who had just come on duty. He gave him a knowing look, the fatigue of the long day already painted on his middle-aged features. Without a word, Martinez went up the worn old stairs until he reached the bullpen at the top. Scattered throughout, inspectors' desks overflowed with paperwork and half-drunk coffee mugs. A steady stream of phone calls echoed through the room, answered by those who had previously signed on for their shift.

Alvarez's desk stood unoccupied, when normally he would already be hunched over a file, preparing for the first case of the day. Martinez went by the lieutenant's closed office door, past the interview rooms and then to the lockers. Maybe Alvarez was in the can or getting dressed.

The locker room was empty. So were the toilet stalls, not so much as a grunt stemming from his partner grappling with his morning crap. Martinez popped his lunch pail in his locker and walked back out, stopping by the lieutenant's door. He knocked.

"Come in," the voice carried from the other side.

Martinez entered to find the station's lieutenant at his desk. Not much older than Martinez, the senior officer was flipping through a stack of documents.

"What is it, Martinez?"

"It's Alvarez. I can't seem to see him anywhere."

"He's called in sick."

"He what?"

"Apparently he's feeling under the weather." His superior shrugged. "Needed twenty-four hours to fight it."

"Sir, Alvarez hasn't had sick leave since the Spanish Flu of 1918."

The lieutenant smirked, suppressing a chuckle at the ageist jest. "What are you getting at?"

Martinez pondered before voicing his suspicion, instead straightening his posture. "I guess it shows he's human, after all."

"Indeed." The lieutenant waved him over the threshold and handed him a folder. "We've got a homicide on Grape Street. The morning shift at a packing factory found two bullet wounds in the victim. One in the chest. One in the head."

Martinez examined the preliminary details. "Dealers?"

"Looks like it. Since Alvarez is off, I want you to take Miggy."

Martinez went to protest, but thought better of it. "Of course. We'll head straight out."

"Thanks, Martinez."

"Is there anything else, sir?"

He shook his head. Martinez stepped from the office, closing the door and surveying the bullpen. Miggy stood by the photocopier with a cup of coffee in his hand, prodding at the controls. The man had only received his shield two months ago. And it showed.

"Looks like you're coming with me today." He gave Miggy the folder. "Sign a car out of the motor pool and I'll join you shortly."

Miggy drained his coffee, tucking the documents under his arm. "Uh, okay."

Martinez departed the bullpen while his temporary partner went in the other direction. He returned to the locker room, securing the door behind him, and took out his cell. He dialed the second most called number on his list, just below his wife's. The phone rang and someone answered.

"Martinez."

He strained his hearing, catching another sound in the background. He was not at home curled up in bed. Alvarez was on the road, the cabin noise unmistakable. "Where are you?"

"I'm sick."

"No, you're not. You're in your car."

"Just heading to the doctors."

"You don't go to the doctors."

There was a brief silence before Alvarez's voice crackled. "Nothing gets past you, does it? That inspector work is really paying off."

Martinez leaned against his locker, propping the sole of his foot against the one below. "What have you got yourself into?"

"Nothing yet."

"Yet?"

Alvarez sighed. "I was up all night wondering about this situation with Dane Winter. The more I think about it, the more I worry about Maria and Ruben Pineda. I've decided to search for them, just in case the cartel makes a move on them."

"How do you know where they'll be?"

"I don't, but I went back to the station last night and did a little digging. Let's just say I'm going off a hunch."

"Your hunches are pretty accurate."

"Yeah, usually."

The whine of creaky brakes and the click of blinkers sounded.

"Do you want help?" Martinez asked. "I could—"

"No, I'm doing this on the down low. If you happen to be 'sick' too, the lieutenant and the chief might get suspicious. I'd rather go this alone. I'm sure you've got work to do, anyway."

"Yeah, there's a drug-related homicide in the inner-west."

"Who they partnering you up with?"

"Miggy."

Brief silence filtered through the phone. "My condolences."

"I guess I'll finally know how you feel every shift."

"You're a hell of an inspector. Don't think for a moment that I'm not proud of how far you've come."

A lump formed in Martinez's throat, his mentor's praise catching him off guard. "Hey, you be careful out there. I expect you to return, okay? I can't have Miggy as my permanent partner."

"Don't worry about me. I've been doing this long enough to know how to watch my back."

"I guess you have. If you need anything, you know who to call."

"I appreciate it, Martinez."

The line went dead and Martinez returned the phone to his pocket. He tapped his fist against his locker in frustration and headed back to the bullpen, finding Miggy awkwardly fumbling with a pair of radios.

It was not the kind of day he was looking forward to. A homicide. A rookie. And a friend getting himself into trouble.

41

Winter tossed the last gummy bear into his mouth, chewing it slowly to savor the flavor, and crumpled the empty packet under his leg. His supply of snacks was exhausted. So was most of his water, only a few sips remaining in the bottle next to him.

He raised his binoculars and peered out at the road. It was quiet, as it had been for most of the day. In more than nine hours of lying vigil, aside from the few times he had gone for a leak, he had seen little in terms of traffic.

That morning, three vehicles had passed his position. Two were heavy-duty SUVs. Likely locals. The third was a taxi, probably from out of town, its navigation system sending them astray down the beaten path.

Around midday, four dirt bike riders tore past in one direction and then the other, using the road as their own personal racetrack. The dust they kicked up lingered long after they were gone, along with the high-pitched buzz of their engines, which eventually faded in to the distance.

Winter was silently thankful of the breeze which had stirred through the forest. It had been a sweltering morning and even hotter afternoon. He dreaded to think what it must have felt like in the city, trapped in the heat of the concrete, steel and asphalt sprawl. And of course, the unforgiving desert beyond. If the stories were to be believed, there was little wonder the cartel buried their victims in the vast wasteland. For the living, death was not just a possibility. It was an inevitability in the expanse.

Winter wiped the sweat from his forehead and unscrewed the cap from his water bottle, taking the smallest of sips. He had not seen a single vehicle pass his position in more than three hours. The truck was due. Overdue, in fact. His mind churned.

Had he been too confident in the discovery he had made yesterday? Perhaps the pickup points were altered daily to throw off anyone investigating. Maybe there were no regular pickups at all, and some of the barrels were decoys. There was also another possibility. What if he had misread the entire situation from the start?

Hector may have just wanted to keep his kitchen clean. The truck driver could have simply been a reckless soul, confident in his abilities to take a shortcut through the wilderness. Or, as Colby had suggested, perhaps the guy needed to relieve himself and figured the middle of the woods was as good a place as any.

Winter frowned. If any of the scenarios were true, he was back to square one. He would have to get to the cartel in another manner. With the way Berrera ran his organization, that would be no simple task. It could take much longer, too.

Suddenly, a noise sounded in the distance. An engine. A diesel engine. It closed, dust spewing up over the crest until a vehicle appeared. It was a truck.

Winter closed his eyes for a moment, savoring his stroke of good fortune. It slowed to a crawl in the center of the road, its bulk barely fitting between its craggy edges. The driver put on his brakes and jumped from the cab. This time without a clipboard in hand. Unlike his other stops, he was not on official business. He walked to the rear of his ride and activated the tailgate. As it descended with a groan, another sound echoed beyond his position.

It was high-pitched. A screaming drone, similar to the dirt bikes from earlier. Winter gripped his binoculars tighter, scanning the area more intently. The vegetation on the other side of the road wavered and parted, snapping the driver's attention to some visitors on approach.

Four quad bikes emerged, their riders circling the truck and its lone driver. He did not flinch at their arrival, remaining calm and hopping onto the tailgate, raising it again to access the cargo area. From Winter's obscured vantage point, the commotion from inside was obvious: the driver was shifting a barrel. It was followed by the thump of the lid being removed.

The quad bike riders, all clad in black, turned off their engines and dismounted. Three of the men, each heavily armed with an automatic rifle slung over their shoulders, quickly assumed defensive positions around the truck. To avoid being spotted, Winter lowered himself further.

The lone unarmed rider moved to the rear of his quad bike and opened a plastic container. He removed several tightly wrapped packages and tossed them to the driver. Even from a distance, Winter recognized them immediately. Crystal meth. Several thuds and bumps followed in the cargo bed as the driver sealed the barrel up with the narcotics inside.

Without so much as a word, the deal was done. The driver returned to the ground and lifted the tailgate. The riders then disappeared into the forest as swiftly as they had appeared. The driver re-entered the cab and started the engine, rolling the truck away to his next more legitimate job.

Winter waited for the dust to settle and the last echoes of the engines to wane into the distance. He used the time to allow himself a moment of satisfaction. He had been right all along. The cartel in Tlapetla was using the drop point to funnel meth through the city and beyond. If the logic followed, somewhere in the hills where those quad bikes had come from was the production facility.

Winter rose and gathered his trash, slipping it into a side compartment of his bag. He finished the rest of his water and clinched the straps of his backpack tight over his shoulders. Setting off, he crossed the now empty road, leaping over some deep tire grooves and vanishing into the brush across the way.

With his assault rifle in hand, Winter looked over the terrain. It did not take too long to discover the path used by the quad bike riders. While it was not a track found on any map, or one suitable for many styles of vehicles, there were definite signs of use, the flattened grass and deep tire imprints making it obvious. Keeping his distance, he veered a hundred yards to the right. Slowly ascending the hill, he crouched where he could and hid behind various trees as he went.

He stopped at one a little further up and spotted movement. He took a moment to collect himself and snuck a look. The guard, dressed in black, stood motionless, casually holding an automatic rifle in his right hand and a cigarette in the left.

Winter smiled. He had found the road to the fortress.

Now it was time to breach the gates.

42

Alvarez had never set foot in Playa Azul before. For most of his life, he had barely strayed from the streets of San Yetaxa. The only exceptions were for work, when a lead would take him beyond Tlapetla into another state, forcing him to collaborate with the local authorities of that region to crack a case involving multiple jurisdictions.

Playa Azul had not been one of those places. Located more than six hundred kilometers from his home, the beach town was a quaint, unspoiled retreat, hugging the gorgeous azure coastline. It did not resemble the glittering images of Mexico's most famous resorts, but it did have a charming quality to it. Modest dwellings dotted the water, while further inland was a scattering of small businesses lining the streets. It was a place for the most part which was yet to be touched by civilization, the usual apartment buildings and massive hotels catering to rich Americans thankfully absent.

Alvarez drove through the heart of town, passing by many locals who were going about their day shopping in the narrow avenues at the market and down the rickety boardwalk along the seaside. Local tourists, too, appeared to be out in force, running around in bright swimwear, while others lugged surfboards ranging from flashy and expensive to battered and scarred.

With one hand, Alvarez flipped open the notepad where he had jotted the address, making a right turn. What little traffic there was dwindled further, and he soon found himself on the trail alone, flanked by beach houses on either side. He wondered what life would have been like living in such a place. Playa Azul undoubtedly had its own police department.

What crimes could they possibly investigate? He wagered they did not have to deal with homicides on a daily basis. As he cruised by more of the homes, he speculated on their price tags. Retirement was coming. Just because he had spent his whole life in San Yetaxa did not mean he had to stay there. A quieter and simpler existence was very appealing.

He shook his head at the thought, dismissing it as fantasy. His pension would barely be enough to keep him afloat once he packed it all in. Moving to Playa Azul was a dream he could not afford. Maybe those in the cartel had the right idea. Get rich off the back of others less fortunate than you and settle in for the easy life.

Alvarez frowned, the brief thought a lapse in his lofty ideals. Life, as his father had always told him, was not fair. Those who did good often went unnoticed. But when the time came, and you reached Heaven's gates, there would be no bargains to make. No one could bribe their way in.

Another street loomed ahead, and Alvarez steered the car left, the Nissan's brakes squealing in protest as he did. He appreciated the old girl, amazed it had made the entire journey. At the end of the road, he brought the vehicle to a halt, easing it into a spot between two other cars, alongside the curb.

With another quick glance at his notepad, he read the number aloud. "Thirty-three."

It matched the numerals on the mailbox at the front of the beach house a little further down the avenue. He stepped out of his car and navigated around a young family heading to the sand. The father lugged a large umbrella over his shoulder, while the mother and two children carried their towels. As he passed them, he caught a distinct look from the adults.

It was the way he was dressed. Though he was not as formally attired as he would have been if he were on duty in San Yetaxa, his dark clothes and hat stood out against the stark neon colors of those around the town enjoying the sun. He paid the stares little mind and pushed onto the beach house.

It was clad with weathered timber boards, the soft yellow paint peeling in patches, and the green door dull from the relentless sunshine. One had to have some money to have a second home in such a location, but the condition told a different story. While they were wealthy enough to afford the escape in the summer months, there was clearly little left to invest in its upkeep.

Alvarez went up the small steps, each of them bowing under his feet. He looked upward at the humble two-story house, and through the windows, their curtains drawn tight to keep out the light. He continued to the door and reached for the brass knocker, which was barely hanging on, its screws about to pop loose. He grunted and used his fist instead, the sound noisy enough to draw someone's attention from inside.

No one came.

He tried again. Louder this time. So much so that it shuddered the door, the surrounding frame grumbling at the abuse.

No answer.

Alvarez went over to the window and cupped his hands

around his eyes to shield them from the harsh glare to get a better look inside. It was empty, the interior bare, with no sign of movement between the slit of the curtains. He put his hands on his hips and noticed a walkway down the side of the house. He went back down the steps, making his way to the rear of the property.

Beyond stretched a magnificent view of the beach, the sea gleaming a bright blue under the afternoon sun. Those on the shore reveled in what it had to offer. A few sunbathed, some splashed in the water, and others made sandcastles. Alvarez imagined a young Ruben and Maria Pineda playing with their cousins on the expanse several years earlier, carefree and full of joy. Time had a horrible way of changing things, and rarely for the better.

He climbed another set of poorly maintained steps and announced himself again with a firm knock. Just like at the front, no one answered. Through the corner of his eyes, he observed a flutter in the curtains. It may have been a breeze drifting from a cracked window somewhere in the house. Then again, it might not.

He sighed and sat on the top step, removing his hat and waving it to cool himself down.

"Look, I understand your concerns," he began, loud enough that someone inside might hear him. "I really do. If I were in your position, I'd probably think twice about opening that door too. You're wondering if I'm on the level or not. Am I a cop you can trust? Let me tell you, Doctor Pineda, I've been truthful about everything I've told you. I wanted to protect you and Maria. I admit there's some bad police officers going around, but I assure you I'm not one of them."

He placed his hat back on his head. "I started serving on the force before either of you were born. I've seen what crime has done to our city. And what the cartel is capable of. That's why I'm here. I want to help you. It's likely that they might still come look-ing. If I could find you, you better believe they could too. Please—"

A faint mumbling muttered on the other side of the door.

Alvarez stood, trying to make out the voices. Suddenly, the door opened with a loud creak. There, standing at the threshold, were Ruben and Maria Pineda.

43

Winter stood, pressed behind the tree, his breathing steady. He had examined the entire rise through his binoculars. Three guards were posted at different points. They were in his way and would have to be taken out. All with the greatest of care, so that he could remain obscured on his ascent.

The first man lit another cigarette, his eyes weary from the boredom of his job. It was likely not his first time on watch duty. He would have grown accustomed to the tediousness of his lonely post, never expecting an intruder to breach his zone.

That was about to change.

Winter craned his neck around the tree to confirm that the man was still puffing away. He returned to his cover and cupped his hands over his mouth, pursing his lips and letting out a piercing shriek. The imitation of a primate's call was a pretty good one, if he did say so himself.

Winter stopped and listened for any sign of movement. Nothing. No approaching footfalls. No rustling of long grass. He made the noise a second time. Louder and more desperate. He even kicked at the brush at his feet to pull the guard's attention.

Finally, the faint sound of boots sifting through the under-growth reached Winter's ears. He hollered again to make sure the man would continue moving in his direction. Winter's muscles tightened as the cartel lackey edged ever closer.

The guard's gun was the first part of him to break through the shadows beyond the tree. Winter shot his hand for it, snatching it from his grasp before he had a chance to react. In the same instance, the man catapulted to the ground from the vine Winter had rigged across his path, his cigarette spilling from his mouth and his face planting into the soil.

Winter drove his knee into his back and shoved his head further into the ground. The pressure quelled any screams or calls for help. His limbs flailed for a few moments until he weak-ened, the man finally giving up and suffocating in the dirt of the forest floor.

Winter remained crouched and reached for a nearby leafy branch which had fallen. He tossed it over the guard, concealing his handiwork. Without a second glance, he pressed on and made his way further up the incline through the brush.

The next guard appeared more alert, his eyes sweeping one way and then back to the other. Winter used the thicker grass as cover and crawled closer to his position, off to the left. He outflanked the guard and hid between a tree approximately ten yards at his rear.

Winter removed the combat knife from his sheath and took careful steps toward him.

Eight yards... Five yards... Three yards...

A snap sounded underfoot and Winter peered downward, his heart skipping at the sight of the twig broken under his feet. The guard's head whipped around in a state of shock. He brought his rifle to bear, but Winter lunged, closing the gap, jerking the barrel of the gun away with one hand and slicing the blade through the air with the other. It fashioned a horizontal path, carving into the man's neck. He dropped his weapon and clutched at the wound, gushing with blood.

Winter slammed the guard onto his back and yanked his arms to keep him from stemming the tide of the gash. As the crimson flood bubbled from his throat, he gasped with ragged breaths, his eyes revealing the horror of the attack. Like his comrade only minutes earlier, his hold on life diminished, and he fell eerily still in the silence of the forest.

Winter stood and rolled the lifeless body onto the grass, the streaks of blood left behind all that remained of his second kill. He gazed up at his next target, who remained facing the other direction, oblivious to what had just happened. Winter wasted no time and crisscrossed his way up the hill, careful to avoid any open ground while remaining in the shadows of the great mahogany trees.

With each step, he closed, noting the surroundings of the last guard. The terrain offered Winter no cover, the grass sparse under foot. Winter would have to come at him head-on. And do so without a gun. If a single shot cracked in the woods, one henchman at the top of the hill would be the least of his problems.

Winter approached the final tree between him and the cartel thug and slipped behind it, gauging the distance between them. Twenty, maybe twenty-two feet. A sidearm with a silencer would have been his preferred ally in the situation. Unfortunately, though the arms dealer was well stocked, some of the more refined gear was absent from his shop window.

He unsheathed his bloody combat knife again, weighing it up in his hands. He never received knife-throwing training in the Marines. It was not until he joined Colonel Dawson at Redwind that he began taking courses in the art and honing the skill.

There were many issues with the practice, including low stopping power and the lack of lethality.

Range would be an issue, the distance from his target far from comfortable. Ideally, he would never throw a blade over fifteen feet. Here, he had little choice. Winter took a breath, steadying himself. His aim would have to be perfect and the throw good enough to carry speed and force to land the blow with maximum impact. He counted down.

Three... Two... One...

He hurtled from the tree, his eyes locking with the Mexican. In those breathless microseconds, time seemed to slow. The guard swung his rifle in Winter's direction, the barrel sweeping from right to left. Winter wound up his shoulder and tossed the knife, gripping the blade instead of the handle for greater power over the longer distance.

As it soared through the air, the gunman zeroed in on his target, his finger tightening on the trigger. The sight aligned with Winter, ready to fire. But before he could shoot, the blade made contact, right in the middle of his chest. He lurched backward, his expression contorted with agony, the rifle in his hands pointing skyward.

Winter's heartrate pulsed, fear rising within that his victim might accidentally squeeze off a round. It never came, the man's body thumping to the ground. Winter rushed to his side to find both hands around the blade handle, the knife still embedded in blood and bone. The gunman stared into the forest canopy above, the last glimpses of life at least more serene than the seconds before it.

Winter crouched beside him and exhaled. His gamble had paid off, the adrenaline continuing to flow through him. He took another moment to regain his focus and pushed himself to his feet, creeping over the crest. His mission objective lay beyond in all its industrial glory. Constructed under the thick forest canopy stood a three-story structure—the crown jewel of the Tlapetla cartel and heart of its methamphetamine production which fueled its power in the region.

Winter gave his backpack an extra tug to confirm it still sat securely on his shoulders. He then stepped toward his target.

There was no turning back now.

44

Maria walked into the living area and handed Alvarez a steaming hot mug of coffee from the kitchen. He attempted to get comfortable on the dusty old sofa, resting the drink on his lap, while Maria joined her half-brother on the chairs opposite.

They stared at him, not in expectation of his verdict of the brew, but because their thoughts were swirling wildly. It was a look Alvarez was all too familiar with.

He sipped his coffee and placed it on the side table. "Thank you, Maria, that's very nice."

"I wasn't sure the kettle would still work," she admitted.

"I imagine it's been some time since this place was last lived in."

Cobwebs clung to the corners of the walls where they met ceiling and floor, the stench of rodents and damp heavy in the air. Filth coated every surface, undisturbed for who knows how long. The curtains were also infested and probably only needed a shake to fill the rooms with dust.

"Our uncle died about ten years ago." Maria frowned. "And

our aunt's in aged care. I don't think our cousins have come here since they were teenagers."

"It certainly shows." Alvarez pursed his lips. "I guess it's a roof over your heads. For now, at least."

"Are you saying we're not safe here?"

"I do worry that if the cartel comes looking for you, they'll use the same methods I have."

"Which was what exactly?" Ruben asked.

"I was able to link you to other family members and search their residences with our police files. It made sense for you to come here instead of your cousins' primary home. You didn't tell them you were coming here, right?"

"We didn't want to get them in trouble. The spare key was in the same place it always was."

"Good."

Maria straightened in her chair. "But why should we fear the cartel now? After we did the swap at the hospital, they surely know Winter's on his own. Why come after us, when he's the one they want?"

"That's a fair point, Ms. Pineda." Alvarez reached for the mug again to enjoy more of his coffee. "My main concern is if Winter's not willing to be found."

"What do you mean?"

"If I may ask you a question, before I answer that?"

"Okay."

"Do you know if he's still in San Yetaxa?"

Maria went silent, her eyes evading his.

"Please, Ms. Pineda, it's very important."

She sighed and her gaze lifted. "He told me he wanted to teach them a lesson for what they'd done to his friends."

"I was afraid of that." Alvarez exhaled deeply. "Everything I've read on Dane Winter paints him as a professional in his field. If he seeks to ruffle some feathers, he'll find a way to do it. That's only going to piss the cartel off."

"So you think they might use us to get to him?"

"Yes. In answer to your previous question, that's precisely what I'm saying."

"Can you be sure?" Ruben asked.

"I've been in this business for a very long time, Doctor." Alvarez put his coffee back on the side table. "Ms. Pineda, I've got a few more questions, if you're able to indulge me?"

She nodded.

"Your brother did his best to inform us of everything that happened when you rescued Winter at Sanchez's fundraiser, but there are a lot of gaps I've been unable to piece together. For instance, did Winter tell you why the cartel were after him? Did he let you know how he got involved with them?"

She shook her head. "He had no idea why they tried to kill him."

Alvarez raised an eyebrow. "So he didn't know they were coming for him either?"

"That's right."

"You're absolutely sure about that?"

"That's what he said."

"Hmm. That means he's just as dumfounded about this as I am." Alvarez fell into the plush cushions of the sofa and pondered. "The night the assassin came to your house. Did you get a visual on him?"

She gulped, closing her eyes, as if going back in time. "He wore a mask. The same ones worn by those who attacked Gilberto Sanchez's estate."

"Any other distinguishing marks? Was he muscular, fat, skinny—"

"He was tall and slim. But not weak if you know what I mean?"

Alvarez's mind flashed with the image of Cruz sitting in his interview room, his gangly legs beneath the table. The partial ID would not cut it in court, but it was enough to confirm his suspicion that he had been sent to kill Winter from the beginning. "What about how they found Winter? Do you have any idea how they might've tracked him down at your house?"

Maria opened her eyes and shook her head.

"They couldn't have followed you from Sanchez's. If they had, they'd have taken him out a lot earlier." Alvarez stood and paced between them. "After not discovering him in the ashes, they could've gone door knocking at potential places he might be holed up. But that's unlikely. The guest and staff list for the fundraiser was extensive."

"Inspector."

Alvarez halted at the sound of Ruben's voice. "Yes, sorry, Doctor."

"You've made it abundantly clear that we're still in danger. What are you going to do about it?"

Alvarez returned to the sofa and sat. "I think we should get you locked into the Protected Witness Program."

"And leave our lives behind in San Yetaxa?"

"At the moment, there's very little left for you there."

Maria crossed her arms. "Dane told me he'd take care of the cartel so we could return."

Alvarez shifted his gaze to her. "That was a very naïve claim for him to make. It's more likely he'll get himself killed."

"You said he was a professional."

"I did; however, the weight of numbers aren't in his favor. Eventually—"

"Inspector, you have to accept we're both wary of any government program designed to protect us. You yourself admitted that there are those in the police force who aren't as trustworthy as you. What would stop our new locations being leaked to the cartel?"

Alvarez hesitated in front of the forthright woman. She was right. There were never any guarantees. Just as he was about to formulate a response that might offer some reassurance, the hum of an engine sounded outside on the quiet street. He rose and went to the window to investigate through the slit in the drawn curtain.

A black SUV parked on the curb in front of the beach house and its front doors sprung open. A duo stepped out. The first was unfamiliar. Stocky but muscular. And bald. Probably close to his mid-forties. The second, however, Alvarez recognized. Taller, younger, a full head of hair with a ponytail knot, and tattoos down the left side of his face.

Roberto Cruz.

45

Winter remained low, scouting the terrain beyond the brush. The cartel setup was impressive. The land had been cleared with the best of earth-moving vehicles, followed by gravel being laid down, and the warehouse erected, all under the cover of the trees. No satellite or surveillance flyover had any chance of uncovering the operation. The money required would have been substantial to have constructed it in such secrecy.

Berrera and El Maestro would have needed a trusted team to level the area and remove just enough trees to keep the facility covered. They would also have required construction workers who would not rat. Outsourcing the job was out of the question, so they were likely all on the cartel's books, probably still being paid to this day to guarantee their silence.

Then there was the equipment inside, which churned out a steady supply of their product for daily shipments. On top of that, there were the ongoing costs of those tasked with creating the meth, the round-the-clock security, and transport overheads. It spoke to the sheer scale of the business in Tlapetla and how deeply lined Berrera and El Maestro's pockets were.

Winter scanned over the scene with his binoculars to take in every detail. Cars and quad bikes were parked in front of the facility, while guards patrolled the perimeter. He scoped out a weak point at the back of the compound. An area likely left unguarded due to the lack of obvious entry. There was, however, a downpipe, which descended from the spouting above the third floor, running the full distance to the ground.

The windows stretching along the third story were a tempting invitation. One he was determined to take.

Winter waited until the guards all congregated at the front of the warehouse, giving him a clear path to the rear. He lifted himself up and propelled across the short grass, forty yards to the facility. He kept his SIG-Sauer pointed ahead, just in case of trouble.

It never came.

Winter closed on the wall and lunged for it, pressing his back against the cool metal cladding. He darted his eyes in opposing directions to ensure he made it without setting off any alarms. Silence. No shouts for help or the pounding of boots on the ground in search of a disturbance.

He turned his attention to the downpipe. It was sturdy, reinforced with braces spaced every two feet to the ceiling. Perfect footholds. He tightened the strap of his rifle to his shoulder so that it would not make a sound against the cladding and gripped the first brace.

Step by step, he pulled himself up the side of the warehouse. The ground floor passed by, then the second. Near the third story, the rhythmic humming of machinery seeped through the outer walls. The vibrations were steady and hypnotic. If there had been any doubt before, there was none now. He had come to the right place.

He pushed onward until he reached the window, his fingers

brushing the narrow sill. The glass was clouded, a sticky layer of dust coating it from the outside, obscuring his view of the interior. He leaned across and pulled the latch, sliding it open in a single motion. Winter moved quickly, throwing one leg over the other and entering in silence.

He found himself at the top of the warehouse on a catwalk that wrapped around the perimeter of the third floor, with a series of railings for safety. He closed the window, careful to stay out of sight should anyone have noticed the faint disturbance, and crouched at one of the metal supports to get a glimpse of the lower levels.

The operation was as immense as he had imagined. What initially struck him was the stench, a harsh odor of ammonia wafting through the building along with a pale haze of vapors simmering from the machinery on the lowest level.

Two main areas seemed to make up the production floor. The first was the laboratory where technicians clad in blue protective suits and black gas masks roamed between benches and equipment, including large vats which bubbled with their wares.

The second section was dedicated to storage, not just of the finished product, but the ingredients. They were stored in crates and barrels. Winter mentally calculated how much could be cooked with the displayed supplies. He was no expert in chemistry, but knew enough to realize hundreds of millions of dollars' worth was not out of the question.

He wiped his brow, the thick humidity pressing his clothes to his skin. Along with the noxious fumes swirling in the air, the conditions were not inviting. He could not stay there for long. To commence his plan, however, he would need to get closer. Much closer.

He glanced to his right, where a row of hooks lined the wall. Tucked over some of the empty ones hung a spare blue protective suit and a gas mask. Perfect. He stripped off the green fatigues and donned his new disguise. With the mask snugly affixed to his face, he completed the masquerade.

What to do with the camo backpack?

He could forgo the rifle, but he could not leave behind his explosives. He set his gaze upon a table to his left at the plastic container on it filled with paperwork. Winter upended it, scattering the documents in a tornado of white and yellow. He unzipped his backpack and transferred the explosives inside. With everything secured, he snapped the lid shut and proceeded to the steps to the bottom floor.

The noise further down was much louder, the whine and moan of the machinery as constant as the lab technicians working together in sync to produce their next batch. Winter stayed as far away from them as possible, not wanting to draw attention. Even with the disguise, the techs had likely worked long enough with each other to know when something did not smell right.

He ambled by a weighing station and slipped behind a bench stacked with vacuum-sealed bags. He surveyed the area as best he could, figuring out the ideal spots to place his explosives. With the collection of dangerous equipment, he was sure to create one hell of a bang, making the attack on Gilberto Sanchez's house look like child's play.

Winter stepped into the shadows behind the largest of the vats and placed the container on the polished concrete floor. He unclipped each side and removed the first of the plastic explosive pouches, adhering a liberal amount of it to the shiny metal surface of the vat. Next came the RF detonator, which he planted inside it.

His second target was the barrel of methylamine sitting on a pallet in the storage area. He squeezed out more of the pliable compound and smeared it over the face. Another RF detonator came out of the container and Winter stood back to admire his handiwork.

Footsteps sounded from behind and he froze at the dark shadow falling across him. A hand grasped his back and spun him around.

"Hey, what are you doing!"

46

Alvarez spun around from the window and rushed over to Maria, a deep-seated urgency sharpening on his older features.

"Is there anywhere we can hide?" he asked. "One's heading for the front door, the other for the back."

Maria sprang from her chair, grabbing her brother by the arm in the process. She looked at him for a moment, a flood of childhood memories replaying in her thoughts. The summers spent with her cousins. The laughter. The joy. The fun. Nostalgia gave way to her quickened pulse, and she pointed up the stairs through the dusty interior of the beach house.

"The attic." The words left Maria's and Ruben's lips in perfect unison.

Ruben guided everyone to the steps, while Maria's mind continued to swirl with the childhood rounds of hide-and-seek played in the house. The attic had been her favorite place to disappear.

Unfortunately, she was not playing a game anymore.

Ruben stopped in the hallway on the second floor, his hand reaching for the string dangling from the ceiling. He tugged at it and the hidden staircase unfolded, offering them their sanctuary against the brutes about to enter the home. Maria went first, followed by the inspector. Ruben rounded out the trio and heaved up the steps to seal the hatch with a quiet thud.

It was dark, the dim light from the stained window on the roadside wall of the attic casting faint beams throughout. It was just as dust riddled as the rest of the house, if not more so. Forgotten furniture cluttered the small room, draped in faded sheets, while banged-up old cupboards and timeworn storage units overflowed with books half eaten by silverfish.

Two loud cracks thundered from downstairs, the front and back doors breaking under forced entry, their uninvited quests announcing themselves inside the beach house.

Maria brushed a hand through her disheveled hair. "You weren't kidding when you said they might come looking for us, were you?"

Alvarez frowned. "I had my suspicions."

"Unless you led them here."

Maria and Alvarez turned to Ruben, who had found a wooden chair to sit on. He raised an eyebrow, appearing ready to double-down on his accusation.

"You claimed you were one of the good guys, but minutes after you arrive, here they are, coming for us," he said. "A bit of a coincidence, isn't it?"

Maria considered her brother's words, allowing them to sink in. He was not wrong. Ruben was amongst the most trusting people she'd ever known. He would not make the allegation lightly.

"And that's just what it is. A coincidence," Alvarez shot back. "I never told anyone I was coming to this house. Not even my partner. And no one tailed me. Believe me, it took long enough to get here."

"Then how do you explain those two men?"

Alvarez appeared at a loss, his expression confirming confusion and frustration. Downstairs, more crashes and bangs sounded, the assassins turning the vacation getaway inside out. Maria thought about her own home, its remains now ashes. Would they ravage this house too, leaving another blaze in their wake? Another beautiful memory from her past reduced to nothing.

"We have to get out of here," she said.

Her brother stood and threw an accusatory finger at the inspector. "Not until I have answers from him."

Alvarez approached Ruben and grabbed him by the scruff of the neck. "Listen to me, and listen closely, Doctor. I don't have the answers to your questions, but what I can tell you is that those two cartel heavies are going to tear this place apart until they find us. And I promise when they do it won't be just the house that gets torn to pieces."

Ruben gulped.

Alvarez pointed to the window. "Where does that lead to?"

Maria stepped in and removed the inspector's hand from her brother's collar. "There's a small roof above the doorway. We should be able to use it to get down to the ground level."

"Only if we're quick enough. Please, open it, Doctor."

Ruben shook off the rough handling and went over to the window, unclipping the latch and swinging it ajar, allowing the hot afternoon air to rush in.

Footfalls sounded from below and Alvarez crouched down, the two assassins now on the second floor. Frustration laced their voices as they slammed their way through the hallway. Maria joined the inspector to better make out the conversation.

"Maybe they're not here," one said.

"They're here," the other replied. "I know it."

"If they aren't downstairs, or up here—"

"They are elusive prey. But we'll find them."

The inspector pressed a finger to his lips and gestured silently to the window. Maria made the leap through first, landing on the roof above the door. Ruben came next. Then Alvarez. They shimmied down the support post to the ground and dashed up the avenue to the inspector's battered old car.

They hopped in and he started it up, the engine hesitating and the battery struggling. Finally, it turned over and Alvarez swung onto the street, pressing down on the gas and barreling them down the road.

Maria placed her phone on the dash, the new cell, much too big for her old pink case, bursting from the seams. It was only a matter of time until the rubber broke. "How do you think they found us?"

"Probably the same way I found you," Alvarez said. "Used their dirty contacts in the police department to trace your family and their addresses. I hope you can believe me, Doctor."

Ruben said nothing as Alvarez drove them to the edge of town, his gaze finding Maria's phone.

"What's with the cover?" he asked.

"Hmm? Oh." Maria clutched the cell in her grasp. "Before we left San Yetaxa, Dane told us to ditch our old phones. He figured that if the cartel wanted to come after us, now that they knew who we were, they could use our previous numbers to trace us."

"Burner phones. Smart."

"That's why this cover doesn't fit properly. I'll have to get a new one at some point."

Alvarez took the next corner and pulled them onto the main highway, providing their escape from Playa Azul. As he planted his foot on the gas, his gaze again fell on the phone, his eyebrows working overtime with thought.

"What is it?" Maria asked.

"I need to ask you another question, Ms. Pineda," he said. "And I want you to think really hard about it, okay?"

"Of course."

"When Dane Winter was at your house, did he make any calls?"

She replayed her time with him, the images of him in bed and at the dinner table vivid in her mind. "He did."

"With whose phone?"

"Mine. He lost his in the attack at Sanchez's estate."

Alvarez pushed down the gas pedal, the old car coughing its way to one hundred and twenty kilometers an hour. "How many calls?"

"Just the one."

"Do you know who he called?"

"I'm pretty sure it was his boss."

"At Redwind?"

"I think so. What's all this about, Inspector?"

Alvarez pondered for another moment before answering. "I've been trying to figure out how the cartel traced Winter to your house. I think the cartel somehow used your cell phone."

"But how would they know to track him with my cell? No one knew he was with me apart from Ruben."

"His phone call. That's what tipped them off."

Ruben poked his face between them from the rear again. "Are you telling me the cartel has got the Mexican cellular network bugged?"

"No." Alvarez shook his head. "Nothing that elaborate. It could be much simpler than that. If I'm right, it means Winter doesn't just have enemies in Mexico. They might also be closer to home."

47

Winter turned slowly, shielding the explosive he had planted on the barrel. Before him, a technician stood, decked head to toe in blue protective gear. The gas mask obscured his face, though Winter imagined the puzzled expression beneath. Had he recognized he was different from the others in some way? Had he done the math and was wondering why there was a seventh technician in the lab?

"You're not supposed to be in the storage section without a second person," he finally said to Winter.

Winter thanked his lucky stars his gas mask had concealed his surprise. He was in trouble, just not as much as he had feared.

"I'm sorry," he replied in Spanish through the mask, hoping the breathing apparatus adequately filtered his voice to avoid being recognized as an intruder. "I got caught up checking levels. Must be these fumes."

The tech stared at him. Had Winter's bluff worked? If it had not, he would have seconds before the other man ratted him out. One loud shout or a dash in the other direction meant Winter's mission was over. Along with his life.

He peered past the tech at the vat behind him, their position hidden by any prying eyes. "While you're here, could you help me with something?"

The man wavered as if sensing danger. But he complied regardless, stepping forward.

Winter sidestepped to reveal the explosives he had set. "I bet you're wishing you called in sick today."

Before the tech could speak or react, Winter grasped him by the neck and yanked him downward, slamming his skull into the top of the barrel. The impact, muffled by the hum of the surrounding machines, was forceful enough to send him sprawling onto his back and knocking him unconscious.

Winter scanned the immediate vicinity. No witnesses. He opened the lid of a nearby barrel and peered inside, discovering there was enough space to stash the body. Winter hoisted him up and tossed him in, sealing the lid shut.

He set the rest of the explosives—two more on the containers of hazardous chemicals, another on the second vat, and the last on the generator which was used to power the facility. Each was rigged with an RF detonator.

Winter inched into the shadows behind a work station and retrieved the final component from his container. A small hand-held control tablet. He linked the frequencies of all the detonators to one command. A single press of the button would be all that was needed to reduce the warehouse to rubble. He tucked the tablet into the back of his protective suit belt and prepared to return to the top floor and escape the way he had entered.

As he took the first step, the crackle of a radio echoed outside the door. Winter had no time to react. Two guards barged in to the center of the lab, their assault rifles raised.

"We're going into lockdown!" one of the men yelled. "Everybody by the bench over there!"

The techs abandoned their tasks and allowed themselves to be corralled to the corner of the lab, clipboards clattering on the tables and equipment clanking on the floor.

"What's happening?" the tallest of the group asked.

The cartel thugs offered no response, instead darting their eyes around the inside of the warehouse. It was obvious they thought of the cooks as nobodies who deserved no answers, despite their skills. Winter understood what was going on, however. They had found the result of his handiwork in the forest.

He had hoped to have more time.

He joined the others at the work bench, and they exchanged wary glances with each other through their gas masks.

The sizzle of more walkie-talkie traffic filtered over the radios between the men inside the warehouse and those scattered around the perimeter of the facility. Winter deduced the others were preparing to do a wider search of the area. One of the guards in front of them acknowledged a call and disappeared out the door to help, leaving them with only a single lowly goon.

Strategy cranked in Winter's mind. Plan A had been blown. There was no escaping the way he had come. Detonating the explosives while he stood within the warehouse was an option as Plan B, but not an appetizing one should he want to live. The reason he was doing this was not just to destroy the cartel's means of production, but to discover why they wanted him dead.

He needed a Plan C. And fast.

Winter shuffled closer to the bench next to the other techs and glanced over his shoulder at a box cutter sitting within reach. He crept his fingers toward it and hid it in the palm of his hand, taking a step forward and presenting as the leader of the team.

"We need to know what's going on here." He gestured around the lab. "If we wait too long, the batch will spoil."

Winter's temporary colleagues looked at one another. Was it that they did not recognize his voice, or because he had the audacity to speak up against someone with a gun pointed at them?

"Hey, I'm speaking to you!" Winter said. "You better believe that if we have to toss all this out and start the process again, it'll be on you!"

The guard gritted his teeth but restrained himself.

"Just because you hold a gun in your hands doesn't mean you're stupid, does it?"

The guard's temper frayed and he stepped toward Winter, a flare of anger flashing in his eyes. Winter seized his opportunity, locked the man's rifle against his body, pointing the muzzle away, and slashed the box cutter across his throat. It was not as sharp as his combat knife, but it did enough to maim and stun the man. Winter wrenched the gun from his grasp and drove his head into the side of the bench, kicking away the radio in a single motion.

"You can't do that!" one tech said.

"Who are you?" another asked, finally catching on.

Winter ignored them and tossed the bloody box cutter to the floor. He dashed to the door with a rifle in his hand and pulled off his gas mask, inhaling some much-welcomed fresh air. As expected, most of the guards had bolted into the forest to search for their fallen comrades.

Some, however, remained.

Winter locked his sights on the first, who appeared momentarily perplexed. He processed the situation and swung his gun in Winter's direction.

Winter was faster, unleashing a burst of fire at him and slashing his chest open, sending him to the ground in a gruesome heap.

A pair of others rushed from the side of the facility, their weapons raised to strike back. Winter edged toward the quadbike, which sat by the end of the track by the two stationary cars, firing a spray of bullets at them. One went down; the other returned serve with a shower of rounds. They struck the rear windshield of a vehicle, the blasts shattering the glass over the ground.

Winter took cover for a moment and waited for his opportunity, peeking from the obstacle and finding his mark, the second guard collapsing against the metal cladding of the meth facility.

The commotion had drawn the attention from those searching in the forest, a group of half a dozen rushing to the scene. Winter removed his sleeves from his protective suit, revealing the grenades he had affixed earlier. He unclipped them and pulled the pins, lobbing them softly through the windows of the cars.

Gunfire spat his way from his new pursuers and he sprinted for the quad bike. Then, just as they arrived near the vehicles to take another shot at him, the grenades exploded and the vehicles lurched upward, both engulfed by massive fireballs.

Winter glanced backward at the twin pillars of billowing smoke. The blasts had taken out all six of those on his tail. But more still flowed from the forest.

He hopped on the quad bike and kicked it into gear, roaring away down the dirt trail. He took the control tablet from his belt and did a quick computation at the distance between him and the facility. As bullets whipped by him and splintered the trees either side of his gauntlet of escape, he pressed the button.

Successive explosions milliseconds apart detonated in the warehouse. The roof lifted into the air and the outer cladding burst outward in a violent display of force. The blaze was the color of the sun, and the shockwave so fierce it rattled Winter's bones.

He skidded to a stop to take in the inferno.

The structure was gone, while those who were inside and around it were nothing more than ash dispersed in the rubble. With a smirk, he turned his back on the wreckage and left the destruction in his wake.

48

Alvarez roared past the sign, welcoming the trio back to San Yetaxa, the city unfurling before them under the inky nighttime canvas of stars. Headlights pierced the evening, the traffic flowing in both directions in and out of town.

The journey from Playa Azul had been quieter than expected. After the initial flurry of conversations replaying everything that had transpired, they settled into an uneasy silence. Alvarez had taken the long way home, avoiding the usual route of the Camino Sin Vuelta Astras, in case Cruz and his colleague might catch up to them. The last thing he wanted was to come up against them in his unreliable car.

He glanced into the back seat at Ruben Pineda, who was fast asleep, the man having succumbed to slumber well before sundown. Next to Alvarez, Maria sat with her eyes wide open. He could not help but think he was making a mistake. Returning them to San Yetaxa was a gamble. The smart thing to do would have been to drive them to Mexico City and get them quickly admitted into the Protected Witness Program. With the contacts he had cultivated over the years, they would have been at the front of the queue in no time.

But he had to take their wishes into account. Neither had any intention of running. While San Yetaxa had its flaws, it remained their home. Just as it was his.

Of the pair, Maria was especially stubborn. She refused to be scared, clinging to the hope that everything would be all right. Was it Dane Winter who had put that belief in her? Had she truly believed him when he told her he would take care of the cartel?

Alvarez held back a chuckle, recalling their many conversations on the subject. One man against an army. Good luck. He wondered how long it would take before he fished Winter's corpse out of the waterway. Then again, the cartel was not a sloppy operation. The most likely scenario was that the American would vanish once they got their hands on him.

"Where are you taking us?"

Maria's voice broke the silence, her first words for hours.

"Somewhere safe. At least for a little while." Alvarez continued down the main road of town until finally peeling off into the suburbs. The traffic thinned and the urban disorder gave way to quiet streets lined with homes. Some were decades old, their facades sun-bleached and cracked, while others were more recent constructions built with shoddy techniques and cheap materials. Though it was still San Yetaxa at heart, it felt a world away from the hellfire of the inner-west and the wealthy enclaves in the hills.

Alvarez steered his car down a familiar avenue and parked out the front of a house he was well acquainted with. Lights continued to shine through the curtains even at the late hour. A good sign. "Come on, let's go."

Maria woke up her brother and everyone stepped out of the crumbling sedan. Alvarez led them up the path to the door and rapped the fake gold knocker. A rumble of footsteps sounded inside the home, the person no doubt taking pause to check through the peephole at their visitors. The door swung open and revealed his friend and partner. The only man Alvarez could trust to keep them safe.

"Hello, Martinez."

"Alvarez! What happened? Where did you—"

Alvarez stood aside to reveal Maria and Ruben. "Can we come inside?"

Martinez hesitated for a moment, and quickly ushered them in. "Yeah, of course."

His wife ducked her head up from the sofa in the living area. She paused the program on the TV and locked eyes with Alvarez, her silent welcome anything but warm. Her gaze then fell upon her husband, who gave her an apologetic shrug. Without so much as a word, she walked from the room to the other end of the house, closing the bedroom door with a slam.

"I'm sorry to put you out like this, Martinez," Alvarez said. "I didn't know where to go."

"It's okay." Martinez gestured to the kitchen. "Does anyone want something to drink?"

Maria and Ruben nodded, and the group went to the dining table. Martinez prepared coffee and handed a mug to both of them. Alvarez gave a subtle gesture to his partner, requesting he join him in the hallway.

"Where did you find them?" Martinez whispered.

"Playa Azul. I tracked down their only living relatives. An aunt and two cousins. When I discovered they owned a beach house, it didn't take too long to figure out where they might be."

"They were lucky, then. If the cartel had come looking—"

"They did come looking."

Martinez raised his eyebrows.

"It was Roberto Cruz."

"They must be still searching for Winter."

Alvarez nodded. "Seems they wanted to use our friends in there to help lure him in."

"They should be grateful that they've got you on their side. You're nothing if not dedicated."

Alvarez grunted. "Did you happen to check the roster when you left work? Did you see if Bautista was on shift tonight?"

Martinez pondered. "I think so. Why?"

"Another hunch." Alvarez took out his phone and dialed the station house. "Yes, this is Inspector Alvarez. Can you patch me through to Inspector Bautista please."

"Connecting you through to him now."

"Thank you."

A click sounded over the line and a different voice materialized. "This is Bautista."

"Hi, Emilio. It's Alvarez."

"Alvarez? You feeling better? Heard you were under the weather today."

"I'm fine. I should be in tomorrow."

"Good to hear."

"I was wondering if you could do me a favor."

"Sure. Anything."

Alvarez leaned against the wall while Martinez eyed him with a curious stare. "I need you to look into some phone records for me. I'll text you the number."

"What kind of time range?"

"Let's go back four days."

"Okay. Is there anything specific I should be looking for?"

"I suspect an outside party has used the cell to ping its GPS."

"Oh... Sounds interesting."

"Yeah. Do a deep dive on everything. The text messages, the data, the audio, to see what you can track down."

"I'll get right onto it."

"I appreciate that, Emilio."

"I'll talk to you soon."

The call ended and Alvarez returned his phone to his pocket.

Martinez smiled. "What's your theory on the GPS?"

"I have a feeling the cartel used Maria Pineda's cell to track down Winter at her home before they shot the joint up and burned it to the ground."

"How do you know?"

"Just something in my bones. You'll get that feeling one day when you've been around as long as I have."

Martinez chuckled. "What, arthritis?"

Alvarez rolled his eyes and peered into the kitchen. "I know Angela will hate me, but do you think we can stay here the night? I don't want to risk going back to my place with Maria and Ruben just in case I was sighted with them at Playa Azul."

"Well—"

"We'll be out of your hair before sunrise. I promise."

Martinez nodded, reluctance lacing his youthful features. "Of course. What are partners for?"

49

The taxi rolled into the hospital drop-off zone, the tires barely scraping the curb before Winter had the door open. He jumped out and tossed a wad of cash into the passenger seat next to the driver, leaving a much larger fare than had been demanded. Winter was sure the cabbie did not mind.

"Keep the change," he said.

The driver, to his credit, noticed the need for urgency and popped the trunk release quickly, allowing Winter to remove his bags with ease. In the same motion, he broke into a stride across the road, in front of oncoming cars in both directions, avoiding them with just enough time to spare.

Beyond the entrance, the lobby, though quiet for the evening, was far from empty. While most of the visitors were gone, a steady stream of admitted patients roamed around in their pajamas or rolled themselves about in their wheelchairs. Nurses and orderlies moved between departments, stealing what little free time they had to converse with colleagues during a well-earned break.

Winter rushed to the reception area, the desk decked in faux holly bunting at its edges and wreaths hanging on each end. The receptionist, wearing a red and white Santa-themed shirt and reindeer antlers on her head, glanced up from her screen.

"Where can I find Sara King?" Winter asked before she could get a word out.

The polite smile she had put on for their interaction faded as she checked for Sara's location on the computer. "She's in surgery. Fourth floor."

Winter broke into a sprint, spotting the first available elevator and bounding inside. He pressed the button and the car surged upward. A choir-style version of "Silent Night" played over the speaker, the trip stretching into an eternity.

A faint ding finally signaled his arrival, and the doors opened, revealing one of the hospital's upper levels. He hurried out, accidentally barging past an unsuspecting man in his haste. Apologizing with a wave, he continued until he reached another reception desk and waiting area. There sitting among the handful of people was Jessica—Sara's best friend.

Her face was red, her eyes swollen from the endless tears she had already shed. Their gazes locked, a silent dread passing between them. She attempted to speak, her mouth quivering at its corners, but no words came out.

Winter pushed on past the desk into a corridor lined with surgical theatres. Most were empty, the equipment within them dormant. He stopped at those that were lit with fluorescent lights, dreading what he might find.

He did not recognize Sara in the first two rooms, breezing by them to continue his search. At the third, however, his boots skidded beneath him. He dropped his bags on the floor and inched toward the glass, pressing both his palms against the window.

Sara.

She laid motionless with a respirator covering her nose and mouth. Gashes marred one side of her pale face while the rest of her body was obscured by a group of six surgeons and nurses working in frantic yet precise movements to keep her alive.

The rhythmic beat of her cardiac monitor rang through the commotion. It was slow. Too slow.

Winter slumped to the floor, his legs giving out. He collapsed on the cold tiles, and the memories of every death he had ever witnessed flooded back to him. With an unsteady hand, he reached for the front compartment of his backpack, unzipping it and taking out the plastic pouch containing the engagement ring he had bought at Heathrow Airport.

The box slipped from his grasp, and the three-diamond white gold ring hit the floor with a metallic clink.

* * *

Winter eased his car to a halt at the verge of the desert road and turned off the engine. He flung the door open and stepped into the night, the cool evening enveloping around him. If there was one thing that he had got accustomed to during his days south of the border, it was the relentless cycle of climatic extremes in the near lawless corner of Mexico.

Then there was the beauty. To the left were the foothills to the San Yetaxa hills, where those with wealth, like Gilberto Sanchez, overlooked the city on one side and the desert on the other. To his right was the very wasteland that bled into the abyss beyond the lush hills. It was a mighty expanse, the unforgiving landscape a collection of sand, vegetation, and death.

Winter proceeded to the trunk and retrieved a pair of night-vision goggles. The arms dealer who had supplied him with his goods had not disappointed. The quality of the goggles was no exception. He closed the rear and secured them over his head, the view around him transforming into a world of green clarity. He homed in on the cliff sitting on the desert side of the road.

Perched atop it was a sprawling mansion like those that dotted the hills opposite. Unlike the others, this one stood alone. The construction was nothing short of impressive, the techniques used shaping the rock to support the house instead of the other way around. The wealthy individual who called it home obviously enjoyed their privacy.

Of course they did. The residence belonged to Alfonso Berrera.

He scanned the considerable estate and zoomed in on the magnificent structure. The two-story home sat at its tallest point at the edge of the cliff, its massive glass windows offering views of its surroundings. On the bottom side were its well-kept gardens, and beyond, a wide driveway where guests could park.

Winter had been scoping out the property from various vantage points since he left the wreckage of the meth lab behind in the forest. Initially, there had been little activity at Berrera's home. But steadily as the afternoon stretched on, a slow procession of cars came and went. And though the faces were unrecognizable to him, they shared the same distinct expression.

Panic.

The cartel were rattled. With their prized possession out of commission, someone had to pay the consequences.

More vehicles had arrived since he had last viewed the mansion. No doubt meetings were proceeding inside the walls, where Berrera was not only admonishing those for what had happened to his operation but also asking for suggestions to recoup all the money they were about to lose.

Winter placed the night-vision goggles on his forehead, taking out a crumpled piece of paper. He fumbled with a small flashlight and ran the beam over the hand-drawn map he had sketched of

Alfonso Berrera's property. It was a fortress, with high metal fences surrounding it on all sides, apart from the rear, near the precipice. To get inside, he would have to enter through its weakest point, unsighted, unless he wanted to be shot before even reaching the perimeter.

He put the plans into his pocket and peered back out at the cliff, noticing a fresh pair of headlights cutting through the darkness. Winter re-affixed his night vision goggles and zeroed in on the vehicle, waiting for the headlights to point in the other direction so that he could get a good look at it. It was different from the others, which had been a mix of modern SUVs and older style sedans.

This was a limousine.

It approached Berrera's home, and the gates opened without the usual security precautions Winter had noted of everyone else who had arrived. Was this the moment he had been waiting for? Were the risks he had taken to destroy the meth facility about to pay off? Was he about to set his eyes upon the elusive El Maestro?

Was he the chief of police? A judge? A politician? Perhaps another enigmatic figure?

The limo stopped in the parking area amongst the other cars that had already arrived. The doors at the rear opened and Winter zoomed in as far as the headset would allow. The first person to step out appeared to be tall, with broad shoulders and formidable bulk. The second mirrored him, just as imposing.

A third figure then emerged. He was shorter than the others. Older, and wearing an impressive black suit. His hair was thinning on top. As he nudged the door behind him, Winter got a view of his face.

His jaw dropped at the revelation. The person he had smoked out of obscurity was no stranger.

El Maestro was none other than Gilberto Sanchez.

50

Maria stared at the glass of tequila resting on the dining table in front of her. Shortly after they finished their coffees, it was as if the bottle had appeared out of thin air. No one said no to the harder substance. She, along with Ruben and the inspectors, kicked back, allowing the moment of reprieve to act as a release.

It was not working.

Perhaps she needed to drink more.

Maria took another sip, giving it time to burn down her throat as Alvarez and Martinez's voices swirled into a haze of police jargon. It was not that she did not understand what they were saying. She did. She simply did not care anymore. All Maria wanted to do was to go home.

Home...

Where was home now?

Her thoughts drifted to the man at the heart of it all. The reason her life would never be the same. Where was he? Was he still alive? And if he was, could he keep his promise to her? Perhaps she was being foolish, believing that he might make a difference. Maybe it was the part of her that cared for him, more than she was willing to admit, that was twisting her perception of everything happening around her.

"Maria?"

Her name got lost in the chatter of the inspectors.

"Maria?" her brother repeated.

She slowly turned to him, his image blurring through her fatigued eyes. "Yes?"

"Are you okay?"

Maria gazed at Ruben, his sunken demeanor revealing a man who felt just as empty as she did. Someone who had seen his life flash before him, having no idea what the future held. "No. Not really."

He reached out, his hand oddly steady, and she grasped it, taking solace in the warmth of his palm. He was all she had left. Her father, who she saw as invincible, would never come to her rescue again. Never again would she feel the calming embrace of her mother. They were two souls on their own now.

"We'll get through this."

She wanted to believe his words. And though she loved Ruben, his promise felt hollow. Even the inspectors across the table, who had vowed to keep them safe, seemed distant. How could she trust either of them? Even if they were sincere, how far did their power truly go in San Yetaxa?

Maria finished the rest of the tequila and went for the bottle again, pouring more. Alvarez noticed and set his concerned gaze upon her. He exuded an unexpected softness in his harsh features. It reminded her of her father.

A ringtone blasted over the quiet ambiance of the kitchen, jolting her from her thoughts. Alvarez patted his pocket for his phone and slid it out. He rose and excused himself, heading to the hallway. Martinez accompanied him into the darkness and the two spoke with whoever was on the other end of the inspector's cell.

Ruben went to say something, but Maria silenced him with a shush. He buttoned his lips, and she did her best to eavesdrop on the conversation. Alvarez was canny. His voice was just low enough for neither her nor her brother to make out the full exchange. Some words did, however, slip through.

"Cell... GPS... Tracking... Ping... Winter... Cartel..."

Maria processed the fragments of the chat. Alvarez was talking with someone about how her phone could have been used to track Winter. Had the inspectors stumbled upon the answer to his question?

The conversation pressed on for several minutes until finally both men reappeared in the kitchen. They sat at the dining table, neither saying a word.

"Okay, let's hear it," Maria said.

Alvarez tilted his head. "I don't—"

"We're all adults here. I'm aware you've been investigating what happened to my phone. How did the cartel use it to find Dane?"

He conferred with Martinez for a moment with a simple look. "I suppose it's only fair that you get told."

"You're damn right."

Before Alvarez could speak, the knocker sounded at the front door. "You're not expecting any guests, are you?" he asked his partner.

Martinez appeared just as confused. He stood from the table and the pair went into the hallway. As they did, a crash echoed through the corridor. Ruben jumped from his seat, the chair clattering behind him. A rapid exchange of words shot back and forth through the air. Some were Alvarez's. Others were Martinez's. And then there were those of the unexpected guests.

A dark shadow fell over the kitchen door and Alvarez reentered, his hands raised with a gun pointed at his head. Two men followed him into the room. The one with the pistol was unremarkable. A stocky bald man with a harsh glower. The other, however, exuded a sinister aura. Tall, slender, a ponytail, and facial tattoos.

Martinez made his way into his kitchen behind them, the absence of weapons trained on him disconcerting. Alvarez locked onto him with a sharp stare.

"I never would've guessed you'd be on the cartel payroll," he spat at Martinez.

The younger cop sighed with genuine remorse. "You brought them to my house. What was I supposed to—"

"You're dead to me."

Martinez frowned at Alvarez's words and left the kitchen.

The tall tattooed man closed on Maria, and her heart thudded from his icy gaze. Nothing else needed to be said. All she could do was brace herself for what would come next.

51

Berrera stood at the end of the table, the long ornate mahogany piece the finest furniture in his house. Majestic knots twisted through the surface, resulting in a genuine work of art and craftmanship.

Thirty feet away at the other end sat El Maestro, his presence commanding. He drummed his fingers against the polished wood. Thumb first, followed by the index finger, then the rest. The rhythm was constant and unchanging, the sound creating an echo within the space which acted as a makeshift conference room.

Sanchez's eyes remained locked on his. He had stared at Berrera with the two enforcers behind him ever since his arrival. Berrera met his gaze and smiled awkwardly. Saying nothing, he shot up from his chair and walked to his bodyguard at the door.

"Where the hell's Angelo?" he whispered.

His man peered beyond the threshold. "On his way now, sir."

Berrera breathed a sigh of relief, even though he understood the feeling would be fleeting. The meeting that was about to take place would not be pleasant. The rage simmering within was enough to bear. He dreaded to think what Sanchez was feeling beneath the surface. As it was, he'd not shown a flicker of emotion. It was only a matter of time before that changed. While face-to-face encounters were few and far between the two men, Berrera knew Sanchez enough. He was a powder keg about to ignite when things went wrong.

Angelo appeared, offering Berrera an apologetic grin. He hurried to the projector system stationed in the middle of the table and flipped open the outer casing. He played with the inner workings. A press here, a flip there, and the machine whirred to life, a bright blue glow materializing on the adjacent wall for all to see. Angelo returned to Berrera with a small remote control. He handed it to him and made a swift exit.

"I apologize, El Maestro," Berrera said. "Technology and all... you know?"

Sanchez remained silent, instead continuing the incessant tap of his fingers.

Berrera cleared his throat and clicked the first slide in the presentation. "These were the initial photographs taken after word came through of the attack."

The image was a wide shot of the destruction in the hills. The facility had been obliterated. All that remained was rubble and the twisted metal of the support structures. The blast zone was immense, the devastation stretching for several dozen yards in all directions, the cladding of the building nothing more than silver confetti. More pictures flashed on the wall of the wreckage and the corpses caught in the chaos. At least what was left of them.

Sanchez stopped drumming his fingers and straightened in his chair. "It looks like a bomb was dropped."

"It was definitely explosives." Berrera paused on what

appeared to be remnants of the lab. "Plastic explosives, to be precise."

"And they were planted inside the warehouse?"

"That's our assumption."

"You're telling me that someone not only found our production facility but managed to destroy it? And they did this in broad daylight?"

Berrera went to speak, but the words became a tangle in his mouth. He glanced at his bodyguard, who caught his silent cue and re-opened the door, admitting a new member to the room. The young man hobbled in on crutches, his legs bandaged and his face disfigured with bloody scars. Every step was the personification of pain as he came to a halt next to Berrera.

"This is Iglesias, El Maestro. He was the only survivor of the attack," he said. "He'll be able to better describe the event."

Sanchez rose and ambled toward Iglesias. His eyes were a sea of calm, the fire within momentarily extinguished. "How are you feeling, Iglesias?"

The man's stiff posture softened, likely surprised at the concern and the revelation of who his real boss was. "I'm okay, sir. I'll heal."

"Good man." Sanchez frowned. "What took place out there this afternoon?"

"I didn't see it all—"

"Just tell me whatever you can."

Iglesias shifted his weight on the crutches, no doubt uncomfortable due to the strain of standing. "Something happened out in the forest. A radio call was put out to one of the sentries. He didn't answer. A few more attempts were made until it was decided to go looking for him. When we got there, we found him dead."

"Dead?"

"A knife through the chest." Iglesias's eyes glazed over for a moment. "The lab was locked down and more radio calls were relayed to the other sentries. None responded up the east side of the hill. A search party was sent out."

"Were you on the search party?" Sanchez asked.

Iglesias nodded. "Not long later, we heard gunshots at the lab. We rushed back as quick as we could and found guards dead at the entrance."

"Who killed them? What did he look like?"

Iglesias narrowed his eyes, a crease forming in his forehead. "He had dark hair, wore green fatigues on top, and protective blue pants."

"Blue pants?" Sanchez turned to Berrera. "What the technicians wear?"

Berrera nodded. "If Iglesias is correct, it stands to reason our saboteur killed the sentries and snuck into the warehouse from the perimeter. He probably disguised himself as a lab technician and planted the explosives without suspicion."

Sanchez opened a button on his fine black suit and removed a small photograph from his breast pocket. "Is this him?"

Iglesias tilted his head, examining the image. "I think it was. Yes. Yeah, that's him."

"You did well to survive." Sanchez dropped the photo in front of Berrera and patted the young guard softly on his shoulder. He returned to his end of the table and sat. A subtle nod was all it took for one of his guards to draw his gun from his holster and fire.

The bark of the bullet echoed through the dining room, almost deafening Berrera in the process as he flinched from the shot, nearly falling from the chair. He regained his composure and peered downward at Iglesias twisted in his crutches with an entry wound through his skull.

Berrera exchanged a look with his own bodyguard, the command to clean up the mess clear. The bodyguard grabbed him by his legs and dragged him across the floor, leaving a bloody stain soaking into the freshly laid carpet. Berrera swiveled, noticing Sanchez had resumed his finger drumming. He considered if he should speak first. If he did, what would he say? How many times could he apologize for what had taken place?

Sanchez's eyes burned red hot once again. "Do you have an explanation for this?"

"I—"

"I instructed you to eliminate the American."

"Yes, well—"

"I gave you his GPS location."

"The thing about—"

"Why isn't Dane Winter dead?"

Berrera took a breath. "The man I dispatched on that assignment failed to—"

"Who does he answer to?" Sanchez interjected.

"Uh, ultimately to me. I—"

"I want to see him."

Berrera smiled weakly. "It just so happens he's heading here now."

"I'm not a patient person, Berrera."

That much was certain. Berrera stood and exited, following the crimson-stained path out the door to where his bodyguard had returned.

"Where the hell is Cruz?"

The bodyguard got onto his radio and chatted briefly with the security staff on the gate. "He's just arriving."

"I want him here now!"

His bodyguard rushed off, leaving Berrera alone, paralyzed in thought. As he stared at the blood, he wondered if he would leave the room in the same manner as Iglesias. He pushed the thought aside and nudged the door ajar.

The tap, tap, tap of Sanchez's fingers welcomed him. Berrera slid into his chair and waited. Just as he was about to get up and check to see why Cruz was dawdling, the door opened with an almighty heave. The lengthy shadow of his best assassin loomed over him for a moment before he confidently strode in, taking his station in the puddle of blood.

"El Maestro, may I present to you Roberto Cruz."

Sanchez studied the ramrod straight form of the enforcer. "This was who you sent to kill Winter?"

"Yes, sir."

Sanchez chuckled. "He resembles a sideshow from the carnival."

Cruz walked down the other end of the room toward Sanchez. As he did, one of Sanchez's bodyguards moved in sync toward him to intercept. The pair came together in a blur, but Cruz was so much quicker. He seized the bulk of the muscular man and planted his face clean into the edge of Berrera's prized table, a sizeable dent contouring the mahogany, and knocked out the goon cold at his feet.

Sanchez sat, stunned, as if he had seen nothing like it before. Suddenly, a grin spread across his thin lips. "Impressive. It doesn't, however, alter the fact that Winter's still alive or that our meth lab was destroyed by a man I'd marked for death."

"He is challenging prey," Berrera said. "Of that, I can only apologize."

"Apologize? Do you know how much money—"

Cruz held up a halting hand, the motionless palm an audacious gesture at El Maestro. "His end is temporarily on hold. Until I can take care of him, please take these gifts to use as you see fit."

Cruz gestured to the bodyguard at the door and he stepped

aside to reveal three individuals. Berrera recognized the older man at the center. Inspector Alvarez. He'd had many conversations at the station house with the grisly investigator over the years. Flanking him were two others, the faces matching those from photos Cruz had given him during his hunt for Winter.

The siblings—Maria and Ruben Pineda.

52

The climb was grueling. Each grip achieved and every foothold taken was a minor victory against gravity. Every one of them a triumph that he had chanced his luck and survived. In the dark, with no harness from the top of the cliff, he relied on anchor points created with pitons and leather gloves purchased from a climbing store on the outskirts of San Yetaxa.

His backpack, full of the essentials, made the ascent that much more perilous. Every spike he hammered into the rock held the burden of all his weight. He had no choice but to trust the elements, using the small LED light on his helmet to ensure he placed the pitons in the strongest of spots to allow the rope to hold him.

Though he was not afraid of heights, he was glad it was night. Anyone would have been fearful of pulling off what he had set out to achieve, and in a strange sort of way, the obscurity helped keep him moving at a steady pace.

He concentrated on the lip of the precipice, his barrier between the abyss and Berrera's home. Could he have figured out a way to breach his house through the front gate? Potentially.

Would he have still had the element of surprise if he did? Unlikely. Everything hinged on being able to work unseen. And now, with El Maestro in the open and exposed, it was his time to strike.

He could not afford to miss his chance. Keeping that in mind and that of his own safety, he hammered in the next anchor above his head, allowing it to bite into the rock. He threaded the rope through, securing it to his harness and detaching it from the lower piton.

Step by step, he approached the edge, the final artificial spike piercing the rock and drawing him closer. His breaths were ragged. He was not as fit as he used to be. If Colonel Dawson had been watching, he would have ordered him back to the bottom and made him go through the relentless climb again.

His thoughts drifted to the man he called mentor. The father-like figure had been in his life longer than his own dad had. What would he have thought of everything that had happened? He was grieving, no doubt. In his own way, of course. Watts. Middleton. Lynch. Sidhu. All slain. And for what?

For Sanchez?

Winter fumed at the image of the man forming in his mind. Since sighting him hopping out of his limo, he had tried to make sense of it all, the pieces finally falling into place. He had played everyone for fools. A con job of epic proportions. Winter anticipated their next meeting.

El Maestro was soon going to pay.

At the cliff's edge, he gripped the lip with his right hand, followed by the left. He peeked over the top at his target. Though the house was only two stories high, it appeared as a tower against the night sky. He scanned for any sign of security, which might end his mission before it had begun. Satisfied, he heaved the rest of his body up and collapsed onto his side, the stinging burn of the climb pulsing through every fiber of his being.

Realizing he could not linger, he sat upright and went to his backpack. He unhooked the rope from his clip and tossed the remaining climbing gear over the edge. Having made himself lighter, he crouched low and took in a view of the estate. With a final sweep of the rear, he crept across the fence line on the western side of the property, obscuring himself in the impressive garden.

He froze at the perimeter, spotting a guard ahead, his back turned to Winter, his assault rifle firmly in hand. The man surveyed the area and continued on, allowing Winter to press on to the front of the manor. En route, he came across more of Berrera's security personnel. Like him, they wore black. The difference was, they belonged there, and he didn't.

In the clear, once again, Winter slipped past the entrance of the house. The estate's brick façade yielded to a spacious parking area surrounded by well-maintained gardens. And beyond that, a closed gate.

Sanchez's limousine was where he had left it, flanked by a handful of other cars, including one that had not been there before Winter began his ascent. Guards roamed at the gate and the front door, their conversations low between the puffs of their cigarettes. Everything was quiet, just as Winter had hoped.

He retraced his steps the way he had come, collating all the intel he had gathered from a closer look at Berrera's house. Every detail mattered. The general layout, potential routes of escape, and the guards' movements within the fences. They patrolled with a standard pattern, but one tighter than the thugs who kept watch at the meth facility.

It had been Berrera's fatal mistake. He had assigned his best men to protect him, instead of the investment that made him millions. For Winter, it had worked in his favor. Now he had to be more careful with professionals to counter. Luckily for him, he enjoyed working in the darkness.

Winter crouched near the wall of the house at an exterior hatch to what appeared to be the basement. He removed his backpack and opened it, revealing his arsenal. More explosives, grenades, his assault rifle, two sidearms, a pair of combat knives and extra ammo, should he need it.

He knew he would.

The castle had been breached. Now it was time to smoke out those inside it.

53

Winter emerged from the basement into the night and closed the small door behind him, tossing his backpack aside. What he had left for the mission ahead, he carried.

He prowled back through the shadows, melding into the rustling bushes of the garden, noting the systemic pattern of the guards moving about the grounds. They were methodical, yet predictable. If his previous viewing of their patrol matched their current one, he would have a clear path to the rear door of the house, needing to only dispatch two guards to gain entry.

That was the easy part. What waited inside would be his most demanding challenge. He had scanned through the windows, his night vision goggles offering a glimpse of the movement beyond the walls. He was sure to encounter surprises.

Winter would need to be careful. Silent. Deadly.

He lowered his goggles from his forehead, clicking them into place over his eyes. The green highlighted perspective gave him the best view of the battlefield. One guard passed by, cigarette in mouth but alert. He made his way to the front of the property, vanishing beyond a nearby hedge.

Winter was clear.

He edged from behind a manicured shrub and gripped his rifle, hurrying to the exterior wall. He pressed against the brick façade and peeked around the corner, spotting his first target. The man stood with his back to Winter, scanning the far side of the estate.

Winter slinked out from his cover and flicked his eyes left and right. With quick yet silent strides, he closed the distance to the guard. He positioned himself at the optimal angle and struck at the skull with the stock of his rifle. The sound of bone, wood and metal collided, combined with a frightful crack. Winter fell to his knees by his victim's side and gripped the man's head, rapidly jolting it sideways with another snap that filled the silence.

He rose and proceeded to the next wall, concealing himself again. Around the corner stood a guard by the door, surveying the area, his casual stature confirming Winter had dispatched his first victim quietly.

Winter held his rifle in the left hand and unsheathed his combat knife with the right, judging his yardage to the target.

He needed to be closer.

Winter waited until the guard's sight shifted, figuring he would have three, maybe four seconds to reach a safe distance. He readied the blade with a relaxed grip and prepared to run.

The man turned in the other direction, opening Winter's window of opportunity.

He sprinted.

Four... Three... Two... One...

The guard's focus returned, his eyes widening at the force of nature that was Dane Winter powering toward him. The guard swung the barrel of his rifle at him, his finger poised on the trigger in a last-ditch effort to save himself.

Winter took one more massive stride, closing a few more yards, and flung the knife.

It fizzed with speed and accuracy, the blade embedding into the chest of the unsuspecting guard. His gun fell from his grip and he gasped, stumbling backward into the wall. Winter moved in, slicing across the guard's neck to finish the job, mashing his face into the soil of the nearby garden bed.

Winter wiped the knife clean with his pants and opened the door with a twist of the handle. More darkness greeted him, the lights off, but his night-vision goggles presented the scene as if it were day.

A blur of movement shimmered in the room to the left, and a figure emerged.

"Hey, what are you doing in here?" they said. "You should—"

Realization dawned on the guard and his posture shifted to defense, recognizing Winter was no friend. Winter struck, thrusting the knife into his jugular. Blood spurted from the laceration, the scarlet jetting out and showering the floor at their feet. Winter shoved him backward, holding on to the blade and kicking the door shut behind him.

He stepped down the long corridor tiled with chiseled stone. At the end, light spilled from the living space near the front of the house. It was vast, scattered with irregular furniture and a staircase that twisted to an upper level.

He shuffled toward it and removed his night-vision goggles with one hand, his rifle ready in the other. A flash of movement caught his attention ahead, a figure appearing adjacent to the front door. They stopped, peering down the corridor at the shadow that was Winter closing. The goon was smart. Instead of assuming it was a colleague approaching, he flipped on the lights to be sure, flooding illumination not just down the hall, but throughout the living area.

Winter cursed.

The guard's jaw tightened. He went for his sidearm, snapping it from his holster, and shouted for help beyond Winter's line of sight.

Winter had no choice but to transform from silent predator to brash killing machine. In a single action, he dropped his knife and brought his rifle to bear, spitting a series of rounds at his new targets.

The first fell before he could even lift his gun; the other faltered, caught unawares. Winter unloaded a second volley and the guard quickly crumbled onto his friend.

Bright lights flickered on from outside, the radiance beaming through the half-drawn curtains. A chorus of panicked voices sounded in the evening, his cover well and truly blown.

Winter sighed. He had hoped to be a little closer to Berrera and El Maestro before it had come to this. He always preferred stealth to a frontal assault. Regardless, he would play the hand he was dealt. If that meant wading through a bloody gauntlet to get there, so be it.

He pushed on to the end of the living area and stopped at the sound of a crash from the entrance. A stream of guards flooded over the threshold. Winter grabbed for the control tablet and pressed the first of the small red buttons on the touchscreen. He took cover behind the doorframe of the adjacent room and waited.

There was no lag in the transmission to the RF detonator.

A boom erupted from the parking area at the front of the estate, the plastic explosives Winter had planted under El Maestro's limousine exploding with a terrifying force. The windows shattered, showering glass over the ornate furniture, sending the cavalry of guards through the air in a hail of shrapnel.

Winter sprang from his position to survey the scene of debris and twisted bodies strewn before him. The explosion had been bigger than anticipated. A curtain rail fell from its braces and the door dislodged from the hinges with a slam only punctuating the devastation.

The silence lasted mere seconds.

More shouts rang out from upstairs and at the other end of the house, a collection of footfalls moved closer to him with each passing second.

Four guards appeared at the top of the stairs to investigate the disturbance. Their expressions were frozen in shock. Not on the carnage, but that Winter was waiting for them. He aimed and fired, sweeping the rifle from left to right. The first collapsed against the safety railing. The second crumpled awkwardly attempting to retreat. The next tumbled down the steps. And the last plummeted over the railing, the carved wooden frame giving way, his body landing with a thump at the bottom.

More footsteps approached from the left, echoing from a hallway, which appeared to lead to a kitchen. Winter unclipped a grenade dangling from his belt and tossed it. The three incoming guards slid across the floor, their boots crunching on broken glass as they came to a halt.

The metallic ting of the grenade striking the stone tiles was the only warning they got.

It detonated with a roar, their shrieks filling the space and the lights above their heads shattering in a cascade of sparks.

Winter stood, allowing the brief hush to settle over him. But only for a moment.

There was still much to do.

54

"Put them in the back!"

Berrera jabbed his finger at Alvarez and the Pineda duo, barking the order at his bodyguard. His enforcer took his gun from his shoulder holster and motioned them to the other end of the conference room. As he nudged them along, the foundations of the house rocked beneath them from another bone-quaking explosion.

What was happening to his beloved home? The paintings. The furniture. The expertly carved sculptures. His symbols of wealth and power. Everything he had saved for. In mere minutes it was turning to ruins.

The bodyguard shoved their three captors into the side room, which acted normally as a storage space. The windowless area, with only one way in or out, made for the perfect cell. With a final push of the inspector's back over the threshold, and a slam of the door, they were trapped.

Berrera smiled, remembering all the interrogations Alvarez had conducted in those grimy downtown interview rooms. Like Moby Dick hunting his white whale, the cop could never let him go. Berrera had always been smarter. He never left proof behind and was confident of that. Having the best legal team in San Yetaxa and half the justice system on his side helped too.

Another explosion jerked the house, forcing him to clutch the back of the chair to stay on his feet. Dust rained from the ceiling, his fleeting moment of victory vanishing in a flash. His empire was crumbling, and he needed someone to blame.

As if on cue, the door to the conference room opened with the help of the protection detail on the other side. Another of his bodyguards, Casas, stepped in, his face bloodied from a shrapnel wound and his hair matted with sweat. His rifle dangled from his fingertips, the weight of the battle evident in his stooped posture and heavy breaths.

"What the hell's going on out there!" Berrera barked.

"He's blown up the front of the house. All the cars have been destroyed. We've got at least fifteen men down." He took a moment to inhale some oxygen and gather himself. "It's like we're fighting a ghost out there."

Berrera slapped him across his face, bloodying him further. "Pull yourself together!"

The man straightened, wiping away the fresh cut on his lip. "Sorry, sir."

"Did you get a look at him?"

"Only for a second. We tried to ambush him near the solarium, but when we did, the floor exploded, taking out two of my men."

Berrera mourned, burying the anguish within. His home had become a warzone, the intruder leaving only carnage in his wake. He clenched the photograph of Dane Winter and shoved it in Casas's face. "Is this him?"

The guard stepped backward and studied the image. A shudder ran through him, and he nodded. Berrera scrunched it up and lobbed it into Cruz's chest, who remained standing nearby, the photo falling at his feet and sticking to the puddle of blood left from earlier.

He glowered at the assassin. "How did he get in here?"

Cruz furrowed his brow. "I don't know."

"Maybe he stowed away in your car."

"He did not."

Gunfire erupted, the cracks of the assault rifles moving ever closer to the conference room. Shouts followed, along with more bullets firing in a rapid clatter and a cascade of screams.

Berrera grabbed Cruz by his shirt, the immovable iron object not so much as flinching. "I want to know how Winter—"

"I told you he was no ordinary prey. He's resilient—"

"Oh, shut the hell up!" Berrera released him and his attention fell to Sanchez sitting at the head of the table. El Maestro, silent since the beginning of the attack, let out a low chuckle. The sound was sinister, laced with a dark irony as if he were the only one to understand the joke.

"He's smarter than you, Berrera," he said. "Your sideshow clown's right. Winter's intelligent. We're not dealing with some gangbanger here. He's a soldier. A machine built for death."

Berrera gritted his teeth. "One man..."

"You failed." Sanchez gestured to the assassin. "He failed. And now we all have to suffer the consequences."

Before Berrera could speak, Sanchez continued. "He watched his friends die in my house. He should've perished too. Against all odds, he survived. That's what this is all about, Berrera. Revenge. Cold-blooded revenge. Think about it. He destroyed our meth facility because he not only wanted to hit us where it hurt but he also wanted to draw me out. He knew I'd come here for answers. And now he's got both of us exactly where he wants us."

Berrera took a deep breath and turned to Casas. The man's

eyes remained wide, reflecting on the terror he had already witnessed. "You're to go back out there and stop him."

He nodded at the command as another explosion went off somewhere, no doubt destroying more of Berrera's prized possessions.

"And you." Sanchez pointed at Cruz. "You'll go too. These gifts of yours don't make up for your failure. Bring me Winter's head or don't return at all."

The assassin pivoted, grabbing Casas by the arm. He dragged him toward the door and they disappeared beyond.

55

Winter landed the grenade at the feet of the advancing guards. They attempted to disperse, but were much too slow. It detonated, ripping up the tiles from under them into jagged shards of death. Drywall disintegrated into blinding dust and the timber doorframes splintered into lethal projectiles.

Winter peered through the haze, waiting for it to subside. The estate fell quiet. Aside from the groan of the structure straining under the weight of his destruction, there were no more rushing footsteps. No more shouts. No more screams.

Had he wiped out Berrera's entire army?

Winter took mental stock of the explosives he had set under the house and around its exterior. What remained was still primed to go. His personal ordnance was lighter than when he began, having already swapped out his rifle for one of his fallen enemy's. But the ammo in the magazine was full, along with his sidearm, remaining holstered. Two grenades were accounted for as well. One standard, the other of the "stun" variety, which he would have preferred to save.

The dust settled over the wreckage in his way, and he inched through it, roaming the hallway of the upper part of the home. He had planned to make his approach on Berrera and Sanchez downstairs but had cut himself off with an explosive he had planted beneath the floor, collapsing the path to the cartel leaders.

Judging by the configuration of the house from his exterior viewing, he calculated the upstairs section would lead to another staircase to the back of the estate, hopefully taking him straight to his prize.

At the end of the corridor, a sound broke the eerie silence. It came from below. Winter tensed and took more steps to the opening of the hallway, the other set of stairs he had hoped for unfurling before him. It was narrower than the one at the entrance. The atrium, though smaller, was no less striking, defined by ceiling-high glass windows, which offered a view of the back garden and the cliff face he had climbed.

Winter halted at the top, the sound of thumping echoing around him.

Footsteps?

A hail of gunfire peppered the upper level. Winter threw himself backward from the ambush of those on the ground floor as bullets tattered the timber railings and minced a pair of marble sculptures flanking the steps.

From behind the cover of a nearby doorframe, he waited for another strike. A voice uttered a sound below, too faint to make out. Footfalls followed.

He glanced at the sculptures, both still very much intact despite their wounds. He pondered and smirked, shuffling to the nearest one. With a heavy shove, he toppled it and sent it careening down the staircase, marble meeting wood with a crash.

Automatic fire erupted at the new target. Winter hurried behind the sculpture still standing and watched the other one tear apart the timber steps and railings. Beyond were the glow of gun muzzles flashing in the darkness. As the poor stone lady reached the ground level, he pulled the pin on his last standard grenade and threw it onto his enemy's position.

It sailed, as if in slow motion, through the air.

A frantic scramble of feet followed by those at the bottom realizing their impending doom. Winter took the initiative and surged from the sculpture. The explosion rocked the ground floor of the house, giving him his signal to attack.

He moved to the top of the steps and ran down them, aiming his rifle and launching a wave of fire on the shooters' last sighted position. At the bottom, he found a dead body ripped apart by the shrapnel of his grenade.

There had to be at least one more.

Where were they?

Winter turned his gaze to the corridor to his left, a blur crossing the faint light emanating from the other end. His instincts screamed at him, and he took heed of them, ducking just in the nick of time for a storm of assault rifle fire to rain across him.

He crawled behind one of Berrera's odd sofas, waiting his opponent out. Winter listened and figured from the line of attack they were somewhere down the corridor, using an open door to conceal themself. The upholstery turned into an eruption of leather dancing in the air until finally the last shell was spent.

With the opening afforded to him, Winter bolted, unloading a haphazard spray of rounds to cover his move. He reached the side of the wall and hid again, the next salvo from his attacker bursting forth.

Winter kept his breathing steady and peered past the edge at the window about ten feet down. In the dim light, he spotted his opponent's reflection. As expected, he stood with his body protected by a doorframe. Even in the gloom, Winter could make out the shape of the gunman, along with the tasteless tattoos painted on his face.

Winter's mind flashed to their first tussle together at Ruben Pineda's house. Previously, he had managed to outwit his foe, but only because he had the element of surprise. The tables had turned. Winter would have to take him down for good this time around.

He fired at the window, shattering the glass, using it as a distraction. Confusing the assassin, he hustled to the other side of the corridor and launched a barrage his way. The young Mexican dove for cover into the nearby room, closing the door in on himself.

Winter dashed to it and fired, each round ripping hole after hole through the timber finish, turning the entryway into a Swiss cheese banquet. He emptied the magazine and tossed the rifle aside, reaching for his pistol.

As he did, a crash burst from the door, the lithe yet powerful killer bounding through the debris and diving for Winter. The force sent the gun flying and the duo lurching to the floor, tumbling end over end with each other. Fists flew, elbows swung, and knees jabbed, the moves a blur of raw muscle.

Winter slammed against the wall, collecting a barrage of punches to his face. He dodged a haymaker aimed at his jaw and flung himself sideways, wrenching from the assassin's grasp. But his opponent was relentless, his counterassault quick on the mark.

Winter stumbled to his feet and backed up, nearly tripping on the remnants of the door. The fighting pair moved into the bathroom beyond, an opulent space where no expense was spared, the gold fittings gleaming under what light filtered from the window.

The assassin pressed him to the wall, winding his fists for another round. Winter bounced further back and inadvertently brushed a switch, bathing the room and the lavish white Italian tiles in a warm yellow glow. The illumination gave him a clearer view of his rival, his eyes filled with rage and his cheeks marred from grenade shrapnel from the earlier attack.

Winter sidestepped the right hook, the fist instead making contact with the mirror and shattering it into a spiderweb of cracks. Winter spied a towel to his side on a hamper. He grabbed it and flung it into the other man's face. The unexpected move blinded him momentarily, and Winter pounced, getting a quick jab-hook combo in before he recovered.

The assassin pitched the towel away and countered, the two men entangling like wrestlers. They slammed into the walls, until finally crashing sideways into the shower, the bulk of their frames breaking the glass. The shards rained over them, and Winter employed the shock of the moment to reach for his knife.

His foe kicked Winter in the knee and swatted the blade away with the back of his hand, getting another kick in and slamming Winter against the mirror. He weaved under one more heavy hook and tackled him like a linebacker, using his momentum against him and knocking him off his feet into the bath.

A fancy automatic sensor kicked in, sealing the drain with a plug and filling the curved white tub with water from the high-pressure tap. Winter threw his weight on top of him and pinned him under the lake forming. His attacker thrashed his arms and legs out, his movements a plea for freedom. But Winter held firm at the rising torrent, submerging the other man inch by inch.

The water turned pink from their bloody wounds while the assassin continued struggling against Winter's grip. As the seconds passed, little by little, the tall man's resistance weakened. His legs stopped kicking and his arms slackened. His neck gave one feeble jerk before it slumped. A final desperate gurgle escaped his lips, signaling his end. Winter fell from the bathtub onto the tiles, gasping for air from the deadly confrontation.

He looked to the door, visualizing his other targets.

It was Berrera and El Maestro's turn next.

56

Winter tossed the stun grenade through the gap in the door. He slammed it shut and anticipated the inevitable.

The panicked shrieks hit like clockwork, the group within the room blinded by the weapon, leaving them disorientated, but more importantly, easy pickings for him. He barged the door open with his sidearm and leveled it at what awaited him.

Five men stood at the far end of a long table. One was Gilberto Sanchez. Instantly recognizable. Another was Alfonso Berrera, the image burned into Winter's mind from his research into the cartel boss. The other three appeared to be bodyguards, all trying to figure out what was more important—to fire their guns in a wayward spray in Winter's direction or cover their eyes from the lingering smoke of the grenade.

Winter gave them no time to decide, squeezing the trigger three times and downing the trio at the feet of the cartel heavies.

Winter frisked the two remaining gentlemen, removing their weapons and shoving them into some plush chairs, the functional business seats oddly out of place in the house cluttered with bizarre, mismatched furniture.

Winter leaned against the edge of the table and waited for the effects of the stun grenade to wear off his hosts. He kept his sidearm steady in his hands, his posture confident, though a little weary from the fight waged. Sanchez was the first to regain his senses, his eyes fluttering, no doubt the blur filling his vision gradually sharpening into the recognizable shape of Winter before him.

"Good evening, Mr. Sanchez, or should I call you El Maestro?"

The man frowned and brushed his unkempt, thinning hair. "Hello, Mr. Winter. It would seem you've done what no other person has. Do you know how many officers of San Yetaxa's finest have been trying to remove my mask over the years?"

"Sometimes it just takes a little outside help."

Berrera's sight returned next, and he flinched. Before he could make a rash move, Sanchez shot out a hand, stopping him from doing anything stupid.

"And you must be Alfonso Berrera. El Maestro's patsy. For a pawn, I must say you've got a very nice home. I hope you enjoyed my renovations." Before Berrera could counter, Winter returned his attention to Sanchez. "You obviously pay him well."

"I look after my employees."

"But for how much longer? Losing your warehouse in the hills. That's got to sting, doesn't it?"

Sanchez shrugged. "A minor inconvenience."

"Really? There's about to be quite the shortage in your territories over the border. Those who enjoy your product are going to be very upset when it becomes a scarce commodity. Where will they get their next hit from?"

"Business comes and goes, Mr. Winter. One takes opportunities when presented and fights for new ones on the horizon. I know what I'm doing. I've been at this a very long time."

Winter could tell he was hurt by what happened through the

forced show of confidence. His self-assurance, however, was disconcerting. "I admire your optimism, Sanchez. In fact, I admire almost everything about you. This whole scheme of yours was genius. When I was figuring out where the facility was located, I did a lot of reading. I remember our discussion about Ciro Lugo, your rival in the governorship race. You told me he was an empty suit. That isn't entirely accurate though, is it?"

He waited for an answer to the question. Sanchez did not play ball. Winter continued. "He's more than an empty suit. He's actually on the straight and narrow, unlike a lot of Tlapetla's former governors. They say he can't be bought out. That's what you were afraid of, wasn't it? Sure, the cartel could have had him assassinated, but in this day and age that kind of drama would draw too much attention. You needed another plan. You required someone to become governor, who would allow your cushy operation to run without interruption."

Winter pointed at Berrera. "You couldn't very well pick him, could you? While never convicted as the cartel front in San Yetaxa, everyone knows who he really is. But Gilberto Sanchez— you're a different story. A wealthy retail magnate. You have your face in magazines, newspapers and on TV commercials. You were the trusted man to take it to Lugo and win the people's vote. No one could possibly imagine you being El Maestro.

"So, you entered the race, putting aside your mask. But the polls were too close to call. You needed something big to sway the swing voters. How about an assassination attempt? Perhaps one at your very own home. A party no less. A battle royale.

"To keep the cartel in business, you sacrificed your house. You orchestrated it beautifully. Have a fundraiser, pack it with guests, and have your own goons attack. Naturally, you just get away by the skin of your teeth, but your house goes up in flames. You end up looking like a hero—a phoenix rising from the ashes—as you tell the people of Tlapetla that you won't be swayed by the ambush. The polls then flow in your favor. Lugo doesn't have a prayer. As for that delightful home of yours, well, you've got plenty more, don't you?"

Sanchez nodded. "When you spell it out, it really does sound like a virtuoso performance."

"Ah, but then there was Redwind. You needed a security force to act as cannon fodder to make it all look real. Naturally, you have your campaign manager killed in a cartel hit, giving you the excuse of requiring outside help. So, you call us. Why not? We're a well-regarded protection service. But even we didn't stand a chance. You gave your people the codes to the gates and provided them the intel to our positions in your home. We were overwhelmed." Winter held aloft a hand with outstretched fingers. "Poof. All gone. All except me, of course."

Winter leaned forward. "I have to ask why. After you found out I survived the attack, why did you send your people after me?"

The smarmy smile returned to his weathered features. "Not so smart now, are you? You've pieced everything together so eloquently but have failed to understand the loose thread that is Dane Winter. One might call that ironic."

Winter lunged, grabbing him by the collar and driving his pistol into the man's neck. "I'm not playing games here."

"Oh, of that I'm certain." Sanchez remained confident. Frustratingly so. "It seems the person who wanted you dead wasn't playing games either."

Winter narrowed his eyes and let him go, composing himself back on the table.

"Have you ever wondered how we tracked you that night at Ms. Pineda's house?"

It was indeed a question Winter had pondered but had been unable to answer.

"Do you remember making a phone call that day?" Sanchez asked.

Winter recalled his time recuperating with Maria at her home. "I made contact with Redwind. To Colonel Dawson."

"That's right, you did. That's how we found you, Mr. Winter. The GPS coordinates were relayed to us by Redwind because they were paying me to do a job."

"What?"

"You obviously have enemies back in the United States, Mr. Winter." The cartel boss shrugged. "When I contacted Redwind, before the party, to have them send a protection team down here, they were more than happy to provide. Not long after, I received another phone message from them. They wanted to do a trade of sorts. They would protect me at my fundraiser, but in exchange I would need to ensure that you and your four friends never left Mexico. It was a ballsy request from someone who didn't know my true identity. The way I saw it, it fit into my plans perfectly. Even before that call, you were going to perish as part of my orchestrated chaos anyway. So I informed your people at Redwind that I accepted their offer."

Winter shook his head. "You're lying."

"I'm not."

"Tell me the truth or I'll kill both of you."

"Who's lying now, Mr. Winter?" Sanchez's façade darkened. "You were never intending to spare us. You're here to avenge your friends' deaths. I admire that. But please don't pretend to barter for our lives."

He clapped his hands and the door near them creaked open. One by one, they were marched out. Maria, Ruben, and the police inspector who had got himself entangled in their affairs. A guard followed behind them with his assault rifle trained on their backs should anyone make even the slightest of moves.

57

Alvarez wrestled with the ropes cutting into his wrists, his muscles straining with all their might against the bindings. The knots at his ankles were just as unforgiving. His chances of freeing himself were slim, but that did not stop him from making the attempt.

On either side of him, Maria and Ruben Pineda struggled to escape as he did. Dane Winter, though, sat still, his face carved from stone. Alvarez could see through it. A storm was brewing behind the calm front. He was recalling the conversation with Sanchez before the cartel heavies blindsided him with their hostages.

The revelation that Colonel Dawson had contracted Sanchez to kill Winter and his friends was obviously a tough pill to swallow. But it was one Alvarez knew was true from his investigation with the phone records from Maria's phone.

Alvarez gazed at Berrera, Sanchez, and their lone bodyguard, conversing with one another at the other end of the conference room. He attempted to eavesdrop on their conversation. Though he could make out none of their words, it was obvious what they were discussing. The fate of their four captives.

Winter's death was a certainty, the contract still needing to be completed. Ruben and Maria were also too deeply involved to escape the consequences. Then there was Alvarez. An inspector of the San Yetaxa police department. His execution was much more delicate. Ultimately, it all came down to Sanchez. His true identity as El Maestro could never see the light of day. All four of them would soon be dead. The question was, how?

"How are you going there?" Alvarez asked Ruben.

The doctor shook his head. "All I'm doing is burning my wrists."

"What about you, Ms. Pineda?"

"Same," she said.

"Mr. Winter?"

The American did not respond straight away, still lost in thought. Maria gave him a nudge to get his attention.

He jolted, turning toward them. "Sorry, what?"

"Have you had any luck loosening the ropes?" Alvarez asked.

"Uh, no. Can't say that I have."

"Perhaps you could try rather than wallowing in self-pity."

"What's that supposed to mean?"

"I think that's pretty obvious. You were ambushed by the fact your own people back home betrayed you. And instead of trying to escape, you've decided to feel sorry for yourself."

"You don't know me at all, Inspector. And if those are the skills you've relied on during your career, I pity you. Besides, Colonel Dawson didn't sell me out."

He said the statement with such an unsettling calm that it threw Alvarez off. He wanted to light a fire under the American, to make him understand the situation for what it was. There had to be a way to break through. Their lives depended on it.

"You're wrong. We listened to the conversation you had with Sanchez through the door. I'm sorry to say, Mr. Winter, he's right. Those inspector skills I have. I put them to use. I looked into the phone call you made to Redwind, and discovered it was your Colonel Dawson who sent the GPS coordinates to the cartel."

"You don't know what you're talking about."

"Really? And you do?"

"Dawson would not have ordered a hit on me. There's more to it than this."

"Fine. Let's say that there is. How will we determine that when we're all about to be killed?"

"I'm prepared for death, Inspector."

Alvarez narrowed his eyes. He recognized bravado when he saw it. "Are Ruben and Maria?"

Winter glanced at the pair. Particularly at Maria. It was a look Alvarez knew all too well. The slight flush in the American's face, and the way his pupils dilated. It was a tale as old as time. If he did not care about himself, he would surely do his darndest to save her.

Winter refocused on Alvarez, his eyes showing some spark. Some anger. Exactly what Alvarez was hoping for. "When the moment comes, Inspector, you'll know what to do."

Before he could press Winter on his cryptic remark, approaching footsteps interrupted their discussion. Sanchez, Berrera and their bodyguard trudged toward them, stopping just short of where they sat near the door.

Berrera taunted Alvarez with a smug grin, the man no doubt savoring his moment in a position of power over him. Their relationship stretched over decades, the pair sparring over the battlefield that was San Yetaxa. Alvarez had desperately wanted to bring him to justice, chasing him only for the bastard to slip through his fingers time after time. Bribery and brutality had been the cartel boss's ally. The death toll he had accumulated, both directly and indirectly, was his biggest legacy. It seemed Alvarez was going to become another statistic.

Sanchez was a different story. There was no joy on his face. Not even the glimmer of satisfaction. No triumph. No gloating. Alvarez would have given anything to peel away at the layers of the man he now knew as El Maestro.

"Well, gentlemen. And lady." Sanchez nodded at Maria. "We've reached that moment where tough decisions must be made. You've all been quite the thorn in our side long enough."

"Come on, Sanchez, I was hoping we could spar a little more," Winter said. "I've been enjoying this."

Sanchez chuckled. "I have a contract to complete, Mr. Winter. Besides, you've given me and my reputation too much of a bloody nose for retaliation not to be served. A statement of my own has to be made. As we speak, I have people digging your graves in the desert."

"That would be a mistake."

"And why's that?"

"Because there's still information I have that you might find useful."

"I very much doubt that."

"I'm surprised you'd be so blasé about this, Sanchez. You've seen what I'm capable of. Don't you want to know about what other tricks I've got up my sleeve?"

A loud beep suddenly sounded from the cache of weapons on the table that Winter had been relieved of.

"Thirty seconds," Winter said.

Sanchez's serene and confident demeanor faltered, as did Berrera's arrogance. The duo hurried to the table, where the sound continued to originate.

"All those explosives that I planted around the house,

Sanchez. Did you not think that I might have some more?"
Winter smiled. "I'll let you in on a little secret. There's one left.
Twenty seconds."

The bodyguard aimed his rifle at Winter, while Berrera
fumbled for the control tablet, revealing the screen to Sanchez.
Their eyes widened.

"When you took that off me, I activated a kill switch setting,"
Winter informed them. "In ten minutes, if I didn't come back into
contact with it, a thirty-second countdown would be set."

Sanchez's facial features contorted, strong emotions playing
across his face for the first time. "You son of—"

"Ten seconds. Where do you think I put the last explosives?"
Winter's eyes shifted downward to Sanchez's feet, a broad grin
again curling at his lips. "Five seconds, El Maestro."

Sanchez grasped the hint and sprinted to the door, betraying
his usual composure. Berrera and the bodyguard followed, their
footsteps heavy as they galloped down the hallway.

"Two seconds, Inspector," Winter said.

Alvarez, too, understood the suggestion and covered Ruben as
best he could despite the restraints, Winter doing the same for
Maria.

A spine-jangling boom discharged from the other side of the
door, the shockwave from the detonation seeming to twist the
very air around them. Timber and steel buckled in the cacophony
of the destruction. For a split second, the voices of those caught
up in the blast pleaded for mercy before they were consumed.

The remnants of the explosion blew through the door,
sending fragments of decimated drywall bursting through it like
shrapnel. The walls of the conference room quaked, and the table
shuddered. The weapons stacked on top tilted over the edge and
clattered to the floor.

Then silence.

Alvarez peeled himself away from Ruben and tipped himself sideways to get a view of the hallway where the three corpses of their captors lay slumped in the debris, the explosion having gone off right under their feet.

He looked over to Winter, who remained as calm as he had earlier, his gambit working perfectly. The American reached awkwardly for the knife which had dropped from the table and sliced himself free from his ropes.

He shrugged at Alvarez. "I guess I forgot which floor I'd set the explosives under."

58

Maria enjoyed her scrambled eggs, the warmth of the breakfast comforting her after the night she'd had at the hands of Gilberto Sanchez and Alfonso Berrera. On either side of her, her brother slurped a large cola through a straw and Inspector Alvarez sipped at his black coffee. Winter sat opposite, motionless, his plate untouched.

She smiled. He had done it. He had kept his promise. And though he returned the smile, she could tell the pain he carried. His friends. The colonel. His journey was far from over. There were still unanswered questions.

A familiar commotion sounded in the kitchen. One Maria knew all too well. Hector had arrived at work, deciding to take his frustrations out on somebody out the back. The door opened, and he emerged on the restaurant floor. He dulled his fierce expression, hiding it from the customers, and zeroed in on Maria.

He stomped over to her and put his hands on his hips, leaning in, his words quiet but unforgiving, "I don't pay you to eat, Maria. I pay you to work. Where the hell have you been the past few days?"

"I was... busy."

"Busy? What's that supposed to mean?" He motioned to the door. "Get out there now and start your shift."

"No."

"No?"

"You heard me, Hector."

"If you don't want a job here, that's fine. I can fire you right here—"

"I doubt you'll be doing that, either."

Silence fell at her boldness, her boss no doubt attempting to decipher what she meant.

Inspector Alvarez picked up his phone from the table and dialed a number. "Yes," he said into the receiver. "He's here."

In an instant, the entrance to the diner smashed open, the abruptness of the police officers storming inside rippling shock through the other customers. The cops made a beeline for Hector, who barely had a moment to react, a set of shiny new cuffs clicking into place over his wrists.

"What's this all about!" he demanded.

"Hector Ramirez, you are under arrest on the charge of aiding and abetting the Tlapetla cartel," the senior officer began. He then read him his rights, his defiance crushed in seconds. The officers dragged the man from the diner while he whimpered and threw him into the back of a waiting police cruiser.

"Maybe working here won't be so bad after all." Maria finished her scrambled eggs and slid the plate to the middle of the table. "Thank you, Inspector."

"Just doing my job." Alvarez had more of his coffee and popped it down next to the remnants of his meal. "Now that El Maestro's been outed and killed alongside Alfonso Berrera, it'll be like rats fleeing a sinking ship. I'll be a very busy man in the coming months."

"Aren't you concerned it might create a power vacuum in San Yetaxa?" Ruben asked.

"I've got no doubt we'll see some kind of turf war. Many parties will want to take control. My job will be to ensure that it doesn't happen."

"What about your partner?"

Alvarez went quiet, momentarily lost in his thoughts. "I'll take care of Martinez in my own way."

A ringtone sounded and everyone's gaze shifted to Winter, who retrieved his cell from his pocket. He glanced at the screen.

"If you'll excuse me." He stood and walked through the exit, answering the call in the parking lot near Hector's police ride downtown.

Maria stared at him as he became absorbed in his conversation on the other end of the line. She could not read lips, but understood from his stiffened posture and furrowed brow line that it was a serious talk.

"Maria?"

The sound of a familiar female voice startled her, and she peered up at Juliana holding a pot of coffee in her hand.

"Would you like a top up?"

"Uh..." Maria looked at her empty mug. "Yeah, thanks."

As it filled, Maria redirected her gaze to Winter, still focused on his call. Shocking those at the table, she dashed from her chair, nearly toppling it over, and rushed out to him.

"If you could send the coordinates through, that'd be great. I appreciate it." He ended the discussion, turning, startled at Maria's arrival.

"Everything okay?" she asked.

He hesitated for a moment, as if deliberating his next words. He sighed and relented. "That was a friend back in the States at the Nevada State Police. I got him to have a look at that phone call I made to Colonel Dawson at your house a few days ago. They put their best experts on it."

"And?"

"They discovered that Dawson's voice had been cloned."

"As in, it was a fake?"

Winter nodded. "It wasn't him I spoke with that day at your house. It was someone pretending to be him."

"Why would they do that?"

"Because they wanted to gain my trust. They needed me to talk long enough for them to trace my position."

"Does that mean that Dawson wasn't the one behind the contract on your life?"

Winter nodded. "He never was."

"What are you going to do now?"

Winter's phone bleeped with a notification. He held it aloft. "The authorities haven't been able to find the colonel back at Camp Redwind, or his right-hand man, Eric Bridges. The last time both were together was in San Yetaxa when they were summoned by the police after the attack on Gilberto Sanchez's home."

Maria raised an eyebrow. "So, they never left Mexico."

"They never even left San Yetaxa." Winter checked the pinned GPS location. "These coordinates are on the outskirts of town."

She examined the map, recognizing the area on the southern side of the city. "You're going to go looking for him, aren't you?"

"I owe him my life a thousand times over." Winter gestured to the trunk of his car and they rested on the back of it. "Finishing up in the service was a hard time for me. I lost two soldiers under my command on my final mission. Sergeant Hicks and Corporal Collins. Both young men. Good Marines. They weren't the first deaths I'd had to come to terms with, but because they were the last, it hit harder. When I flew home, I took an engagement ring with me. I was going to propose to my girlfriend. Between tours, we'd built something worth holding on to. She'd waited for me. When I returned, I wanted her to know that I was done with that existence."

Silence lingered, and he gathered his words.

"Sara was in a high-speed car accident on the way to the airport. She didn't make it. From that moment on, nothing mattered anymore. I left the hospital and wandered. I must've traveled across half the country, just drifting. Then out of the blue one day, Colonel Dawson appeared. In an Arizona bar of all places. He saved me. If he's in danger, I owe it to him to return the favor."

A tear ran down Maria's cheek. "At least let me come with you."

"I have to do this alone."

She shook her head, the weight of what he had said settling in her chest. Before she could speak, he wrapped his arms around her and their lips met in a kiss. Like their previous passionate embrace, the world slowed, the moment stretching into infinity.

He eventually withdrew, his eyes filled with determination. Without another word, he opened the car door and slipped into the driver's seat. The engine roared and he passed the surrounding police cars, pulling away fast and disappearing into the distance.

She trudged into the diner, her steps heavy underfoot. She sat back at the table and stared beyond the other men who were finishing their breakfasts.

"Where did Winter go?" her brother asked.

She said nothing.

Alvarez must have spotted something in her silent expression and reached out with his hand, his callous riddled digits scratching against her soft palm. "Ms. Pineda? Where's Winter gone?"

59

Winter scanned the basement of the Rattlesnake Watering Hole, letting the noise and stink of the place wash over him. The crowd had swelled around the illegal poker game which he had found his way into. The air beneath the high ceiling was soured by the stench of stale beer, strong tobacco, and the ripe tang of body odor.

He grabbed his beer bottle and gulped what remained inside. A burp slipped out. He was unable to remember the last time he had not been drunk. Or at least hovering close to the line. He wondered how long it would be until he put himself in an early grave.

Shrugging off the dark reflection, he shifted his thoughts to the mountain of chips at the center of the table. Thousands of dollars sat in the heap, waiting to be won or lost.

"Hey, we haven't got all day here!"

Winter ignored the jibe from somewhere in the crowd of the packed basement and locked his attention on the man across the table from him. His opponent was older, with long, unwashed hair, his face carved by hard years. The kind of person who did not just frequent basements like this one, but belonged to them. Winter was merely a guest in his underworld.

Winter examined his hidden cards, sliding them up ever so slightly so that only he could eye them. He had a big decision to make, one that was going to score him good money or force him to leave with nothing but the clothes on his back.

He placed them down and checked the community cards laid out next to the pot, which were available to all the players. There was a potential flush and full house on the board. Winter had a strong hand. But he knew his opponent did, too. He stared across at the man who had put him all in and tried to assess his poker face. He gave Winter nothing, glaring at the pot before them, his breathing steady. Once upon a time Winter would have gleaned a tell. Of late, those skills had forsaken him. Now it was down to mathematics and luck.

His concentration broke at the sound of boots thudding down the rickety staircase from the bar above. The crowd remained absorbed in the game, but Winter looked up. The new arrival at the foot of the steps did not say a word. He did not need to. His imposing size was impossible to ignore.

Colonel Joseph Dawson.

Their gazes met inside the smoky room, and the two men shared a silent moment. How long had it been? Since the desert. Since the war. It might as well have been another life.

Winter focused back on the play, ignoring the ghost from his past. The chips piled up in front of him were substantial. But he would have to wager it all to match the man opposite him if he wanted to take it all.

Winter slid his hand under his shirt, finding the three-diamond engagement ring which hung from the chain around his neck. He brushed it lightly with his fingertips, the jewelry a tether to the past he could not forget. He took a breath and let it dangle, placing both hands firmly in front of him. With a push, he shoved his chips into the middle, the pot almost overflowing the edges of the table. His opponent rose and threw his cards down, revealing a full house, his smile smug and triumphant.

Winter edged his chair backward, the feet screeching along the timber floor. Everyone watched him in anticipation as he stood. He chucked the cards onto the top of the chips. But instead of showing a winning hand, he tossed them face down, mucking them into the pot.

He had lost.

A riotous roar burst from his opponent and his supporters around the table. Winter tossed his chair and reached for the large olive-green backpack behind him, slinging it over his shoulders, and shoved his way through the mob, who mocked him as he went. He brushed past Dawson as if he were not there and climbed the stairs, his steps echoing through the dank basement.

At the bar, he opened his threadbare wallet and scrounged a crinkled note for the bartender. A beer materialized on the counter with the top popped. Winter took it, walking by Dawson, who had appeared from behind. He walked by the colonel and moved into the men's bathroom. Dawson tailed him. Inside, Winter placed his bottle on the shelf above and pissed into the old trough-style urinal.

"What are you doing here, Colonel?" he asked.

Dawson crossed his arms and leaned against the back wall. "For a moment there, I thought you didn't recognize me. What'd you have? A flush? On a paired board?"

Winter did not answer.

"I assumed as much. That was a terrible call, Dane."

"What are you doing here?" he questioned Dawson again.

"I've come to see you."

"How'd you find me?"

"I have my ways. Been keeping my eye on you for a few weeks. In that time, you've traveled by bus from Louisiana to Arizona."

Winter finished and zipped up his pants, grabbing his beer and walking out of the bathroom. Dawson went with him, the pair ending up out the front of the Rattlesnake Watering Hole through its batwing doors. Winter pulled a pack of cigarettes from his pocket and lit one up.

"I tried to find you when I came back from the Middle East," Dawson said. "You were nowhere to be found. It was as if you'd just fallen off the map."

"Yes, well, with everything that happened..."

"I know. I'm sorry about Sara, Dane. It can't have been an easy time. I wish I'd been there for you." Dawson paced in front of him. "But I'm here now."

Winter exhaled a puff of smoke. "What do you want?"

"I want you."

"I'm not returning to the service."

Dawson let out a dry chuckle. "Neither am I."

Winter arched his brow.

Dawson leaned on the timber next to him. "I've retired."

"I would've never taken you for the retiring type."

"You're not wrong. I got bored. Started up a business about six months ago—Redwind Security."

Winter smirked. "What, for like shopping malls?"

"Not exactly. Redwind's a global firm. Our clients are more... important."

"And you'd like me to join you?"

Dawson spread out his arms. "This isn't the life for you. Drifting from town to town, getting yourself into trouble, gambling, drinking, and smoking what little you have away."

Winter took a swig of his beer. "If that's what you think of me, why would you want a drunk, chain-smoking gambler to work for you?"

"Because you were the best goddamn Marine I ever served with. And I know somewhere beneath it all that man still exists."

Winter twirled his cigarette between his fingers.

"With that said, I can't afford to take on a charity case. I've got too much invested in Redwind to do that." Dawson spoke in the same tone he used back in the service. "You'll have to shape up. The jobs we deal *with aren't a walk in the park. That's why I pay well. Is that something you'd be interested in?"*

Winter drew on his cigarette. "Honestly, Colonel, I don't know."

Dawson took out a card from his breast pocket with his phone number on it and handed it to him. "Think about it. I'm building a facility out in Nevada. Won't take too long to get to by bus."

Dawson grasped him firmly on the shoulder and left without saying another word. His car skidded on the dirt road by the tavern, kicking up dust before vanishing over the horizon.

Winter drained his beer and stared at the card in his hand, pondering the offer. He turned to the clink of glasses echoing inside the bar.

It was not a decision that could be made without having another drink.

* * *

Winter opened the trunk of his car and removed the assault rifle resting inside. He slung it over his shoulder and reached for a holstered pistol secured in its pouch. He extracted the gun and tucked it into his waistband at the small of his back.

With a clunk, he closed the trunk and peered out at his surroundings. It was desolate, the ground little more than grit stretching in every direction, broken only by tufts of brittle grass and the odd spindly cactus. The road which had carried him there had transformed from asphalt to dirt miles back, leaving only a hardened but broken trail leading to the property, enclosed by a shabby rabbit-proof fence.

He stepped from the car and made his way to the heart of the land another half-mile away where an old farmhouse had been built at least a hundred years earlier. It was a wreck, falling apart at the seams from the weight of time, the timber boards warped and fractured, while what remained was overgrown with the yellow shrubs.

About fifty yards east, a barn stood in a similar state of disrepair. The main door lay in a heap on the ground, long torn from its hinges, while above was another opening where hay would once have been hoisted inside the loft. All that thrived now were weeds, along with a collection of rusty farming implements scattered across the dirt.

Winter swept his rifle over the scene. The morning sun had arrived with a vengeance, its scorching heat forcing him to wipe away the perspiration gathering on his forehead. He brushed his skin with the back of his hand and dived into his pocket. He swiped his phone open to check the map application to ensure he was at the right coordinates. A brief examination confirmed the pinned area.

He narrowed his eyes over the deserted landscape. Long since abandoned and untouched. Not a soul in sight. The only movement, if any, came from the slither of an unseen snake.

He pressed on past the house, taking a glance through the windows, confirming the lack of human life. He then moved beyond the barn, which Winter imagined had once been a field where livestock grazed during wetter times. Now, it was a mess, more akin to the inhospitable plains of Mars.

"Colonel!"

His voice carried over the emptiness, echoing off the rock formations in the distance.

"Colonel Dawson!" he called out again.

No answer.

He went for his phone and dialed the man's number. While most numbers blurred as one with the convenience of contact lists, he never forgot Dawson's. He pressed the green button and lifted the device to his ear.

A dial tone sounded.

Winter waited.

Nothing.

He lowered the cell and pricked up his ears at another sound.
A ringtone...

He followed the melody across the expanse, the noise of the
other cell getting louder with each step. His pulse quickened with
the certainty that he was no longer alone.

Then he stopped.

The call rang out and went to Dawson's voicemail.

He redialed, and the ringtone blared again.

Winter spun around on the spot, then peered at the soil
beneath him. It was not hardened like the rest of the land.
Someone had recently disturbed it. He kicked at the loose dust
and dropped to his stomach, pressing his ear to the ground.

His heart sank.

"Oh, hell..."

Winter sprang to his feet and rushed off to the barn, skidding
to a stop inside. He picked up a rusty shovel and sprinted back to
the sound of the ringtone, tossing his rifle aside and driving the
shovel into the disturbed earth. Each scoop sent clods of dirt
flying behind him, a new heap piling up. The heat beat down on
him, suffocating him as he worked.

Winter dug furiously, his lower back and arms burning from
the speed of every movement. The world around him lowered as
he started to make progress.

One foot down... Two feet... Three feet.

He kept going, refusing to stop, even redialing the number
repeatedly to confirm he was on the right track. The sound only
got louder, the ringtone matching the beat of his heart pounding.

Four feet... Five feet... Six feet...

A hollow clunk reverberated inside the crypt he had dug out.

He struck it again, the same ominous noise echoing. Throwing the shovel next to him, he got onto his hands and knees and brushed away a thin layer of soil. He uncovered something.

Wood.

The timber was fresh. He excavated around it and revealed a box. It was rectangular and in such a size there could be no illusions about what it was.

He hammered the blade of the shovel at the corners until the lid loosened and cracked open, creating a space for his fingers. He drove his hands inside, wrenching it apart with all his might, the nails popping free one by one and revealing what lay within.

Winter collapsed to his knees at the sight.

There, lying before him, was Colonel Dawson, his once sharp eyes now closed, and a bullet wound marring the center of his forehead. His arms were crossed one over the other in rest, his grayed features in stark contrast to what would have been a brutal end.

Winter dialed the number again, and the ringtone emanated from the colonel's pants pocket. He reached inside for it and took out the cell, the screen showing his own number on it, along with a list of missed calls. Winter pressed the two buttons on the side of the handset and switched off the phone for the final time.

He sighed and rested a hand on Dawson's arm. In a dark way, part of him had wished Inspector Alvarez had been right. He would have preferred the colonel had ordered a hit on him and his friends. At least then Dawson would still be alive. Winter had always seen the man as a giant. Indestructible. Staring at his lifeless form, he could not shirk the questions that had arisen. Who was behind all of this? Who wanted them all dead, and why?

A lump formed in his throat, his grief twisting into vengeance. He let go of Dawson's arm. As it shifted, he spotted something shiny beneath the sleeve. He picked up the elbow and took a better look.

A medal.

A Bronze Star.

Winter unfastened it from the shirt and turned it over to read the engraved words on the other side.

"Corporal Jeremy Collins..."

The name was like a punch in the gut. He instantly recognized it as one of the two Marines who had died on his last mission in the Taktur Mountains before leaving the service. He furrowed his brow and took the medal in his hand, climbing to the precipice of the hole he had excavated.

At the top, he dropped the Bronze Star over the lip and used the strength of his arms to push himself to freedom. He stood and froze at a figure standing twenty feet away from him, an aberration in the silence surrounding him. An assault rifle sat nestled in his hands, the same one Winter had discarded on the ground before beginning the dig.

In the quiet of the Mexican desert, with the bare whispers of a breeze kicking up the dirt, stood Dawson's right-hand man. Redwind's chief financial officer—Mr. Bean—the bean counter himself.

"Eric Bridges..."

He gave Winter a slight nod, his face stern and his eyes cold. He appeared more like a commando than the bumbling accountant he remembered. "Remove the weapon in your waistband, Captain."

Bridges had never addressed him by his former Marine rank before. He did it in a way that was so natural. Winter did as he was instructed and reached back for his sidearm and dropped it to the ground.

"Kick it away, please."

Winter gave it a swift punt with the side of his boot, sending it spiraling next to a spiky cactus. "What's this all about, Bridges?"

"I'd be surprised if you haven't begun to piece it together yourself."

Winter glanced at the Bronze Star in the dirt. "Corporal Jeremy Collins. He was awarded this posthumously after his final mission. This was the medal sitting on your wall in your office..."

Bridges nodded. "Jeremy was my son."

"Your son...?" Winter stood straighter. "Then you're not—"

"No, my name's not really Bridges. It's Collins."

Winter's mind raced as he tried to decipher it all, mouthing silent words. As he did, his gaze remained fixed on Bridges—Collins—whatever his name was.

The man's expression faltered, his eyes wandering. "He never deserved to die in those mountains."

It all began to make sense to Winter. "How long have you been planning your revenge?"

"Ever since you sent me that letter telling me that he'd died in the service of his country." Collins refocused. "When Colonel Dawson returned to the United States and started up Redwind, I saw my chance."

"That's when you changed your name?"

Collins nodded. "It took a while, but eventually I gained employment with Redwind. It was the best way to get close to him. I was never sure how I was planning to do it, to be honest. Then Gilberto Sanchez came along."

Winter stood silent, allowing him to connect the final pieces.

"When he requested Redwind's services for his fundraiser, I knew Dawson would send his best. You. Lynch. Middleton. Watts. Sidhu. Those he holds so dear." Collins took a step forward, the barrel of his gun never wavering. "Afterward, I contacted Sanchez and made him a deal."

"Let me guess. You offered him more money if he guaranteed we'd all be killed in his little piece of theatre."

"It didn't take much convincing."

"And the cash came out of Redwind's coffers, no doubt?"

"Right."

"How did you know Gilberto Sanchez was El Maestro and that he was planning to attack his own party?"

"You fight your wars with weapons, Captain. My battlefield's finance. How it flows. Whose hands it ultimately ends up in." Collins shrugged. "After some digging, I had a fair idea what was happening in San Yetaxa with Sanchez and the cartel. That's when I decided that this would be my play. I was going to make Colonel Dawson pay for his part in my son's death. He might not have had his own children to grieve over, but I knew that losing you and the other four would be payback enough."

Winter glanced over his shoulder at the grave. "And then you killed him?"

"A small mercy he never afforded me."

"Goddammit, Dawson wasn't there, though. He wasn't the ISIS fighter who shot Jeremy. If you want to blame anyone, at the very least, blame me. I led the mission. Why didn't you just come for me?"

"Dawson may not have squeezed the trigger, Captain. He did, however, push the paper that put my son in the line of fire."

"Is this really what Jeremy would have wanted?"

Collins's demeanor darkened further, his eyes staring off at a distant point. "Dawson saw the burned bodies of your friends at Sanchez's home. I was hoping you were there too before I put a bullet in his head. I should've known you'd figure out a way to survive."

"Sorry to disappoint."

"No matter." Collins confirmed his aim at Winter's chest.

"Wait just a minute—"

"That letter you wrote to me after Jeremy's death—it contained all the usual buzz words one would expect." A tear streaked down the older man's cheeks. "Heroism. Courageousness. Honor."

Winter's mind flashed to the moment he'd returned to find the bodies of Collins and Sergeant Hicks killed by ISIS machinegun fire. "You have no idea how sorry I am—"

"Shut up!" Collins took another step closer. "It's time for this to end. Time for his memory to be cleansed."

Winter raised his hands. "This won't make you feel any better."

Collins hesitated.

"It won't. You could kill everyone in the world, but it'll never bring back those you love. Believe me, I know." Winter recalled the past days in San Yetaxa, the ghosts of Lynch, Middleton, Watts, and Sidhu at his side as he tore the cartel to pieces, drenching Tlapetla in blood. "Sometimes we hurt. And we have to live with that. It's the hardest thing we have to do. If we don't face that reality, we'll be just as dead inside as those we lost."

More tears burbled at the corners of Collins's eyes. "I've gotten this far, Captain. Like you, there's no turning back."

His hands steadied, his aim firm. Winter prepared himself, the images of his past cascading into a slideshow. The good and bad. The faces of those who had come and gone. His childhood. His time as a Marine with his brotherhood. The moments with his friends at Redwind.

And Sara...

Then there was a crack.

The shot echoed across the barren plains.

Winter looked down at his chest.

He expected to see a pool of blood gushing from it.

There was no pain. No wound.

He turned his attention to Collins. The man's eyes, once full of suffering and rage, were now empty. A single round had found its mark in the side of his head. His rifle dropped first, hitting the dirt before the rest of his body crumpled in a staggered heap on top of it.

Winter's heart heaved as he searched his surroundings for the shooter until finally spotting a familiar figure perched in the loft of the old barn.

Inspector Alvarez.

He tipped his hat at Winter in acknowledgment.

Winter picked up the Bronze Star and dusted it off, stepping toward Collins and placing it on top of his dead body. The finality of everything left Winter cold in the brutal heat. Another meaningless death in a long line of senseless deaths.

Another bloody chapter closed.

60

The memorial went exactly as Winter had expected. Hundreds of mourners had traveled from all over the country. There were current and ex-military personnel who had served with the colonel, Redwind employees not currently deployed on assignment, and a range of dignitaries from different branches of the government.

Dawson's coffin was draped with red, white, and blue. A quiet acceptance filled Winter. Though his mentor was gone, at least now he lay in peace. He was at home on the grounds of Camp Redwind, away from the sun of the Mexican desert.

A hand brushed against his, pulling him back into the pomp of the memorial and the familiar rituals of the military service. He glanced at Maria beside him and smiled weakly, attempting to put a mask on his grieving face. She had traveled with him from Mexico, the gesture one he could not thank her enough for.

Many people spoke, recalling stories from the decades Dawson had served. Though Winter listened to the eulogies, he took in none of the words. Before he knew it, the rifles of a twenty-one-gun salute cracked over the Redwind grounds, followed by the flag-folding ceremony. Dawson's ninety-six-year-old mother, clearly an invalid bound to her wheelchair, but with a fire in her eyes matching her son's, received the stars and stripes.

At the memorial's conclusion, the crowd dispersed and mingled with each other in small groups, the servicemen reconnecting with one another after having been apart for several years.

He led Maria through the grounds, where Dawson could forever look down from atop the hill at what he had built from the ground up. He showed her every corner of the property, pointing out the buildings, the training fields, and barracks. It was an achievement he hoped Dawson had been proud of.

"So, what are you going to do now?"

Winter was lost in thought, unable to register her words.

"Dane?"

He shook off the haze, attempting to push the heaviness of the morning aside. "Oh, uh... Travel for a bit. This won't be the first memorial I'll be attending. I plan to pay my respects to the families of Watts, Middleton, and Lynch. I even intend to go to India to visit Sidhu's parents."

"I think they'd like that."

"It's the least I can do."

"What about Dane Winter?" she asked.

"Hmm?"

"You plan on easing everyone else's pain. What about your own?"

"I don't know." Winter chuckled. "Put it in a box and push it deep inside."

Maria frowned. "That's not what I meant. Where will you go from here? What do you think will happen to Redwind?"

He considered her words. "From what the lawyers are saying,

there's little money left after Collins paid off the cartel. Not that there was a lot to begin with."

"Why's that?"

"Dawson was a fine leader, but he wasn't great with his finances. No one wants to admit it, but he gave too much to his employees. I imagine we'll all get a decent payout and with any luck, Camp Redwind will stay under Dawson's name. Apart from that—"

"You'll be out of a job?"

"It wouldn't be the first time."

"Will you miss it here?"

He let the question hang in the air for a moment. "If there's anything that I've learned, it's that sometimes it's best not to linger on the past. My time in the Marines was what was needed at that point in my life. When Dawson rescued me from the roads of America, Redwind was exactly what I needed then. Perhaps something awaits me on the other side of the horizon."

Winter changed the subject. "What about you? What does the future look like for Maria Pineda?"

She stopped, taking some shade under a tree, the locale giving them a good view of the grounds. "When I was a little girl, all I wished for was to leave San Yetaxa. I wanted my parents to pack our bags and never return. As an adult, I thought such dreams were childish. Now that I know of the big wide world out here..."

"You're going back, aren't you?"

"You've given my people hope, Dane. Now isn't the time to run away. It's time to rebuild San Yetaxa to what it used to be before the cartel turned it into a battlefield."

"It won't be easy. At some point another El Maestro will try to stamp his authority."

"And that's why I have to go back. Perhaps if people like me,

Ruben, and Inspector Alvarez can make a stand, our home could flourish again." Maria reached out for his hand. "You could come with me. Maybe that place you're looking for over the horizon is San Yetaxa."

Winter frowned. "You may be right."

"Then what's stopping you?"

Winter drew her in close. "Because I've still got a lot to give back. I did some horrible things in war. Things that I had to do. Things that will live with me forever. Colonel Dawson gave me an opportunity to repay those debts in a small way. I think there might still be people out there I can help."

She frowned, her eyes averting his, as if knowing what the answer would be. "If that's the case, I hope one day after you've finished helping everyone, you find your happy place. And maybe in the meantime, you'll promise to visit me from time to time."

"I think I'll be able to manage that." Winter leaned in and kissed her. "How long did you say you had until you were flying home?"

"Three days."

"Well, then." He wrapped an arm around her waist and they set forth over the crest and toward the horizon. "Plenty of time to make some very poor decisions before you head off."

* * *

MORE FROM SAM COGLEY

The next instalment in Sam Cogley's Dane Winter series, is available to order now here:

https://mybook.to/DaneWinterBackAd

ABOUT THE AUTHOR

Sam Cogley is the author of popular action thrillers, melding suspense-laden espionage plots with the mesmerising world of high-tech innovations. He writes the high-octane Dane Winter thrillers for Boldwood Books. Sam lives in Victoria, Australia with his wife and children.

Sign up to Sam Cogley's mailing list for news, competitions and updates on future books.

Visit Sam Cogley's website: www.samcogley.com

Follow Sam Cogley on social media here:

f facebook.com/samcogleyauthor

BB bookbub.com/authors/sam-cogley

Boldwood

Boldwood Books is an award-winning fiction publishing company seeking out the best stories from around the world.

Find out more at www.boldwoodbooks.com

Join our reader community for brilliant books, competitions and offers!

Follow us
@BoldwoodBooks
@TheBoldBookClub

Sign up to our weekly
deals newsletter

https://bit.ly/BoldwoodBNewsletter